ALIEN
LOG II
THE NEW WORLD ORDER

By

Robert E. Farrell

Published by: **R. E. FARRELLBOOKS, LLC**
Sun City West, Arizona

R. E. FARRELLBOOKS, LLC
Sun City West, Arizona

www.refarrellbooks.com

ISBN 0-9759116-3-5 / 978-0-9759116-3-1

Cover design by author and Wendy C. Farrell using NASA photo taken by Apollo 8 combined with a composite of cylinder UFOs presented throughout the literature. Photo on page 10 is courtesy of Phillip Treweek and photo on page 16 is courtesy of Sergey Rimsha. Other figures are by the author.

Printed in the United States of America

ACKNOWLEDGMENTS

This book never would have happened had it not been for the help of many people and the encouraging letters from readers of the first book in the series, *Alien Log*. Below is a partial list of credits.

First and foremost, I wish to thank my wife, Linda who stood by me patiently during the years of research and writing that went into this book. This says nothing of the countless hours she spent proofreading the many versions of this book as it evolved. I owe many thanks to my daughter, Wendy, who worked diligently to get this book to market.

Several people were kind enough to read the draft copy of this book and check for content errors and to ensure that the story had a logical flow. I am indebted to Gloria Hawker, Dr. Ruth Hover, Dr. Rebecca Hardcastle, Dr. William J. Harris, David DeBlois, Bobby Mc Gehee, Marion O'Brien, and Hank Brandt for their kind efforts in this regard.

I would like to thank Jeanette Chaplin, Ed.D. and Amelia Sheldon for their superb efforts in copy editing.

A special debt of gratitude is owed to the Writers Round Table of Phoenix for giving me an education in writing fiction. I especially want to thank John Safin (The Grand **Pooh Bah**) whose vision led to the formation of the Writers Round Table of Phoenix and who helped me with the cover design.

Thanks to NASA and those brave astronauts on Apollo 8 who took the first photograph of "Earth Rise" on May 9th, 1969. I felt their photo was an appropriate fit for my cover.

In Loving Memory of My Son

INTRODUCTION

It has been said that good science fiction is based on good science. I have tried to follow that rule in writing this book. As you might well appreciate, it is difficult to find good science in the field of UFOs and ETs. The hard evidence is lacking, at least in the public domain. It is difficult to say how much evidence exists in government warehouses and at top secret bases; they aren't talking.

Once you conclude that the UFO phenomenon is real, you are forced to rethink the entire fabric of your belief system. It now has to be reconciled with the realities of UFOs. This book may cause the reader to do just that.

Prolog

Yucca Flats, Nevada Test Site, Area 3

Tuesday, May 19, 1953
5:03 AM local time

Captain Miller crouched down in his bunker and looked to the north through his field glasses. He focused on the 300 foot tower only one mile away. It was only 30 minutes before the dawn of a new day and the light from the eastern sky caused the tower to have an unearthly glow. The tower cast a long shadow which pointed west-ward like a sinister finger. At the top of the tower was an 8,000 pound gadget. That's what these things were called, not an atomic bomb but a gadget. Perhaps the word gadget made the bomb seem less sinister. No matter, it was a bomb. It was a horrendous method of mass destruction created by humanity in the panic of a world war. The war was over but the gadgets remained and continued to be made and tested, by the hundreds. Now it was a matter of improving the efficiency so the gadgets could be smaller, lighter, and have a higher yield to kill more efficiently. Today's test was predicted to have a yield of 37 kilotons. It would be one and a half times more powerful than the bomb dropped on Hiroshima eight years earlier. That one killed 100,000 people within seconds.

This test, only 80 miles from the growing city of Las Vegas, was the ninth of the planned eleven for the spring of 1953. The test series was code named Upshot-Knothole and the gadget's name was Harry, the most efficient pure fission design ever built with a yield below 100 kilotons. Later, history would refer to this gadget as "Dirty Harry". The unexpected shift in wind would carry the radioactive cloud into Arizona and Utah exposing the "downwinder" residents to a third of the total radiation from all of the tests that would be conducted through to 1958. It would be decades before the residents of the surrounding towns such as St. George, Utah, and Littlefield, Arizona, discovered what had been done to them. At the time, government men in white suites and carrying Geiger counters, told them that everything was okay. Oh what a nasty beast, cancer, with its long, painful, and drawn out death.

Today, Harry would be televised to the whole nation to alleviate the fears of the American people. TV cameras were permitted to view the test from News Nob only 7 miles from ground zero. Mock towns were built with cars, trains, and other equipment placed in different positions around the test site. Troops were dug in at various distances from the deadly tower. Their instructions were to move out of the trenches shortly after the blast and walk toward ground zero. The American people would be able to see for themselves on their TVs that indeed, it was possible to survive a nuclear exchange with Russia. All they had to do was to take a few simple precautions when the A-bombs struck. Duck and hide and all would be well. The gadget was scheduled to go off at 5:05.

"Tee minus one minute." The words echoed across the test site from strategically placed public address speakers. This was the queue, to those with protective goggles, to place them over their eyes. Without these, the initial blast, brighter than the sun, would be blinding. With them on, it was impossible to see in normal light. They were as dark as welding glasses. Captain Miller took one last visual survey of his troops. They did not have goggles but were instructed to cover their eyes with their arm. Television camera crews installed lens caps to protect the sensitive video tubes. For a long moment, Americans watching at home would be blinded.

Perhaps it was the goggles or perhaps it was the sun's early rays, but none of the participants of this show noticed the strange, silver, 32 foot disc-shaped craft moving closer. It was 4,000 feet above the desert and only a mile to the east.

The pilot of the craft chose to stay to the east with the sun directly behind, making it difficult to be seen. This was not the first test this pilot had witnessed. His vessel had been directed to monitor human events in this area. The normal procedure was to lay off three miles to the east and observe. After the explosion, the prevailing winds would bring the fallout to them so it could be sampled. Analysis of the fallout debris would allow them to learn much about the makeup of the bomb and the level of technology the humans had achieved.

Today, something was wrong. The previous tower test was detonated one and a half hour before sunrise. It was now nearly sunrise. *The device must have malfunctioned,* thought the pilot. He decided to move his vessel in closer so he could do an infrared laser scan of the deadly device. In this way he hoped to determine what had caused the failure.

"Tee minus five, four, three, two, one," echoed the loud speakers. At the instant the silver craft was within one thousand yards of the tower, the tower erupted. A new sun was born for an instant. A tremendous electromagnetic pulse raced outward at the speed of light, striping the magnetic shield from the craft and distorting the electromagnetic field controlling the gravitational field propulsion system. An instant later an overpressure shock wave struck the craft. The pilot and three crew members were slammed down onto the control panel as their vessel was tossed eastward several hundred yards.

The pilot struggled to regain control but the radiation had pierced the craft's thin skin, shooting through his body with lethal damage. Skillfully, he turned his vessel eastward toward the Colorado River and to a safe landing spot on a dry lakebed one hundred and sixty miles to the southeast. As the pilot fought off the effects of deadly radiation, the craft began to waver and veered to the south. It had slowed to only 100 miles per hour when it struck the soft ground and came to rest in the mountain foothills 25 miles north of Kingman, Arizona.

At the Kingman Airport, 10 miles north of Kingman, the radar operator had been tracking an unidentified craft which entered his control area from the north-west. He watched with alarm as it lost altitude and disappeared from his screen. "An unidentified craft just went down!" he reported to his superior. Within hours, several jeeps from the local base reached the scene and began the recovery.

Chapter 1
The Pickup

Wednesday, May 14 (present day)
5:46 PM
Twenty-five miles north of Kingman, Arizona

Colonel Joseph "Pete" Mitchell scanned the sky to the east. His strong jaw thrust forward, accenting his graying temples. Pete yelled as he turned to the taller of the two men standing near large boulders twenty yards behind. "He's coming! Corey, help Colonel Andrews get behind those boulders. Be careful of his injured leg." He motioned to the tall attractive young woman standing next to them. "Wendy, you take cover too. I'll direct the chopper in."

The whoop, whoop, whoop of the twin-engine Huey UH-1N grew louder as it angled in to find a good landing spot. The rock-strewn foothill of Long Mountain was not the most ideal place to land. Fortunately, the seven percent grade was within the capabilities of the Huey. The pilot found a spot that was the most level and least cluttered with rocks. His preference would have been to set down two thousand yards to the east where the ground was level.

However, with a wounded man, the better evacuation area was too far away to be considered.

As the chopper was about to touch down, Pete turned his back toward the craft to brace against the rotor's downwash and protect his face from being sandblasted. His tall frame absorbed the buffeting as he went into a partial crouch. The warm air from the downwash blew over Pete's back and filled his nostrils with the smell of burning JP4 jet fuel. Skillfully, the pilot turned the craft so its nose was on the upgrade side of the slope and he delicately set the chopper down. Pete turned and walked over to the boulders where the other three members of his party were taking refuge. He yelled over the whine of the chopper's turbines, "Corey, you and I will carry the colonel over to the chopper. Wendy, you bring the duffle bag."

Dr. Wendy Ahearn nodded in agreement as she tightly clutched a small blue duffle bag. In it was an artifact alien to this planet. It was, in fact, the most important piece of alien technology ever recovered. Contained within the artifact was information key to humanity's survival. It was expected to play a major role in discovering the invasion plans of an alien race. Despite its importance, few people on this planet knew of its existence. It was Pete's hope that it might allow Wendy, a world-renowned linguist, to tap into the aliens' main computer and gain access to technology beyond anyone's dreams.

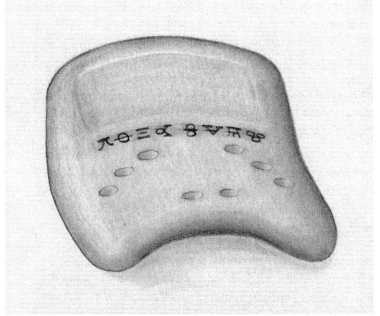

Colonel Andrews was being propped up by thirty-year-old astrophysicist, Dr. Corey Newton, who was nearly half a head taller. With his six-foot-two athletic build, supporting the colonel was no effort. Middle aged, Colonel Andrews' five-eleven frame was slender as he had kept himself trim during his army career. Wendy stood next to Corey. Her tall five-foot-eleven frame appeared dwarfed by his. The chopper's downwash was buffeting her long auburn hair. To the rescuing pilot and the rest of the outside world, Colonel Andrews, base commander, was being rescued from his crashed stealth fighter after a routine mission. Only the trio, Pete and his two team members, Wendy and Corey, knew the real reason for the colonel's flight from their secret base.

As Base Commander for Area 51, Colonel Andrews had stolen the alien artifact and fled the secret base in an F-117A Stealth Fighter. His plane disappeared from the radar screen shortly after takeoff. The other members of the base thought he had simply wandered off course on a flight to

Seattle, Washington. Instead, he had deliberately dropped below the radar detection altitude and changed course, heading instead toward the east, toward Kingman, Arizona. During his escape, he crash-landed in a dry lake known as Red Lake, thirty-two miles north of Kingman and was forced to abandon his craft. Wounded and weak, he made a fifteen-mile trek through the desert toward the Kingman Airport. Ten miles from the airport, he was intercepted by the trio at gunpoint. Ironically, they intercepted him at the same location the artifact had been found nearly six decades earlier, in 1953, during the recovery of a crashed UFO. Perhaps irony was not involved. This was, after all, Colonel Andrews' intended destination.

Pete bent down and studied the colonel's leg. It was a bad laceration but nothing appeared broken. The colonel had lost some blood on his trek through the desert but the bleeding had stopped. "Colonel, when Dr. Newton and I lock fingers, you sit in our locked hands and put your arms around our necks. Can you do that, Colonel?"

"Yes … but … I think I'm feeling well enough now. I can walk on my own." Colonel Andrews groaned. He was still pale from a loss of blood.

"Don't even think of it. You might faint again. You're dehydrated and have lost some blood. It's no problem for us to carry you." Pete shot Corey a glance. "Are you ready, Corey?"

"Yes," Corey said as he locked the fingers of his left hand with those of Pete's right hand. In the few short days he had been on the project with Pete, Corey had learned that he was a leader. When Pete gave a command, it was with firmness, even to civilians such as Corey and Wendy.

Pete was a tall man but still a good two inches shorter than Corey. The two men slid their locked hands under Colonel Andrews' buttocks and lifted him off the ground in a human chair. The one hundred and seventy pound older man was an easy lift for the taller two men. The colonel groaned as he placed his arms around each man's neck.

The chopper pilot who came to rescue them had no clue as to the real situation. In his mind, he was on a mission to save his downed base commander. He exited the Huey and approached the trio of men. "Colonel Andrews," he yelled, as he gave the obligatory salute, "I'm Captain Herber. Glad you're okay. Everyone at the base was worried when we heard your plane went down." Seeing the colonel being carried, he grew concerned. "Do you need medical attention?"

"No, thank you, Captain, I just banged up my leg a bit. It's not a major problem." Colonel Andrews did not betray his misdeeds.

The captain looked at Pete, who was clearly in charge of this rescue. "Colonel Mitchell, if Colonel Andrews doesn't need immediate medical attention, I need to take the chopper back to the Kingman Airport and have the number one engine checked out. The chip light for that engine came on and I was getting a high TOT indication as I flew over here."

"Captain, Colonel Andrews has a bad laceration in his right leg but the bleeding has stopped. I think he can do without medical attention for a while. How long do you think it'll take to have the craft checked out?"

"When the chip light came on, I radioed back to Kingman Air Service and, as luck would have it, they happen to have a good jet mechanic there with experience on T400 series choppers. He was just going off duty but agreed to stay over. I don't think it'll take more than a couple of hours or so for him to make the required repairs."

"That's fine, Captain. Let's get the chopper fixed before we attempt the hour and a half trip back to base. Help us lift the colonel into the chopper. We can put him in the jump seat behind yours."

"Yes, sir," the captain said as he climbed up into the passenger compartment. "Sit him on the floor at the door and I'll help him over to the jump seat."

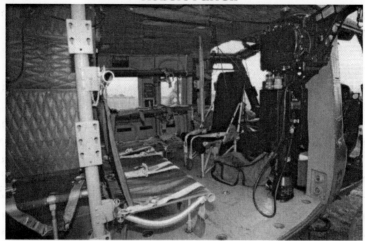

Pete and Corey backed over to the open door on the right side of the craft and set the colonel on the floor of the chopper. Captain Herber helped the colonel to his feet and over to the rear facing jump seat directly behind the pilot's seat.

"Here you go, Colonel. You may want to use the headset hanging next to your seat. You know how noisy it gets in here."

"Thanks, Captain," Colonel Andrews said as he strapped in.

"Colonel Mitchell, would you like to ride in the co-pilot's seat?" the captain asked as he pointed to the left seat in the cockpit.

"No thanks, Captain, if you don't need my assistance, I'll stay back here with the others." Pete knew it was safer to have two pilots in the cockpit, but he didn't want Colonel Andrews out of his sight.

Corey climbed in and turned to help Wendy. Both took the right end of the forward-facing bench seat opposite Colonel Andrews. Wendy sat to Corey's left. Pete climbed in and took the seat next to Wendy on the left side of the craft. She clutched the duffel bag and eyed Colonel Andrews with contempt. The day's stress had taken its toll and she was exhausted. Her apprehension was growing.

She turned to Pete. "Is this helicopter safe to fly?" she asked over the noise of engines as they came up to speed.

"Yes, the plane is safe to fly but we shouldn't try a long flight. A short, ten-minute flight back to the Kingman Airport is fine. The chopper can fly on one engine if need be."

"What's a chip light and a high TOT?" she hollered in a voice of strained apprehension.

"A chip light can come on if the chip sensor detects metallic particles, or chips, in the engine lubrication oil," Pete explained. "That could be a sign of an engine bearing that's failing." Sensing Wendy's apprehension, he decided to elaborate. "Bearing failure is a slow process and can take many hours. As the bearings fail, small specks of metal are released into the lubricating oil. That's what the sensors detect." He looked at her and gave a reassuring smile. "Also, it could just be a faulty indicator. That happens sometimes."

"What about TOT?" she asked.

"TOT means Tail Outlet Temperature and if it's too high, that's not good either."

"Why?"

"If the tail outlet temperature is too high, that means that the turbine blades in the exhaust stream are running too hot and could experience thermal failure," Pete explained.

"Oh." Wendy was beginning to wonder how many things could go wrong and what was the probability everything would go right? *Is this a safe mode of travel?* She wondered, as her anxiety grew.

Pete sensed her growing concern. "I think the captain's correct in wanting to fix the problem now. One of the rules of flying a helicopter is never fly unless you are absolutely sure it will stay in the air until you're ready to land." He smiled again to reassure her. "Everyone on board wants to have a safe trip. The plane can fly with a chip light and high TOT. They are not fatal problems. It can even fly on one engine. It's just standard operating procedures that problems like those get addressed as soon as possible." Pete saw Wendy's body get tense and realized that the word *fatal* was probably a bad choice of words.

"We have a lot of desert terrain to cross in order to get back to our base," he continued to explain. "The trip back to Kingman is much shorter. Also, it'll be dark soon and we don't want to be forced to land in the desert at night. That could be tricky." He read the fear in her face. "Don't worry, we won't be flying very high."

Pete was aware of Wendy's fear of flying. Her dossier had highlighted that fact. When she had been a college student, both of her parents were killed in a plane crash. They were professors at her university and decided to fly to Cancun for spring break. Wendy had a paper to finish and opted to stay at home. Her parents were among the twenty-three passengers killed when the plane crash landed. The death of both parents in a plane accident had taken a toll on her. Whenever she had to travel, she went by ground. She avoided flying if at all possible. After she was recruited for the project, it was necessary to fly Wendy from State College, Pennsylvania, to the base in Nevada in order to maintain secrecy. Pete had flown her on the last leg of her journey and was impressed with her ability to control her fear.

Wendy sat back with a more reassured expression as the pilot finished his engine check and lifted off. Everyone was exhausted after the ordeal in the desert. No other words were spoken during the ten-minute flight to the airport.

***

At Kingman, the captain set the chopper down in the service area next to a large hanger marked KINGMAN AIR SERVICE. After shutting down the engines, he shouted back to Pete, "I'll run in and get the mechanic to check out the engine. You four may want to wait in the café next to the flight line, I think it's still open?"

Pete eyed the other passengers and could see the exhaustion in their faces. "No thanks, Captain, I think we'll stay here. We're all pretty tired. One of us may go over later and get some coffee. If we go, would you like us to grab one for you, Captain?"

"Yes, thank you, sir. I take it black," the captain yelled back as he headed over to the hanger at the edge of the tarmac. The four occupants of the craft sat in silent exhaustion.

Wendy was staring forward through the cockpit window, her eyes unfocused. Her mind began to drift back to a week ago when she was in a safer place—her classroom at the university. She thought about Bob, her boss, mentor, and dear friend. She wondered how he and his wife Lisa and her dog, Tigger, were doing. They were her family now. After she lost her parents, Bob and Lisa had become her guardians and surrogate parents. Bob had guided her education and her career in teaching ever since.

Wendy thought about her parents and the path she had chosen for her life. As much as she loved music, that was not her chosen career even though her mother, who was a professor of musicology at the university, steered her in that direction. Wendy had a natural gift for the piano and was on a par with many professional concert pianists. However, in addition to her musical abilities, she also had the innate ability to translate any form of written text. She dazzled her colleagues by translating texts of various unknown languages. She would simply study the text by reading it over and over. Soon, the meaning would become clear. The process amazed even her. She could not explain how she was able to accomplish such feats. For her, translating was intuitive. Her father, a professor of engineering, recognized her talent for linguistics and encouraged her to follow that path as a career. After entering the field, she quickly established herself. Even at the young age of twenty-seven, she was already recognized world wide for her abilities and had been an invited speaker at many linguistics conferences. Wendy was happy, linguistics required much less travel than was required of a classical pianist.

Yes, teaching linguistics is much safer, she thought. *Yet, here I am, sitting aboard a helicopter. I've been told that God never intended for these things to fly. Yet, as I sit here it's being repaired and hopefully made safe to fly. What have I gotten myself into? What a week this has been. I've spent several days sequestered in a secret underground military base in Nevada; seen strange alien bodies and their craft; been given the daunting task of activating and translating a strange alien artifact to learn what they are up to; and stranger yet, I've been having weird thoughts about them. Why do I keep getting flashes of reptilian looking beings in my mind? Yet . . . I sense that they are our friends who want to help humanity; to save it from destruction. Destruction from what? Strange . . . really strange. No one will ever believe any of this . . . no one . . . except Pete and Corey. Corey is such a charm. Being with him is worth the stress of the project. He's been so strong, yet gentle through all of this.*

Wendy turned her glance toward Corey and admired his strong features. He was sitting next to her with his eyes closed, resting.

Chapter 2
Return to Base

8:52 PM
Kingman Airport

The sun had set and it was getting dark as Captain Herber stood next to the chopper and scanned the repair order on the clipboard the mechanic handed him. "Thank you, Mr. Leonard. I appreciate you working overtime to give us such prompt service." He scribbled his signature on the form. "So, after draining the engine oil, you used the correct mil spec oil, right?"

"Oh, sure. I've changed oil many times on the Bell 212's. That's the civilian version of this craft, as you know."

"Yes, I know," Captain Herber said. "How did the half hour engine burn look?"

"The burn and penalty check looked good," Mr. Leonard said. "Also, I topped off the fuel. This bird is ready to fly. You should be fine now. Is there anything else I can help you with, Captain?"

"No thanks. We'll be on our way now." The Captain peered through the open cockpit door at the four

passengers. "We're all set now, Colonel Mitchell. Thanks
for your patience."

"No problem," Pete said. "I'm sorry but the café was
closed so we couldn't get any coffee."

"That's okay, we'll be back to the base in less than an
hour and a half. I can wait." Captain Herber looked at Pete
apologetically. "I'm sorry, sir, but since it's dark, I will
need you to fly shotgun for me. You're checked out on
these birds aren't you?"

"Yes, I have a few hours." Pete knew this type of craft
was not safe to fly single-handed in low visibility
conditions so he'd have to help the captain by watching the
terrain. As he stood up to exit the craft, he leaned over to
Corey and whispered into his ear. "I have to go forward.
Keep a close eye on the colonel."

Corey nodded as he glanced to his right toward
Colonel Andrews who was sitting with his eyes closed.

Pete climbed down from the chopper's left side, went
forward, and climbed into the co-pilot's seat on the left.
"All set, Captain. What channel do you want me to set into
the VOR/DME?"

Wendy overheard Pete. "What's VOR and DME?"

Pete glanced back over his shoulder at Wendy and pointed toward the instrument panel. "Wendy, VOR is an acronym for Very high frequency Omni-directional radio Range and tells the pilot the direction to whatever VOR station is tuned in. The outbound leg from the station is referred to as the *radial*. DME is the Distance Measuring Equipment. It provides both the distance to the station and the ground speed toward that station.

Captain Herber glanced at Pete. "Colonel, you can set the VOR channel to one-zero-eight-point-eight, channel twenty-five. I plan to take off on runway two-one and fly outbound on three-four-five radial until we're out about thirty nautical miles and then proceed on a heading of three-one-zero back to the base. Set the altimeter for three-four-four-nine feet. We'll cruise at about one thousand feet AGL to clear the mountains to the northwest."

"Roger that," Pete said, as he recalled that AGL meant above ground level.

"Watch out for Mount Tipton," Captain Herber said. "Its peak is over seven thousand feet and should be on our left side as we pass it." Captain Herber knew night flying at low altitudes was always risky. This night was especially dangerous since there would be no moonlight to help light the terrain. "Keep an eye on the radar altimeter for terrain changes." The captain sighed. "I can't imagine flying on a night like this without ground-tracking radar."

Pete picked up a set of goggles with eyepieces that melded into a single, Cyclops-looking lens. He examined them and glanced toward the captain, "Once we get airborne and away from all of these lights, I'll put on these night vision goggles so I can keep an eye on the terrain."

"Good idea. Thank you, sir," the captain said as he started the engines. Within a minute, both engines were running at full power. "No chip light and TOT looks good. I guess we can start back now. Radio check, can you hear me back there?"

"Roger. Five by," Colonel Andrews said in a feeble voice."

"Five by," Pete echoed.

"I hear you," Corey said.

"Me too," said Wendy.

With that, Captain Herber raised the collective, pressed the left pedal, and pushed the cyclic forward. Ever so smoothly, the chopper lifted off the ground and began moving forward. As he climbed to altitude, he made a gentle right turn to a heading of three-six-zero and intercepted the three-four-five radial outbound. At one thousand feet above the terrain he leveled off. Within minutes they were away from the lights of Kingman and Pete slipped on the goggles. The scene below him was glowing with an eerie green tinge as the desert radiated the heat stored during the day.

* * *

The sound inside the helicopter sounded like the combination of a turbine engine and a threshing machine. The rhythm of the beating rotor blades combined with the turbine whine was mesmerizing.

Pete watched through the night vision goggles as the desert hills, in their surreal green glow, slowly drifted by below. His mind went back to the evening he flew Wendy to their secret base. That was less than three days ago.

So much has happened. It's amazing that Wendy was able to get the alien artifact activated in such a short time. And she's learned so much about the aliens already. Truly impressive. If she and Corey can use that device to connect to the alien's central computer then we will have access to fantastic technology. Corey has been a great asset. His technical explanations of Wendy's findings and of the alien craft have helped both Wendy and me gain a much better understanding of the alien technology. I'm so glad he agreed to join the project. He and Wendy have great chemistry . . . maybe more than that.

Those two remind me of Sue and me at that age. I was so in love with her. I still love her even after death do us part. She must know that. I think of her every day . . . and her senseless murder. I've got to put that behind me now and concentrate on the future ... my future ... the future of the project ... the future of humanity.

Pete began to formulate the report he needed to give the President after he returned to base. *The President was surprisingly calm after my last report,* Pete thought. *One would think he would have been more emotional after I told him of the theft of such an important artifact. I guess keeping calm under pressure is what makes for a great leader. Anyway, he was happy and congratulated us on the progress we've made on the project and did offer to pull out the stops to help us get the artifact back. I can imagine how happy he'll be when I report we've tracked down Colonel Andrews and recovered the device. Now, we can return to probing the artifact to release more of its secrets.*

Corey had also been deep in thought. He looked at Colonel Andrews, who was sleeping and slumped against the shoulder restraints. Corey then gazed with unfocused vision out of the side window at the blackness. *My colleagues back at GraviDyne would never believe what I have seen in the past few days,* he thought. *That nerd, James, would think I had been tripping on something. I'd love to show him the craft that I've seen. His ridiculing of my belief in UFOs would end real fast. Oh well, he deserves to be in the dark and remain ignorant. He calls himself a scientist yet he is the epitome of bad science, a scientist that is closed minded.* He felt Wendy move in the seat next to him. *The best part of this experience has been meeting Wendy. Beauty and intelligence.* He wondered how she was holding up and glanced to his left to catch a view of her. Even in the soft red glow of the cabin lights, he could see that she was not at ease. He took her hand and squeezed it tenderly. With headsets on and the overriding noise, private conversations were difficult. "I don't care much for flying either," he mouthed and then gave her a smile.

Wendy stared into his eyes and smiled back, resisting her urge to kiss him. Corey couldn't resist. He gave her a tender kiss to reassure her. Wendy put her head on Corey's shoulder and began gently stroking his other hand as she closed her eyes.

* * *

Pete's head was full of questions he wanted to ask Andrews after they return to base. First, a doctor would need to attend to his wounds, but then the questions could begin. *How did he know the device existed?* Pete wondered. *Who else knows about it? What was he going to do with it? Was he going to give it to a foreign government?* Pete knew that Base Security could make Andrews answer these questions. *They have ways ... very unpleasant ways.* He thought. *No ... I'll have to question him myself. No one else on base must know the artifact exists. I'll have to make him talk. Given the importance of this project, torture is an option.* Pete was well aware of the United Nations' Convention Against Torture. When he attended the War College, he had been required to memorize Article 1 that defined torture. He recalled: *Torture means any act by which severe pain or suffering, whether physical or mental, is intentionally inflicted on a person for such purposes as obtaining from him or a third person information or a confession.* Pete recalled that the United States was not a signatory to the UN Convention Against Torture and in fact he was required to learn interrogation techniques that violated that Convention. Most of the techniques were very unpleasant and extremely distasteful, but, if necessary, he would use them. He also knew that Colonel Andrews attended the same war college and had the same training with regard to interrogation. Pete knew that interrogating him would not be easy ... the colonel would know how to resist.

Glancing over at the DME, Pete noticed they were out thirty miles. *Time to change heading*, he thought. At that moment, the captain turned left to a heading of three-one-zero. Pete could see the mountains nearby to his left through his goggles as the chopper headed north-west. They seemed menacing. He knew now why the captain wanted him to ride shotgun. About a mile ahead, a small dry lake appeared in their flight path. *A good place to land in an emergency, Pete thought.* Suddenly everything went black! He couldn't see anything through his goggles and pulled them off. "These goggles have stopped working. The battery must be dead." he yelled over his mouthpiece as he examined the goggles. *No response from the captain! Our headsets are dead too!* He ripped off his headset and glanced toward his right. Captain Herber was in near panic and struggling to keep the craft level.

"Christ, Colonel!" the captain yelled, "We've got a complete electrical failure! Radar and everything is out! I don't believe it! Not even the battery operated instrument lights are working!" Captain Herber flung off the headsets, realizing they were dead. "I can't read my altimeter!" he yelled over the engine noise. Instinctively, he pulled back on the cyclic to reduce forward airspeed. "It's so goddamn dark out, I can't see the ground!" Captain Herber was approaching a full blown panic. "Hand me those goggles so I can see the ground and keep from flying this damn thing into that mountainside to our left!"

"Captain, they aren't working either!" Pete said as he tried to fight off the panic of the situation. "They went black when the electrical power failed!" Pete tried to regain his composure but the situation was desperate.

"How can that be? They're battery operated!" Captain Herber shouted as he looked out of the windshield and strained to see whatever landmarks he could that would provide visual reference. Only blackness appeared in every direction. Beads of sweat began to run down his forehead and into his eyes. He blinked to clear his vision. The salt burned his eyes. "Check them again while I put this bird into a tight orbit to avoid any mountains that might be in our path!" he yelled. "I need to hold level flight without becoming inverted!"

As Pete fumbled to reset the battery switch, he noticed his watch. Through the glow of the radium dial he could see the hands were spinning backward. "What the hell?" He slid the battery switch on the goggles back to the ON position and held them up to his eyes . . . darkness! "They still don't work, Captain!"

Still straining to find a visual reference, Captain Herber considered his options. "Take that flashlight on your door out of its holster and shine it on the instruments!"

Pete retrieved the flashlight and flicked the switch. No light! He tapped it with his palm. Still no light! "The batteries must be dead on this, too!"

"We're running out of options," Captain Herber yelled over to Pete. Then he remembered. "Colonel, grab some of those glow sticks in that compartment under your seat and activate one! Hurry!" He blinked again to squeeze the salty sweat out of his eyes.

Pete felt under his seat, found the compartment, and withdrew three glow sticks. He bent one, breaking the glass vial inside, releasing the hydrogen peroxide into the solution of phenyl oxalate ester and fluorescent dye. After shaking it once, it began to glow with a ghostly green light.

"Here!" Pete said, as he held it out for Captain Herber.

"Hold it under the instruments so I can see our altitude!" The captain screamed over the roar of the engines. He knew that even with a complete electrical failure, the altimeter would still work since it was based on the pressure difference at altitude compared to ground level. It was like a simple barometer. "I need to try and maintain a constant altitude until I get my bearings!" His plan was to hold the chopper in a tight orbit at constant altitude to avoid the mountains that he knew were approaching in the darkness. "Colonel!" he yelled. "I've got to set this thing down as soon as possible! Light another glow stick and throw it out the window! Perhaps it'll stay intact when it hits the ground and give enough light for me to judge the distance for a safe landing. God, I can't believe it's so damn dark out. Of all the times and places for an electrical failure!"

With his free hand, Pete opened the window on his left and then activated another glow stick. He reached through the open window and dropped the glow stick. It seemed to take an eternity for it to fall to earth. With a fading flash, it hit the ground and burst open. "Damn, it broke!" he yelled. "I'll try another!" He lit another and pulled out a handkerchief from his flight jacket. Holding the glow stick between his knees, he tied the handkerchief to the glow stick to slow its descent and dropped it out the window. Pete watched it as it made a fluttering descent. This time, a persistent green disk formed on the ground. "Good one! Thank God! It survived!" The tension in his voice eased as there now seemed to be hope for their survival.

The captain looked out his side window and, straining to see the ground, spotted the dim green glow. He gently lowered the collective and began descending as he circled around the light below. "Brace yourself, everyone! I don't think this will be one of my smoothest landings!" He knew his distance perception would probably be off in the paleness of the light and if he misjudged they would become a pile of rubble on the desert floor.

The glow from the glow stick formed a circle about twenty feet in diameter. The captain continued to spiral down toward the green spot now only a couple of hundred feet below. Down . . . now to only a hundred feet . . . now only fifty feet. He pulled up on the collective and pressed on the left pedal as the craft began to flare. Too late!

"Oh shit!" Instinctively, the captain and Pete yelled out together. The chopper bounced hard, first on the right skid and then the left. The second bounce caused Pete to strike his head on the side window frame. He wasn't wearing a helmet. Blood oozed from his left temple as his world suddenly became filled with light.

* * *

As Pete began to regain consciousness, he could hear a commotion in the aft cabin. Then, suddenly Wendy screamed, "Oh, God! He grabbed the duffel bag from me and is getting away! I can't get loose from my shoulder harness! Corey, get him!"

Pete, still groggy, turned to look out the window to his left. His vision was blurry but he was able to make out the figure of Colonel Andrews clasping the duffel bag. Half running, half limping he was heading toward a thirty-foot golden circle of light on the desert floor thirty yards to the left of the chopper. *That's strange,* Pete thought. *Why is that light gold? It should be green. The glow stick was green when I threw it out.* Nothing was making sense. He shook his head in an effort to clear his blurry vision. Looking out of the front windshield, to his left he could see the green glow stick and its circle of light only ten yards ahead.

Two circles of light? What is that gold one? He thought as he struggled to make his brain work. Glancing back to his left, he could see the colonel enter the golden circle, look up into the sky, and raise the duffel bag. *Why is he raising that bag?* Pete wondered. Corey was nearly on the colonel and made a flying leap to tackle him. Suddenly, a bluish-white shaft of light shot down from the sky above and froze Corey in flight. Both he and the colonel began to spiral upward in a surreal dance.

"Holy shit! What the hell is happening here?!" Pete screamed. He watched helplessly as both men disappeared upward out of view. He tipped his head back and closer to the left window to look out over his overhead window. That's when he saw it. The most beautiful craft he had ever seen. It was a metallic-looking disk thirty to forty feet in diameter surrounded by a golden glowing haze. It hovered, perfectly stationary, fifty yards above the chopper. Pete watched, dumbfounded, as the two men spiraled up and disappeared into the belly of the craft.

"Did you see that, Captain?!" Pete yelled as he turned to look at the captain. The captain was in shocked awe, staring up through his overhead window. The craft hovering above cast a soft ghostly glow on his face. He looked pale and his mouth was gaping open as if frozen in a scream. The captain said nothing but continued to fix his stare on the strange metallic disk.

Soon, it began to wobble and the blue-white shaft of light went out with a loud zzzit-clap of thunder. In a blink of an eye, the craft was gone, leaving behind a glowing pink vapor trail. Then the darkness returned. All that remained was the green glow on the ground from the

glow stick in front of them. Suddenly, the electrical systems came back up and all the instruments began to activate!

"Corey! Oh no, Corey!" Wendy cried out above the engine noise as she struggled to unbuckle her shoulder harness. It was still stuck. "Pete ... They ... They took Corey! I told him to go ... and now he's gone ... because of me! They took him! We have to get him back!" Finally, she broke loose and still stunned from the crash, she collapsed onto the floor of the craft and began crawling toward the door through which the two men had exited.

Pete unbuckled and climbed out of the chopper. He ran back along the left side to the open door and saw Wendy crawling toward him, sobbing.

He looked at her with a lowered gaze. "Wendy, come here," Pete insisted as he could see she was in a state of shock.

She obeyed. Pete lifted her down from the chopper and wrapped his arms around her. "This wasn't your fault,

Wendy. Corey would have gone after Colonel Andrews whether you said anything or not. He wanted to get the duffel bag back. If anyone's at fault it's me."

"So now he's gone ... and so is the artifact. What are we going to do, Pete? How can we get Corey back?" she sobbed. "We can't get him back. What can we do, Pete?"

Pete hugged her for a moment longer and then walked around to the pilot's side of the chopper and opened the door. "Captain, is this thing flyable?"

The captain regained his composure and scanned his instruments. His voice was shaky. "It seems to be fine now, Colonel. Look, even the flashlight is on. It was a hard landing but the craft seems to be flyable." He saw the blood oozing down Pete's left temple. "Are you okay, Colonel?"

Pete winced as he touched his left temple and examined the blood on his fingers. "Yes, I'm fine." His voice was faint. "Can you fly this thing back to the base without me?"

The captain looked at Pete in disbelief that he would even ask such a question. "No, sir, it's too dangerous. If that power failure had occurred while I was flying single-handed, we would all be dead now."

"Okay then." Pete tried to clear his head. The captain was right, that was a dumb question. He wasn't thinking straight. He shook his head and thought for a moment, trying to figure their next move as he glanced at his watch. It was working now but the time was all wrong; it was reading three-twenty-two. Pete shook his head again to clear his thoughts. He remembered his watch running backward just before the crash. He strained to get his mind functioning properly. *What time did we leave Kingman?* He asked himself. *Yes, I remember! We took off from Kingman at about 2100 hours and were in the air about twenty minutes.* Pete set his watch to twenty-one-thirty. He now had a plan and was ready to put it into action. He looked up at the captain. "Captain, in thirty minutes I want you to radio base and request another chopper. Have them send extra crew to help you fly this one back. I can't explain now, but Dr. Ahearn and I need to get as far away from this craft as we can. We need to disappear into the cover of darkness. Give us a half hour before making the call to the base. Set your watch to twenty-one-thirty and make your call to the base at 2200 hours."

"Yes, sir ... but, Colonel, why don't you both just climb back in. We can fly this thing back to base. It's only about an hour and a half away. I don't understand." The captain was still shaken.

"No, that won't work. I can't explain now. Hand me those night vision goggles and shut down your engines." Pete knew he was asking the captain to become bait as they made their escape, but it was necessary.

"Yes, sir." The captain handed the goggles to Pete and began shutting down the engines. He was not aware of his fate.

Pete turned the goggles on and held them to his eyes. "They work fine now. How long will they operate on battery power?" He tried not to show the emotion that was welling up within him.

"Ten to fifteen hours on a fresh battery pack."

"May I have your flashlight, Captain?" He said in a commanding voice.

"Yes, sir ... here," Captain Herber said as he handed Pete the flashlight and finished shutting down the engines.

Pete reached into the vest pocket of his flight jacket, retrieved a map, and opened it under the light of the flashlight. He studied the map and then pulled his GPS out of another pocket. He turned it on and waited as it acquired some satellites.

"What are our coordinates according to the chopper's GPS, Captain?" he asked, calmly.

"North thirty-five degrees and forty-five minutes. West one fourteen degrees and eleven point five minutes," the captain called out.

"Check," Pete said as he replaced the GPS in his pocket. "Captain, do you have some water rations we can take?"

Captain Herber pulled out a canteen from under his seat and handed it to Pete. "Here you are, sir. Do you think they'll be back?" The captain asked, nervously.

"Who?"

"Them!" the captain said, pointing toward the sky.

"No, I think they're done with us." Pete lied. "Thanks for everything, Captain. Tell the acting base commander, Colonel Weir, *not* to send out a search and rescue party. That's important. I'll explain later. We'll be okay. Tell him I'll contact him later." Pete folded his map and walked quickly around to where Wendy, still in a state of shock, was leaning against the open chopper door.

"Are we ready to leave now, Pete? This place gives me the willies." Wendy stared at the drying blood on Pete's temple visible by the glow of the chopper's cockpit lights.

"Yes, we're ready. Let's get started. We have a long walk. Here, take the canteen."

"Walk! You mean the helicopter is not able to fly?"

Pete gave a commanding stare into her eyes that she saw, even in the faint light. "It can . . . but we can't. We need to put distance between it and us. We don't have much time. I'll explain as we travel. Let's get going," he commanded. Wendy knew it was not the time to question Pete.

He donned the Cyclops-looking goggles and took her hand. "Let's go," he commanded, as they rounded to the pilot's side of the craft and headed east into the dark, away from the safety of the chopper.

The captain watched as the two started jogging toward the low mountains in the east. Within minutes, they were swallowed by the night.

Chapter 3
Where Am I?

The last thing Corey remembered was reaching out to wrap his arms around Colonel Andrews as he made a flying tackle. Suddenly, the world turned a blinding blue-white and he could no longer see. Unable to withstand Corey's momentum, the colonel's leg buckled and he went flying backward with Corey's arms locked around him. They landed with a soft thud as Corey's body pinned the colonel's. Corey felt the warmth of the colonel's body beneath him as he regained consciousness.

"You're not getting away this time, Colonel," Corey groaned, still blinded. The colonel didn't answer as Corey straddled him, belly to belly. Corey pushed up with both hands to lift his chest from the colonel's and as he did, he felt lighter and could feel the smoothness of floor. *Smooth floor!* Corey thought. *I'm in the desert, the desert isn't smooth! Why do I feel so light?*

He shook his head to try and regain his sight. All he could see was the colonel under him and white all around him. He shook his head again to clear his vision. Corey looked at the colonel but there wasn't any movement. Concern overcame him. "Colonel, are you okay?" No response. He placed his hand on the colonel's carotid artery to feel for a pulse. There was one! Corey, breathing easier now, rolled off and sat up.

Gradually the room took on some definition. It was square, about eight feet on a side. The walls transitioned to both the floor and the ceiling with what looked like a three-inch radius. All the surfaces were smoothly blended together as though the room had been molded in one piece. The walls had a soft glow and appeared to have an eggshell texture. The ceiling seemed almost too low for Corey to stand in. He looked around. *There are no doors! How did we get in here?* "Colonel, wake up!" he shouted as he shook him.

"Ohooo . . . waaa . . . whooo . . . ahhhh," the colonel moaned, as he lay on his back and reached for his head.

"Colonel, wake up. Something strange has happened. Wake up. Do you hear me?" Corey's anger toward the colonel waned as he realized they both were now victims.

The colonel rubbed his eyes and rolled over to face Corey. Staring up at him, he tried to regain his senses. "Where are we? This isn't the desert."

"I'm not sure. You tell me where we are. The last thing I remember is taking a flying leap to tackle you. There was this blinding light and here we are. "

Andrews rubbed his eyes again and sat up. He looked around. He remembered now. "Oh, I think we're in an alien ship," he groaned.

"Alien ship!" Corey choked. "What do you mean, alien ship!?"

"Alien ship, alien ship. You know what I mean, Dr. Newton!"

"But, how could this happen?" Corey's mind reeled with intense excitement that ran the gamut between terror and joyous excitement.

"I was supposed to meet them at the old crash site but you got there first and captured me. Remember!" The colonel grew angry as he recalled that his plan had been foiled. "This craft followed us and brought the chopper down at an opportune time. They waited until we were away from civilization. I could see them following us as I looked out the window of our chopper. Didn't you see it?"

"No. It was too dark out," Corey said, as his eyes continued to scan the room.

"Well, Dr. Newton, it looks like you're the one who's captured now," the colonel smirked. Don't worry, they won't hurt you. However, had we made it back to base, I'm sure Colonel Mitchell would not have been as kind to me. He would have felt it his duty to get information from me, no matter how much pain he needed to inflict. I know the procedures. He would just be doing what he was trained to do," Colonel Andrews said sarcastically.

Corey looked at the duffle bag the colonel began clutching. Anger welled up within him. "Colonel, what do you plan to do with that?"

"Give it back," the colonel said matter-of-factly with a tone of satisfaction.

"You can't," Corey said, with an impassioned plea.

Colonel Andrews stared at Corey and smiled. "Of course I can and you will be my witness."

"Don't you realize that by giving that back to the aliens, you ruin any chance we have of finding out what they're up to? We'll have no chance to gain an understanding of their culture or their technology."

Colonel Andrews shook his head. "We aren't ready for their technology. I don't think you realize what a favor I've actually done for humanity." He pointed toward the duffel bag and with an ever increasing voice he continued with conviction. "World leaders would have used this to gain power. In the process, they would have destroyed the earth. I *had* to take it before it was too late.

Corey suddenly heard a slight whooshing sound behind him. He turned to see a portion of the wall open to form a doorway. The colonel stood up and faced the door as though expecting someone to appear. His head was only an inch from the ceiling. Corey jumped to his feet and went into a half crouch position so his head wouldn't hit the ceiling. He turned to face the door. Within moments, a small figure less than four feet tall appeared and stared at both men. It said nothing. It wasn't human!

Corey was startled at first and turned to the colonel in disbelief, his mouth gaping. *That thing looks familiar,* Corey thought. *I saw one in the specimen tank back at base. Pete called it a Gray. This one is alive!*

"Colonel, it's a . . . "

"I know, a Gray," the colonel said before Corey could finish. "It came to get me. Your presence surprised it. It didn't expect to see you here and is not sure what to do with you. Don't worry, it won't hurt you." The colonel looked at the Gray and for a long moment they just stared at each other. Then the Gray turned back and the door closed without leaving a trace. There was no visible seam around the area that had been a door. It just vanished. The colonel turned to Corey. "It wants us to wait here until we get to the mother ship on the back side of the moon. We'll be there in about forty-five minutes."

"How do you know that?"

"The Gray told me that telepathically," the colonel answered. His face was expressionless.

"What do you think will happen when we get there?" Corey asked, with concern. The colonel was on their team and he wasn't.

Colonel Andrews sensed Corey's apprehension. "After I give back the artifact, they'll probably want to question you to find out what you already know." Andrews could see Corey's face grow tense. "Dr. Newton, I assure you they won't harm you in any way. When they're done, we both will be returned to Earth with a memory block. We won't remember anything that happened after our chopper was forced down in the desert."

"Well, that's comforting," Corey said sarcastically. "Never mind that I'll have to watch as you hand the artifact over to the aliens." Corey stared at the colonel for a long moment and then glanced at the duffel bag. "Aren't you worried about what the aliens plan for humanity?"

"Worried? No, should I be?"

"It's Colonel Mitchell's assessment that they might be planning an invasion or something? If you give that back, we'll have no way to know in advance." Corey's eyes were pleading with Andrews.

"What makes him think they're planning an invasion?" The colonel looked at Corey with an expression of incredulity.

"Well, perhaps not an invasion as we know it, Colonel. But aren't you up to date on what abductees are reporting?"

"What *are* they saying?" The colonel said, as he tried to lead Corey down a path of self-discovery.

"Come now, you must be up on this?"

"I believe I am but why don't you tell me what *you* think abductees are saying."

"Okay." Corey hesitated as his eyes scanned the ceiling and he formulated his response. "Under hypnosis, many abductees report that the aliens will disclose themselves soon and make formal contact with us." He pointed toward the duffle bag. "Dr. Ahearn has been able to activate the artifact. She has discovered that by the time disclosure occurs, alien hybrids will be in positions of authority."

Colonel Andrews laughed. "So do you think these hybrids are plotting to take over the Earth?"

"No, from what I understand, they're not aware of being hybrids so they're not plotting anything. However, Dr. Ahearn's finding is that, due to their unique skills, they're now moving into high positions. At the right time, they'll be awakened and informed of their mission. Then, the hybrids will act under the direction of the aliens and unite the world in one world order."

"Is that bad?"

"From what Dr. Ahearn has learned, we will have to fall into step with the alien way of thinking. We will have no choice but to obey since we'll have no defensive technology that can match their weapons. According to Colonel Mitchell, the bottom line is that we'll become their slaves." Corey raised his voice. "Shouldn't that concern you?"

Again, the colonel laughed. "That's a pretty pessimistic view of things. You say that Dr. Ahearn was told all of that?"

"Well … I don't think she was told that. Somehow she got that information from the artifact. That's her understanding. It doesn't matter how she found out. Don't you see, if you give back the artifact, we'll have no way to know," Corey pleaded. "We will not be able to learn more about the aliens."

"Look at the good side. Consider the social benefits when we *are* under one world government. Think of the wonderful technology the aliens will share with us." The colonel's voice grew louder with each sentence he spoke. "Don't you think it's time someone stepped in to keep us from destroying our planet? Don't you think it's time we got some *real* leadership? Our present world leaders only care for themselves and their own pocketbooks. You know that. Economics rule." Andrews waived his arms in disgust. "To hell with the planet and its future."

"Come on, Colonel, I think you're being naïve. Give humanity more credit than that. No one wants to destroy our own planet."

Andrews' brow furrowed. "That's right, no one *wants* to destroy the planet. Human ignorance and passion will destroy the planet. It will be human ignorance of the consequences of their actions and their passion to destroy one another. That's what will destroy the planet." He looked at Corey and shook his head. "The aliens are not ignorant and they do not let passion rule their behavior. They do not have wars that unleash nuclear weapons upon one another to create wholesale slaughter of their own kind and to contaminate the environment. They do not threaten the world's environment by burning thousands of square miles of rainforest every year in the name of *progress*." Andrews paused in his ranting and then, suddenly, smiled at Corey. "Dr. Newton, you are a very highly educated man. You might even be a genius. Do *you* have a plan to lead us away from this path of self destruction?"

Corey shook his head. "No, but today the public is being made aware of the damage we're doing to the environment. More and more scientists are starting to point out the consequences of what we are doing. The world governments will have to listen."

Andrews laughed in disgust. "Come now, Dr. Newton, you know our government will only listen to the scientists who propose plans that are good for short term economics, those that make the politicians look good during their reign. They won't listen to scientists who say we're destroying the environment. Don't forget, the politicians are financed by the same industries that are destroying out planet. Dr. Newton, wake up!"

Corey gave Andrews a hard stare. "Colonel, I guess I have more faith in humanity than you. I truly believe that, long term, the people *will* listen to the scientists and force world leaders to take action."

"That's wishful thinking and time is running out," Andrews rebutted. "Long term ... you say. Will we even have a planet worth living on ... long term?" Andrews began shaking his head. "The information needed for people to make an informed decision is being suppressed every day by the governing powers."

"Colonel, I believe in the power of the media. I'm firmly convinced that world-wide communications will bring us closer together on the important environmental issues."

"Now who's being naïve?" Andrews said, as he eyed Corey. "The media report what they are told to. Surely you must realize that newspapers, radio, and television are being controlled by only a very few people. These people have gained such power that the United States' government stands back and allows the small guys in the news media to be swallowed up by a few giant corporations. Today, it's only a few people at the head of those giant media corporations who decide what the people will read, hear, or see."

Corey knew he was loosing ground in this debate. He had to retrench. "We will eventually work out our own solutions to our problems," He insisted. "I'm afraid that the price for the aliens' help in our problems just might be too high. From the way Dr. Ahearn explains it, we could become enslaved," Corey fired back.

"Enslaved? That's a pretty charged word. A leadership that makes decisions for the good of humankind and the planet instead of themselves would not enslave you. You will always have free will." Andrews smiled with confidence as he knew he was winning.

"Look, Colonel, surely you have to agree there is a chance that once they take over, the aliens could do whatever they wanted to do, despite promises to the contrary. We would have no way to stop them."

"Sure, that's possible but I don't think it will happen because it hasn't happened yet and they've been around longer than we have."

"Well, I for one don't want to risk that," Corey said. "*We* need to be in control of our *own* destiny."
Colonel Andrews winced as the pain in his leg returned. "Well, I find it difficult to carry on this enlightening conversation," he said sarcastically. "You have to do what you have to do and I have to do what I have to do." He stared at Corey. "I believe it was George Orwell who said, 'In a time of universal deceit, telling the truth becomes a revolutionary act.'" With that, Andrews fell silent as he rubbed his leg.

The two men sat quietly, facing one another for the remainder of the trip.

***

Hisss-swish.

Corey turned to face the sound as once again the door appeared in the blank wall. The Gray appeared in the doorway and stared at the colonel for a long moment and then left. The door closed behind him.

"What was that all about? What did he tell you this time?" Corey asked.

"He wants us to move out of the center of the room and over against the wall, right away."

"Why?" Corey asked as he went over to the wall.

"We have reached the mother craft and are entering the ship's hanger. Once inside, the floor will open to provide an exit."

Neither had detected any movement of the craft since waking up. They only noticed what appeared to be a reduced force of gravity. Yet, without any sensation of motion, they had accelerated out of the Earth's atmosphere, traveled to the moon, and docked with the mother ship. No sooner had both men reached the wall when there was a further reduction in the gravitational force. With a hiss, like a truck releasing its air brakes, a rectangular opening appeared in the floor. One end of the rectangle dropped down to form a gangway to the level below. The colonel grabbed the duffel bag and quickly disappeared down the ramp. Corey hesitated but then followed. He had to adjust his walk to compensate for the reduced gravity. *We're on the moon!* He thought. *Gravity is only one sixth of the Earth's.* Corey remembered seeing videos of astronauts walking on the moon. Without effort, they could almost glide over the surface, even with heavy space suits and backpacks. He knew he would have to make adjustments in how he walked.

As he exited the craft down the ramp, Corey almost shot across the walkway at the end of the ramp. He was surrounded by a blue-grey fog that had a strange citrus odor. Within seconds the fog disappeared and he saw his surroundings. They were in what appeared to be a very large hangar. The walls were all white and blended with the floor as he had noticed in the smaller craft. He glanced to his left. Twenty feet away, the colonel was being greeted by a tall human form. *A human!* Corey thought. *What's a human doing here?*

"Colonel Andrews, welcome aboard. I see you brought an unexpected guest," the tall human form said, as he touched Andrews' hand and pointed toward Corey.

He speaks English! Corey suddenly realized. The human form was a handsome blond man about six foot-three with a muscular build. He had the same determined chin as Corey but with high cheekbones. He had a subtle smile that seemed frozen on his face. His complexion was perfect and his skin was as smooth and unwrinkled as that of a teenager. The wisdom in his face made Corey guess that the Nordic-looking man was in his mid-forties. He wore a collarless gold colored single-piece suit that glistened in the diffuse light.

The colonel led the stranger over to Corey.

"Quellin," Andrews said, "this is Dr. Newton. He's part of the team that activated the communicator."

As they approached, Quellin's face suddenly broke into a broad smile. Corey was taken aback as the man bowed slightly and extended his hand toward Corey. As he reached out with his unusually long arms, Quellin touched the palm of Corey's hand. "I am very pleased to meet you, Dr. Newton. We were not expecting you to accompany Colonel Andrews, but since you have . . . welcome. I see you are adjusting to the reduced gravity here on the moon. Soon it will seem normal to you." Quellin stared directly into Corey's eyes. "Do not be afraid, we will not harm you."

Corey reluctantly shook his hand as he eyed the stranger. *Unusual dark blue eyes*, he thought, as the stranger's eyes bore into him.

"From what I understand, you are part of a team put together to activate and translate our communicating device. You are working with Dr. Ahearn, who I understand is a linguist. Is that correct?" Quellin asked.

"Yes," Corey answered hesitantly, "but how did . . . ?"

"Colonel Andrews is aware of your activities," Quellin interrupted. "He *is* the base commander." Quellin leaned closer to Corey and stared into his eyes with a smile. Corey had an uneasy sense that his brain was being turned inside out.

"Please don't do that," Corey snapped as he leaned away. He did not like this man; he was too perfect.

"I'm sorry," Quellin said, apologetically. "It is a bad habit of mine but I find it is the quickest way to understand humans."

"So, what else do you know about me?"

"I know you are a brilliant man with an extreme curiosity and passion about what we do and how our craft work. I know that you are employed by a firm called, I believe, GraviDyne and that you are trying to develop field propulsion drive." Quellin studied Corey for a moment. "Dr. Newton, I want to assure you that you are correct in your assessment of our propulsion system. It is a field drive. In fact, we use both positive and negative fields, depending on the situation. I will explain more about our system later. I thought you might like to take a tour when Colonel Andrews and I are done with business."

Corey was taken aback momentarily by the depth of information this man had and his kindness. He smiled, "That would be very nice, Mr. Quellin. I'll probably have a lot of questions."

"And I will try to answer as many as I can."

"And, what else do you know about me?" Corey was curious about just how much Quellin knew.

"I know that, because of your passion for UFOs, as you call our craft, you were hired for a special project at the secret base. You are to do a technical interpretation of whatever Dr. Ahearn discovers when she translates our communicator. I also sense that you have developed strong feelings for Dr. Ahearn. I believe that her first name is Wendy. Shall I go on?"

"No, you seem well informed," Corey answered. "How do you know all of that?"

"For now, let me just say it is a gift I have."

"Dr. Newton," Colonel Andrews said, with a smile, "Quellin can read your thoughts."

"Yes, yes that is true," Quellin agreed. "But let us not stand here any longer. Come, we will find a place to sit and talk." Quellin turned to Colonel Andrews. "I trust you brought the communicator?"

"Yes. I have it here," Andrews said as he held up the duffel bag.

"Good." Quellin noticed Colonel Andrews' bloody pant leg. A look of concern came over him. "Colonel, are you wounded?"

"Slightly, I hurt my leg when I crash landed the plane I was flying. It is not a serious wound. I'm sure I'll survive."

"We will take care of your leg before you return to Earth. Will you be able to walk for a while?"

"Sure, this reduced gravity helps a lot," Andrews assured him.

Quellin smiled. "Good. Then would you two gentlemen please follow me to our conference room." He turned and led the two men down a narrow passage and through what appeared to be an airlock. They followed him from there down a hallway and past several doors. At one of the doors he stopped, raised his hand, and placed it near a small patch at the side of the door. The door in front of him slid open into the wall, revealing a small windowless room about twelve feet wide and eight feet deep. As Corey followed the two into the room, he noticed this room was similar to the small room in the other craft except that the ceilings appeared to be higher. He guessed they were perhaps seven feet high. The walls were blended into the floor and ceiling as in the other craft. These walls, however, were a plain pastel color. As Corey scanned the room, he noticed that the walls gradually changed colors. *Beautiful,* Corey thought. In the center of the room was a small table with three chairs on each side.

"Gentlemen, have a seat," Quellin said, pointing to two chairs on the back side of the table.

"By the way, Dr. Newton, you can drop the mister and just call me Quellin. We do not go by mister here."

"Oh, sure, I'm sorry. I didn't think," Corey said, feeling foolish about his presumption.

"That is quite all right. I understand." Quellin smiled and then turned to Andrews. "Colonel Andrews, I would like to compliment you on recovering the communicator for us. As you know, we have been waiting for years for it to be activated so we could track it down. It should have been taken to your base along with the damaged craft, back in 1953. It is unfortunate that it was hidden by the American officer. As you realize, it could present many problems for us if it fell into the wrong hands. May I see it please?"

"What do you consider the wrong hands?" Corey asked.

Quellin turned his stare toward Corey. "The wrong hands would be those who wish us harm. It also would be those to whom harm would come if they misused the information acquired through the communicator."

That's interesting, Corey thought. "So, you have enemies?" he asked sarcastically.

"Indeed," Quellin said as a strange smile appeared on his face. "As you will learn soon enough, we have *common* enemies." He looked at Colonel Andrews. "May I see it now?" he said, with a degree of impatience.

Colonel Andrews set the duffel bag on the table and opened it so Quellin could see inside. "There it is," the colonel said, watching Quellin's face for an anticipated smile. Instead, a puzzled expression appeared as Quellin reached inside and extracted a rock the size of a large potato. He held it up and examined it as he turned it in his hands.

"Colonel Andrews, this does not look like any communicator I am aware of," Quellin said, as his brow folded into deep wrinkles.

Colonel Andrews' face became pale. "Quellin, I, I'm sorry, Colonel Mitchell must have switched the communicator with that stone when I wasn't looking."

"Way to go, Pete," Corey said softly to himself as a broad smile stretched across his face.

Chapter 4
Head for the Hills

Pete drew to a halt and looked back at the helicopter through his Cyclops goggles. The craft was now five hundred yards to the west. The twin-engine tailpipes were a brilliant green glow even though the engines were not running. He could clearly make out Captain Herber, who glowed from his own body heat. "I'm sorry, Captain, but this is the way it has to be," Pete said softly under his breath. "You have to be the sacrificial lamb." He took off the Cyclops goggles and the helicopter was barely visible in the darkness. The silhouette of the craft was faint in the green light from the glow stick.

"Wendy, this is far enough." He was breathing hard. "We need to head south-west now."

"Pete, I still don't understand why we had to abandon the helicopter if it's flyable. What are we doing running around in the desert in the middle of the night? I almost tripped over some rocks twice. It's dangerous out here."

"We have to because they'll be coming to get us soon." Pete's voice was strained.

"I know. You told the captain to order a rescue chopper. So why didn't we just stay with the craft. This seems silly . . . and dangerous," Wendy complained.

"Wendy, it's not the rescue chopper who's coming to get us," Pete said in a tone of frustration. "It's the alien craft that will be returning to get us! We have to get out of the open and quickly!" Pete said, as he placed the night vision goggles back on his head.

"Why would the aliens want to come back and get *us*?" Wendy questioned. She paused and thought for a moment. "They got what they were after didn't they?" She asked in a concerned voice.

"No, what you saw was Corey and the colonel, carrying the duffle bag, being beamed up into the craft. The duffle bag did not contain the artifact. I did a switch earlier. They have a rock and I have the device, here," Pete said, with a satisfying smile as he patted the breast pocket of his flight jacket. "I switched it with a rock when no one was watching."

Wendy held her hands up to her face in horror. "Oh my God! You're right! They *will* be back, just as soon as they discover it's not in the bag."

"That's right, they'll track down the chopper again and if it were in the air they would force it down, again. We might not survive that crash. That's why I didn't want to chance flying back to the base." He looked back toward the craft again. It was still glowing a bright green as it gave off heat visible through Pete's goggles. Captain Herber was still sitting at the controls and appeared to be on the radio. "He'll be making the call back to the base soon. It's safer for Captain Herber if he's sitting on the ground when they come back."

"What will they do to him?" Wendy asked with concern.

"I'm hoping they won't harm him but I'm sure, somehow, they'll find out what they want from him. In fact, I'm counting on it."

Wendy's concern grew. "What do you mean? Do you think they'll torture the pilot to make him talk?"

"I don't know but I'm sure they have ways to get the information they want," Pete assured her. I expect him to tell them that we headed out on foot going toward those low mountains in the east." Pete pointed toward the mountains, forgetting that Wendy could not see in the darkness. "That's why we're going to head south-west now. We're far enough away so he won't see us change direction. What he doesn't know, he can't tell them," Pete said with satisfaction as he made a ninety-degree turn to the right. He looked south through the night vision goggles. In the distance, just to the southwest, he could see an outcropping of rocky hills. "I checked the map before we left the chopper. There's a dirt road just south of here that leads through that outcropping of mountains about three miles to the south-west of us." He pointed into the darkness, again, forgetting that Wendy was blinded by the darkness. "That should give us cover."

Wendy held up her hand. She couldn't see her hand in front of her, let alone Pete's hand pointing south. "It's pitch black, so I'm not sure where you're pointing."

"Oh, I'm sorry. Trust me though, the mountains are there."

"How do you think they'll try to track us, body heat?"

"Yes, we'll be conspicuous by our body heat when they search for us with their infrared sensors. Just as I can see with these night vision goggles, they probably can see everything that's warmer than the surrounding terrain. We'll shine like a light bulb." Pete looked at Wendy and had to squint. "Your body heat makes you so bright it's almost painful to look at you through these glasses."

"So, how can we hide?" Wendy's concern grew.

"I know you can't see them, but there are mountains ahead of us and to the right. My plan is to get ourselves into those mountains as quickly as we can," Pete said as he pointed south again. "These goggles have only enough battery power for a few hours or so. I want to be hiding in those mountains before the power gives out. We'll have to continue running at a fast jog. Are you up for it?"

"Yes, I've been keeping up so far despite the fact that I can't see. I follow the sound of your foot falls."

"Stay close behind me. I'll be the eyes for both of us. The road is just south of us about a mile. It'll be easier going, once we reach the road."

"Is it a paved road?"

"No, it's dirt but much smoother and not covered by rocks. I think it's probably an old mining road. There are lots of old mines around here. If I knew where one was, I'd take us there to hide. Since I don't, we'll take the road that leads to a pass through the mountains about four miles away. I'm hoping we can hide there," he explained. Pete took a deep breath. "Are you ready?"

"Yes, let's get out of here," Wendy said in a frightened tone, as she took a deep breath.

"Let's go," Pete commanded.

* * *

Captain Herber sat at the controls of his Huey staring out through the windshield. His eyes were unfocused as he began to formulate how he would report today's mission. How would he explain the abduction of the base commander and a scientist by a UFO? And, just as strange, why did the colonel and the other scientist run off into the desert? He looked at his watch as he saw the faint star to the north of him grow brighter. "They made good time. It's been only an hour since I called for a backup chopper," he said softly to himself with satisfaction.

He switched on his NAV lights. The strobe light would provide a beacon so they could spot him easier. The craft danced strangely over the peaks of the mountains to the north and grew larger and brighter as it approached. Captain Herber strained to hear the familiar chopper sound. Normally the upwind rotor blades create the familiar sound of shock waves as they break the sound barrier during fast forward speed. Within a few seconds the approaching light had loomed to resemble a small moon. The captain still could not hear the familiar beating sound of helicopter blades. There was only silence. Something was not right. As the light approached, its disk shape was almost too bright to look at.

"What the hell ... that's not a ... !" he yelled. Captain Herber realized that what he was looking at was not a helicopter but it was too late.

* * *

"This is it, Wendy," Pete said in between gasps for breath. It had been years since Pete did a four-mile run. At forty-six, he was in good health but not the same excellent shape he had been in his younger days when he used to do five mile runs every morning. He stopped running and began a fast walk. Using the night goggles, Pete had followed the dirt road as it bent around to the right. Just as Pete had guessed, it led to a pass in the rocky hills that now blocked his view of the chopper to the north. Wendy followed closely behind, led as much by Pete's foot falls as by the dim vision she had of him in the darkness. Pete came to an abrupt halt, and Wendy, unable to see, crashed into him.

"Sorry, Wendy, I should have warned you I was stopping," Pete apologized as he surveyed the terrain through his goggles. The road now branched off and made a sharp turn to the left as it headed toward two large mounds of boulders. Pete had stopped at the fork. "This road leads all the way through the pass," he said, pointing straight ahead, forgetting again that Wendy could not see. "If we continued straight, when we come out on the other side, we'll be only about fifteen miles from US Route 93. From there we can head north to Hoover Dam or south to Kingman."

"I thought we were going to hide out in the mountains," Wendy said.

"Yes, we are. We'll decide whether to go north or south tomorrow. For now, let's take this fork to the left and hide up in the mound of boulders at the end of the road." Pete knew Wendy couldn't see what he was talking about but wanted to give her a sense of where she was. "We'll climb up into those rocks and hide in a crevasse or cave, if we can find one. We'll spend the night there and make it out to the highway during daylight."

"Won't they be able to track our body heat tomorrow?"

"Our body heat won't be as conspicuous during the day."

"Your plan sounds fine to me," Wendy said, her voice quivered. "I'm right behind you. Let's go. I'm getting nervous."

Within a few minutes they were at the rocky mound and Pete found a natural cave formed by a pile of boulders that had fallen down the ravine side of the small mountain. Slowly, Wendy followed Pete as they climbed up the rocks and into the cave. "I'll make sure the place is clear of scorpions. We'll stay here tonight," Pete said.

"Scorpions! Great!" Wendy said sarcastically. I definitely did not sign on for this," she complained.

"No one ever said life was easy," Pete countered philosophically, as he surveyed the cave with satisfaction. "They could fly directly over us and still not see our body heat. We're protected by that overhanging ledge rock." He arched his arm over her head and touched the ledge hanging over them.

"I guess this is a good place if you say so," Wendy agreed, as she felt her way around. "You're sure there are no scorpions?"

"Yes, now stay here, I want to climb to the top of this mountain and take a peek back toward the chopper," Pete said, as he left the security of the small cave and began climbing.

"You won't be gone long, will you?" Wendy yelled out, with a tremor in her voice.

"No, not long. I just want to make sure our alien friends take the bait and head east," Pete reassured Wendy.

Within five minutes Pete reached the top and slowly raised his head above the boulder he was behind. Cautiously, peering through the night vision goggles, he began searching the horizon to the north-east. The green glow of the chopper's tail pipes could be seen less than four miles away. Even brighter was the blinking strobe light. Suddenly, a chill went down Pete's spine. Sitting next to the chopper was a disk-shaped object just like the one that had taken Corey and the colonel. He could only imagine what Captain Herber must be going through. Pete knew it was only a matter of minutes before the alien's search for him and Wendy would begin.

Pete's frozen stare was locked on the scene playing out three miles away. He was replaying the escape he and Wendy had made from the chopper. Retracing their path, first to the east of the chopper and then to the south-west. Then it dawned on him. He visualized in his mind, green-glowing footprints leading from the chopper to their hiding place. "I hope to God the heat from our footprints is gone or we're in deep trouble! They'll find us for sure," Pete said to himself under his breath. He continued to watch as the disk began glowing and then lifted off, heading easterly at a low altitude. "Keep going, baby. Don't stop," he said to the craft through his pursed lips. It continued moving eastward, slowly. Then it stopped a few hundred yards from the chopper! Pete could feel his heart pounding as his carotid arteries in his neck began throbbing. He watched more intently now as the craft began a slow circle, heading to the south, right toward him and Wendy! "Oh shit!" Pete watched as it hesitated and then continued in a tight circle, going completely around the chopper. Then, suddenly, the menacing disc streaked off to the mountains in the east.

Pete let his breath out slowly with a sigh of relief. The disk was much smaller now but still visible as he watched it searching the mountains in the distance. An occasional shaft of light beamed down from the distant craft, lighting up the side of the mountain like a silent lightning storm. He watched until he was certain the alien's search would be futile.

* * *

"What did you see? Wendy asked, as Pete climbed back into the cave. "You were gone for a long time. I was beginning to worry that something had happened to you."

"No, nothing happened to me. I was watching our alien friends searching for us," Pete said, as he took off the night vision goggles.

"They came back!"

"Yes, and they stopped by the chopper for a while, just as I thought they might. Then they took off and headed east, toward the mountains," Pete said, with a smile. "They took the bait."

"Good, I guess we gave them the slip," Wendy said, as she relaxed against a wall of the cave.

"Yes, I was afraid they might be able to see the heat from our footprints, but apparently our footprints have cooled enough to become undetectable. Also, it appears that they can't home in on the artifact," said Pete.

"That's an interesting point," Wendy said. "I hadn't thought of that. Apparently, they can only detect the artifact when it's activated. Otherwise, they would have known it was not in the duffel bag."

"Good point."

"You said the general who found the device was able to keep it hidden for over fifty years. He never activated it. Two days ago, we activate it, and it was taken from us."

"Yes, that's true." Pete thought for a moment. "You realize that creates a dilemma for us, don't you?"

"That's right," Wendy agreed. "We have a device that may offer us the only hope for survival from an alien invasion. But, unfortunately, to use it, we have to activate it. If we activate it, they will find us."

"Exactly," Pete said. "I agree with your logic. So, what do we do?"

"Yes, precisely the same question I have."

Pete leaned against a large boulder that formed one side of the cave. "First off, I think we should only return to base if we have a good reason. Based on the past few days' experience, there is no doubt in my mind that the base has been infiltrated by aliens or their agents. The President warned me about that. I think Colonel Andrews might be one of their agents."

"I agree," Wendy said. "I'm not sure I want to return. Actually, there is no reason to return other than to view their craft or other alien artifacts and that's only if I really need to."

Pete thought for a moment. "I think we should keep on the move. When we're ready to activate the device, we should activate it for only short periods of time and then quickly move to a new location."

"What about finding an underground facility that will shield the device from the alien's detectors?" Wendy wondered, out loud.

"I'm not sure being underground will help. Remember, we were in a well fortified top secret base buried within a mountain and somehow they knew we had activated the device."

"Yes, but perhaps the colonel had some type of tracking system that allowed him to sense the artifact when it was turned on. If that's true, then being underground might help."

"Perhaps, but I don't think so. Don't forget, based on your research, Corey determined that the signals from the device were able to pass through the mountain, go all the way to the moon, come back, and pass through the mountain again."

"Yes, that's true," Wendy said, in a trailing voice. She stared out into the darkness. Thoughts of Corey entered her mind now. It was Corey, she remembered, who had figured out that the signal was being relayed from the moon. While they were both aboard the wrecked alien craft back at the base they discovered that the control panel of the craft seemed to respond to key strokes on the artifact. But, there was a time lag. It was Corey who did the calculations and determined that the time lag in the signal represented the distance to the moon. He's the one who concluded the aliens might have a base on the moon.

After a long silence she asked, "Pete, do you think Corey is okay? You don't think the aliens would harm him?" There was another along silence.

"Wendy, I think Corey's okay, but are *you* okay?"

"Waa … Ohhh … Sure. I'm okay. I was just wondering how Corey's doing."

"Well, I know Corey can handle himself in any situation. He's not going to take any guff from anyone, including aliens. He's also smart. His boss at GraviDyne thinks he's a genius. He thinks Corey can walk on water. I think you knew he has been trying to develop gravity drive. He's convinced that the UFOs use gravity as a means of propulsion. Now that he's aboard their craft, he'll have a chance to learn more about their propulsion system. This could turn out to be one of the best things to have happened to him. I'm sure he'll make the most of it."

"What good will that knowledge do if they don't release him … or worse … harm him?" Wendy's voice cracked.

Pete couldn't see the tears streaming down her cheeks, but could tell by her voice that she was crying. He tried desperately to reassure her. "Wendy, from all that I have read about UFOs, and believe me I have read plenty lately, the aliens have never harmed anyone other than, perhaps, in self-defense. And even in those situations, they choose simply to disarm or immobilize their attackers."

"Corey would never attack anyone with the intent to harm them," Wendy said, trying to rationalize Corey's safety.

"Well then, there you go. I truly believe he will be released unharmed when the aliens realize he is of no use to them. Probably he will have no memory of ever being abducted. They seem to have a way to block certain memories."

"I hope you're right," Wendy said sadly.

Pete decided to get Wendy's mind out of her depressed mood by changing the subject. "Do you know how UFOs can cloak themselves?"

"No."

"Well, Corey explained it to me. He said they surround themselves in a magnetic field which acts like a lens that then directs the background light from behind the UFO and around to the front. That makes them invisible . . . they're cloaked. He also explained that they change colors because of the synchrotron radiation given off by the electrons flowing in the superconducting skin of the craft. I tell you, the man is brilliant."

"You don't have to convince me of that," Wendy said, with a whimsical laugh.

"He also warned me," Pete continued, "Radiation given off by UFOs can be extremely harmful.

"Why is that?"

My strategy was working, Pete thought. *She's getting out of her dark mood.* He continued. "UFOs can be harmful because the radiation they give off runs the entire spectrum, including x-rays and gamma radiation which can be lethal if you are near them too long when they're operating."

"Yes, now that you mention it, I do remember Corey telling us about that when we were examining the craft."

Wendy could not see the smile of admiration on Pete's face as he continued to praise Corey. "I couldn't have asked for a better team member than Corey. He is like a walking encyclopedia when it comes to UFOs. He even explained how UFOs can do high rates of acceleration without harming the occupants." Pete paused for a long moment. "I guess we both agree ... Corey is truly brilliant."

"I agree," Wendy said, "I think he's wonderful."

"I've noticed. You two have a thing going." Pete hesitated but then continued. "Aren't you concerned that he may have a girlfriend back in Boston?" He was not sure if he should pursue that issue further but continued anyway. "His doctorate in astrophysics is from MIT and GraviDyne is just down the road from there. He's been there long enough to have an established relationship. He is a very eligible bachelor you know."

"Yes, he is very eligible but we've had some time to talk and I know he doesn't have anyone back in Boston. He was engaged though."

"Oh, I didn't know that." Pete was caught off guard. He thought he had a complete file on Corey. There was nothing in it about his engagement. "What ended his engagement?"

"His fiancé drowned tragically while they were out sailing together."

"Oh, what happened?" Pete asked.

"They were sailing and the boat was capsized by a wind gust. He blames himself for her death. He thinks he should have recognized the unsafe wind condition. Ever since the accident, he has avoided developing new relationships. I told him that he shouldn't blame himself for that. I said he should move on with his life. I think he's beginning to realize that." Wendy's voice trailed off.

"You're absolutely right, Wendy, we have to move on with our lives," Pete agreed. His mind faded back to his own tragic loss. *Such a senseless murder,* he thought to himself with remorse. "We have to move on," he repeated. "Anyway, don't worry about Corey. I don't think they'll harm him. He can take care of himself. He's probably in seventh heaven; like a kid in a candy store, surrounded with all of the advanced technology they're probably showing him," Pete said, in an effort to calm Wendy.

Wendy smiled, "Yes, I think you're right. He *is* in his glory." There was a long silence. She mused, "Pete, you know a lot about Corey and me, but I know very little about you. What made you sign on for this project?"

"To be candid, I'm looking for a promotion to a general officer. This is the project of a lifetime and a guarantee for promotion ... if I don't screw it up. I report directly to the President." Pete paused, "It's also extremely interesting." In the darkness, Wendy could not see the smile on Pete's face.

"You can say that again. What led you to choose the military as a career?"

"Oh, I suppose it was the excitement of being able to fly the best technology on this planet. Also, and this sounds corny," Pete said with a more serious tone, "I do love my country and the military is a great way for someone to serve their country."

"And what does your wife think about the military?"

Pete took a long hard breath. His voice nearly broke as he answered, "My wife loved the service life ... but ... she's ... no longer living." There, he said it.

"Oh, I'm terribly sorry," Wendy said with sincere sorrow. "How long ago did you loose your wife?"

"She was murdered ... two ... no ... three years ago."

"How terrible. I'm so sorry for you. Have they caught the person who did it?"

"No."

Wendy tried to redirect the conversation to a more pleasant vein, "How long were you married?"

"Over twenty-two years."

"Did you have any children?"

"Suzan and I had a son, David. He's twenty now. He's at the Air Force Academy," Pete said proudly. "It's one of those family things, I guess. I went to the Academy and so did my dad. He's a retired brigadier general and keeps asking when I'm going to get my star. He was forty-two when he got his first star. I'm forty-six and still waiting," Pete said with a smile.

"You're reporting directly to the President on this project. That's got to be good," Wendy added.

"Yes, it should be good, but as I said before, as long as I don't screw it up. Loosing this artifact would definitely be a screw up." Pete pressed the button on the side of his watch. The dial glowed a pale green. "It's 23 hundred hours. We probably should try to get some sleep." He took off his flight jacket and put it over Wendy.

"Thank you, Pete. I was starting to get chilled, but what about you? Won't you get cold without your jacket?"

"No. I'm fine," he lied. "I have a tee shirt under my long sleeved shirt. I'll be fine," he reassured her.

"I don't believe you," Wendy said as she moved over next to him and put his jacket over the both of them. "There, now we can share body heat. They must have taught you that in your survival training."

"Yes, they did and you are right. This *is* much better."

They lay there side by side as they both drifted off to sleep. Pete's mind slipped back to happier years with Sue. *Such a senseless murder. Why her? Why her? If only I could turn the clock back. I would have been home to prevent that drifter from getting into our house. I would have protected Sue and she would still be with me.* It was not long before sleep overtook Pete and offered a sweet relief from his exhaustion.

Chapter 5
The Tour Begins

9:38 PM
Aboard an Alien Craft

"Dr. Newton, I want to assure you that we will not harm you," Quellin continued, as he sensed Corey's apprehension. "I have dispatched the scout ship to return to your downed helicopter and find the communicator. It should not take long to track down your team members and recover the communicator. Meanwhile, if you like, I will give you a tour."

Corey was impressed with how tranquil Quellin seemed, given the disappointment he must have felt at not having the device returned. There was not a note of threat in his voice.

Quellin smiled as he perceived Corey's acceptance of him. He looked at Andrews. "Would you like to join us, Colonel? Is your leg well enough to do some walking?"

"Why, yes, I would like to go along if I may. My leg is not so bad that I will let it keep me from the tour," the colonel replied eagerly. "Also, the reduced gravity helps tremendously so it's no problem to stand and walk."

"Well then, shall we start?" Quellin asked, as he led the two out of the small conference room and down a long hall.

"How large is this craft?" Corey asked, as he looked around. Impressed with the size of the craft, he was almost overwhelmed. All his life he had been ridiculed for his belief in UFOs and now he was actually standing in one. It was truly awesome. From his readings, he was aware this class of ship was the one often referred to as a transport ship since it carried several of the smaller scout ships. Some researchers referred to it as the Leviathan.

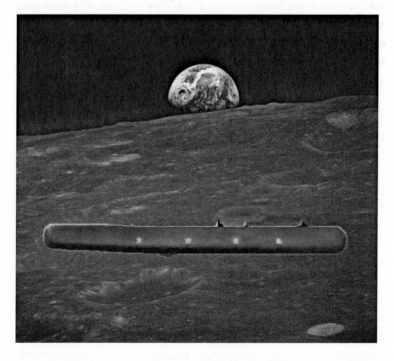

"Well . . . in your measurement system, I would say roughly four hundred meters long and thirty-five meters in diameter," Quellin said, matter-of-factly. "We use it to shuttle our scout ships to strategic locations on Earth and shuttle to our main base here in this planetary system."

This is almost as large as our aircraft carriers, Corey thought. "And where is your main base?" he asked as the two men followed Quellin down the hallway.

Quellin slowed his pace as he prepared his response. He then stopped and turned to Corey. "Dr. Newton, as you know, we have many bases. You know where one is," Quellin smiled. "Dr. Ahearn told you, remember?"

"It's between Mars and Jupiter, in the asteroid belt." Corey said, almost mechanically. He was surprised at the ease with which Quellin got him to pull that out of his memory. *But how did I know that?* He tried to remember a conversation he had recently with Wendy. *Yes, she had told me they were hiding the ship among the millions of asteroids in orbit around the sun. But how did she know that?* He was about to ask why they were located there when he saw a smile appear on Quellin's face.

"We located that base there to avoid detection," Quellin answered without being asked. "Our scientists had determined humans would not have the technology to resolve the difference between our craft and the asteroids in that region. They believed you would not have the ability to detect our craft at that range until we were ready for disclosure."

"How large is that craft?" asked Colonel Andrews.

"Why don't you ask Dr. Newton?" Quellin smiled again.

"It's over eight miles long and two miles in diameter," Corey blurted out. *What am I, a puppet?* Corey's mind screamed. *Wendy told me that, too, just a couple of days ago. Amazing! Quellin's screwing with my mind.* Corey was growing angry but could not stop from completing his description. "That's why it had to be located out there among the asteroids," he continued. "At that range, even using our best telescopes, it would just appear as a blurry asteroid."

Colonel Andrews stared at Corey in amazement. "How do you know all of that?"

"Why don't you ask Quellin?" Corey retorted, angrily. He was tired of Quellin probing his mind and pulling his strings as though he were nothing but a puppet. He turned to Quellin. "I know you know every question I am about to ask, but for the colonel's benefit, I will ask it anyway." He gave Quellin a hard stare. "Is it the nature of *your* species to be so rude?"

"I am terribly sorry, Dr. Newton. That is a bad habit I have when dealing with humans. I did not mean to make you uncomfortable. I will try to refrain from reading your mind. Go ahead and ask your questions."

Corey wanted to keep probing. "You mentioned that by the time we can detect your craft, you will be disclosing your existence to humanity. When will that be?"

Quellin starred intently at Corey. "Dr. Newton, I am not surprised at your inquisitiveness. I would expect no less from you. Surely, you do not expect me to give you a time and date?" His expression was blank.

"It would be nice if you did. I am curious and you will erase my memory anyway," Corey said, with a faint smile. It was his volley. "How about December 21st, 2012? Isn't that the date the Mayan's gave?"

Quellin looked at Corey a long moment and then resumed walking. "Dr. Newton, first of all, we *will* erase your memory of this visit but our experience has been that often it is only temporary. We cannot predict when you might recall some of the memory of your visit here and it could prove embarrassing to us. Second, to answer your question, I am aware that for the Mayans the end of the 13th b'ak'tun in their calendar represents a new beginning or time of re-birth, but I see no connection," he lied.

Corey fired back. "Well, I've been told by a reliable source that on that date the world will be under one government and one religion. Are you going to tell me, that with all of your knowledge, you did not know that?"

Quellin stopped again and stared back at Corey a long moment and then blinked hard before answering. "I will tell you that it will be very soon ... in your lifetime. Humankind will play a large role in determining when disclosure occurs. Surely you must understand that I cannot reveal to you the exact date and time. Our existence must be revealed very carefully. The disclosure process must be gradual to avoid a panic within humanity. I think you can understand that. People must be conditioned."

"Conditioned?" Corey eyed Quellin.

"As you are aware," Quellin explained, "we have been allowing people to see us from time to time as we put on public displays."

"Are you talking about the Phoenix lights display back in March of 1997?" Corey asked.

"Yes, and in Mexico and other parts of the world. More displays like that will occur in the future," Quellin added. Also, we have increased the number of signs we place on the ground."

"Are you talking about crop circles?" Colonel Andrews asked.

"Yes," Quellin answered. "Surely these designs must be raising the level of consciousness of people around the world. They must wonder what it all means."

"Many people are trying to understand them, but unfortunately, most people have been misled into believing they're man-made," Corey added.

"Yes, that is unfortunate and we are aware of that, but some people are beginning to learn how to discern those that are hoaxed. Dr. Newton, I know that you already know."

"Yes, I believe I do." Corey agreed. "I am curious to know how you make them."

"I know you have your own theory," Quellin said. "Would you like to share it with Colonel Andrews?"

Corey turned to Colonel Andrews. "Colonel, one of the most distinguishing features of crop designs that are not hoaxed is that the plant nodes in the affected plants are elongated and often have expulsion cavities. It is as though they were rapidly heated internally before they are laid down. My theory is that they project a microwave field over the design area to heat and soften the plant stems. Then they apply some sort of force field to lay the plants down in a swirling motion. The superheating softens the plants so they're not broken when they're bent down." Corey looked at Quellin. "Am I close on that?"

Quellin stared at Corey. "Dr. Newton, let me ask you a question."

"Sure, go ahead."

"Do the affected plants die after this encounter?"

Corey was puzzled by Quellin's question. "No, but they are affected and exhibit a change in growth pattern."

"Would such microwave heating allow that?" Quellin began to steer Corey to reassess his theory.

Corey hesitated as he considered that question. "Now that you mentioned it, I think the plants would be killed by such intense radiation," He looked at Quellin and smiled. "Okay, so how *do* you do it?"

Quellin laughed for the first time since Corey had met him. "Dr. Newton, do not give up so easily. You know the answer, I'm sure you do. Just think about it. How else could you superheat the water molecules in a plant?"

With Quellin's mention of water molecules, a smile of discovery appeared on Corey's face. "Ultrasound? Yes . . . ultrasound," Corey answered his own question. "Now I remember. People who have been in a field when a crop design was being created reported hearing strange buzzing sounds just before the plants collapsed."

"What kind of buzzing sound?" Colonel Andrews asked.

"Do you know of that device that the Australian aborigines use?" Corey asked.

Colonel Andrews looked puzzled. "I'm not sure."

"You know, the one they whirl around their heads on a string," Corey added.

"Oh yes, now I know what you're talking about. It's called a bora and it makes a funny trill sound. Yes, that is a strange sound," Colonel Andrews admitted.

"Well, that's the sound witnesses have reported who were near a field where a crop design was being made." Corey looked at Quellin, "How do you create such intricate patterns with your sound?"

"I believe you would call it Cymatics," Quellin answered. "It is a simple matter to animate inert substances such as powders, liquids, or even plants into flowing forms of great complexity. A complex pattern of nodes can be created simply by adjusting the frequency and amplitude on any vibrating plane. We can cause these nodes to manifest into any form we desire. After we soften the plant stems with ultrasound, we use sound to position the plants and lay them down."

Corey was spellbound. *Such a simple solution,* he thought.

"Laying down designs in crop fields is only one of the many methods we are using in the conditioning process. We also have begun a controlled release of information that will desensitize humanity to our presence."

"What sort of controlled release?" Corey asked.

"A number of your authors are writing books about us. Television programs and movies are being presented that give balanced views on the possibility of life beyond Earth and of our existence. We believe that more and more humans are ready to accept the discovery of life beyond Earth. Also, books are being written that will cause you to question the dogma of your social and religious leaders. Your social and religious fabric is changing."

"Why do you want us to change our social and religious fabric?" Corey asked. He knew about the increase in UFO material being fed the public through the media, but was not aware of attacks on social and religious institutions.

Quellin resumed his walk down the hall and the two men fell into step. "Your civil and religious leaders have hidden and denied our existence for a long time. A sudden revelation would be too chaotic without first allowing humanity to question and study the evidence. The people must have time to question what they are being told by their leaders. We do not want disclosure to be too disruptive. In order to avoid human panic, we feel it is better to transition you to a new understanding."

This was beginning to sound sinister to Corey. He could not let this pass. "So you're saying that if you were to make your disclosure today, it would be too disruptive and cause world panic. Is that right?"

Quellin stopped again and faced Corey. "Yes it would be very disruptive. However, make no mistake, there will be change, but it will require time. It will be gradual and for the good."

For the good of whom? Corey wondered.

Quellin led them a little farther, stopped in front of a door, and waved his hand in front of the small patch. The door slid open and he led the two men into a small white room similar in size to the conference room they had just left. Again, Corey was impressed. The room looked like it was molded into the ship. It was well lit even though there was no direct evidence of a single light source.

"The light … ," Quellin interrupted himself, turned to Corey, and smiled. "I am sorry, I did it again. Go ahead, Dr. Newton, ask your question."

Corey smirked at Quellin, "Where is the light coming from? I noticed the same thing in the last room." He had noticed that the walls and ceiling seemed to have a diffuse white glow that left no shadows in the room.

"All the surfaces in this craft have the ability to radiate light. In the other room, you noticed, we can change the color if we wish." Quellin panned the room with his hands, "Off-white seems to be the best color for this room."

As Corey's eyes followed Quellin's hands, he could see strange instruments lining both side walls. In the center, he saw what looked like an operating table. Above the table, the ceiling had strange and ominous instruments that extended down over the table. To Corey, they looked like the legs of some giant crab.

"What is this room?" Corey asked apprehensively. He had a bad feeling. From his research, it fit the description of examination rooms described by abductees. *Perhaps Quellin is so willing to answer my questions because he's giving a tour to a condemned man,* Corey thought.

"It is our examining room," Quellin said. He sensed Corey's apprehension and smiled. "I know you are familiar with this room, Dr. Newton, but do not fear. It has a reputation among humans that it does not deserve. For centuries we have been studying and monitoring human development. It is in this room that we take specimen samples of our test subjects."

Specimen samples indeed. Corey thought. He had read the many eyewitness reports by abductees. Samples of body fluids, hair, and flesh had been taken . . . in the most unpleasant ways . . . without anesthesia. "What do you do with the specimens?" Corey asked, with distain.

"Dr. Newton, why do you disapprove of our methods? Do not your own scientists and doctors do the same? They are constantly taking samples for analysis ... from a variety of living organisms . . . including human. Have you not seen on your own Internet what your scientists do to other primates? We monitor your broadcasts and your Internet and we see how dispassionate you are to other species. They are treated as though they do not feel pain. They are terrorized. Surely you must be aware of the facilities on your planet that raise primates and other animals for testing various chemicals. Scientists there say they do it for the benefit of humankind, do they not?"

"Well ... yes," Corey had to admit.

"Well, so do we. We take them so that we can monitor human development," Quellin continued.

"Why do you care?" Corey asked sarcastically. "Are you looking for our weakness?"

"Dr. Newton," Quellin snapped back. "I resent your tone. We are not the enemy you suppose. We are trying to help." His tone softened and he looked at Corey with eyes pleading for understanding. "We want to determine what humans are doing to themselves through the chemicals they add to the environment. We wish to determine how the chemicals you spray in the air and add to the ground and water are affecting your food chain." Quellin studied Corey for signs of understanding. "Are you aware of any test programs that humans are conducting to answer the same question?"

Corey gave Quellin a puzzled look. "Well, I can't cite any at this moment, but I know there are many agencies that test the food we eat to ensure it is okay. Also, there are agencies like the FDA that test new drugs to be sure they're safe before we are allowed to consume them. And then, of course, there is the EPA."

"That is correct but who is monitoring the effects of all the thousands of other chemicals you introduce into the environment. What about fertilizers, weed, and insect killers that leach into the environment and your bodies? Then there is the smoke you inhale, and not least of all, the exhaust from your vehicles and generating plants. Dr. Newton, you surely are aware that some of your medication is applied through your skin, are you not?

"Yes, we call it trans-dermal medication. What about it?

"Would not the chemicals in the soaps, lotions, and deodorants that you apply to your skin also find their way into your body? Has there been a study to determine the long term affects of these chemicals? We do not think so. Dr. Newton, I assure you, we are aware of the testing organizations you mentioned and we monitor them ourselves. I am sorry, but I must say, their methods are much too primitive."

"Are they now?" Corey said, as his Irish heritage surfaced. He could feel the hair on the nape of his neck stand up. "I thought they were quite good. They don't have *your* technology but they do their best with what they have."

"Dr. Newton, it is not just their technology that I criticize; it is their methodology."

"Well...they have limitations that you don't. Studies required for airtight conclusions about long-term effects of chemicals take too long and many of the required tests aren't ethical to carry out."

"Unfortunately, that is not good enough. You cannot continue to allow chemicals that bioaccumulate in humans or other animals to be widely distributed around the planet," Quellin fired back.

"So what's wrong with their methodology?"

"Well, for example, they test single chemicals. They fail to test the effects of the same chemical in combination with others. They fail to recognize that exposures during different stages of life have different impacts. Their studies ignore the fact that developmental processes create windows of vulnerability for specific effects. For example, prenatal exposures can cause abnormalities at birth. This can also impact the adult reproductive function. It is also important that they consider the range of genetic susceptibility that different humans have. None of the studies being done by your own species incorporate the full complement of these considerations."

"And yours do?" Corey fired back.

"Yes," Quellin gave Corey a hard stare. "As I have said, we *are* concerned about your welfare and have taken it upon ourselves to conduct studies. We are not limited by political, religious, or social taboos. Do not think that we are ignorant of your politics, laws, and agencies such as your FDA. For instance, our studies have shown there is a chemical you use in some of your plastics that affect your endocrine systems. Your FDA approved that chemical for human use. No, Dr Newton, our studies are much more thorough and have been going on for centuries. We not only take samples from humans but also take samples from your food chain."

"Do you mean … like, cattle?" Andrews asked.

"Yes, that is one example," Quellin answered.

"Is that why you're mutilating our cattle?" Colonel Andrews asked. "Surely, you must be aware that people are disgusted by what they perceive as senseless mutilations."

"We do take specimens from cattle but it is neither senseless nor mutilation. Mutilation is a strong word. We do no more harm to them than you humans as you butcher them for food. At least we do not slaughter and eat them. Unfortunately, the specimens we must take do result in the animal's death. However, their life is ended in a painless manner first and then we take the specimens we need."

"Why cattle...why not sheep or chickens?" Corey asked.

"The grasses they eat accumulate the chemicals we are monitoring. These chemicals then accumulate in their bodies and are concentrated in their blood and some of their organs such as their utter. You humans consume their milk. Also, your cattle are unique in that their blood is remarkably similar to human blood. Thus, we can monitor the long-term effects that the chemicals you are releasing will have on humans."

"So you simply drain their blood and incise the organs you wish to take?" Corey asked.

"Yes," Quellin said dismissively.

"So, what have you learned after all of this *testing*?" Corey asked.

Quellin's gaze fell to the floor. "Unfortunately, our testing indicates there is a dramatic deterioration in your species."

"What deterioration?" Corey asked with concern.

"Dr. Newton, what is a requirement if a species is to survive?" Quellin asked.

Corey thought for a moment. "Well, it has to reproduce."

"Precisely. Did you know that humans are destroying their ability to reproduce?"

"No," Corey answered with a look of surprise.

"Well, for instance, during the past two generations there has been an alarming decrease in the sperm count in male humans."

Corey was surprised. "How much of a decrease?"

"From sampling we have done in all the developed nations of the Earth, we have detected a fifty percent decrease in sperm quality over the past two human generations."

"Why do you think that is?" Corey asked with alarm.

"We believe the massive amounts of chemicals you have been releasing into the environment have permeated your food chain. This is the same food consumed by pregnant females. Our studies indicate that during the last months of pregnancy the fetus is very susceptible to damage to their reproductive system. As I explained before, there seems to be an endocrine mechanism involved. Both male and female reproductive abilities are being reduced. Also, there are many other negative effects on human health. We have detected an increase in cancers, for example. And now other species on your planet are also beginning to pay the price for humanity's carelessness."

Colonel Andrews jumped in, "Dr. Newton, now do you see what I was telling you?" he said, nodding his head. "We *are* destroying the environment. The CO_2 level is at the highest level ever recorded and the average temperature has increased by a degree. Northern latitudes have seen an even larger increase. The Earth is almost at a tipping point where it will be too late to repair the damage."

"That is correct, Colonel," Quellin agreed with a stern look of concern. "You *are* destroying the environment and in many ways." He turned to Corey. "We cannot allow that. We have too much time and energy invested in this planet *and* humanity. Our scientists have determined that the time has come for us to intercede ... before it is too late. Conditions *have* reached the tipping point. If we wait much longer, the environment *will* be beyond repair. We have seen that happen before in our galaxy where the dominant species developed technology that destroyed the planet."

Corey was not sure how to respond to this. It seems the colonel was right about the environment. A seed of a thought entered Corey's mind. "Quellin, why don't you plant this information into the minds of the people who are researching in these areas?"

Quellin smiled. "That is an excellent idea, Dr. Newton. Do you suppose there would be any social and political constraints placed on those researchers?" he said with a tone of sarcasm.

"Well ... ," Corey could not deny that fact. He got the message. "They probably would have to keep their findings within some sort of acceptable norm. Otherwise they would jeopardize their funding."

"Also, degradation of the environment is not the only problem that humans have caused," Quellin answered.

"What other problems?" Corey asked.

"Many. For one, consider the human development of the atom bomb," Quellin said.

"I'm sure that got your attention," the colonel volunteered.

"Yes, and you can imagine how much that concerned us. At that point you humans not only posed a threat to yourselves but also your planet and, in fact, the Federation. However, fortunately, humanity understood the dangers of self-destruction with atomic weapons and for the most part has taken self-regulating measures to prevent that. We hope that some day humanity will elect to destroy all such weapons of mass destruction. Only rarely have we had to intercede."

"Yes, like the time in 1967 when you disabled our Minuteman nuclear missiles while they were still in their silos at Malmstrom Air Force Base," Colonel Andrews added.

"Yes," Quellin nodded, "But we simply disabled the power source and drained the batteries of those missiles while they were still on the ground. As you know, Colonel, we have monitored your missile fields many times over the years and, I will add, we will continue to monitor them. We also follow and monitor your missiles when they are in flight," Quellin affirmed.

"You did more than that to some," the colonel added. "You blew them up."

"Yes, but no one was harmed," Quellin said dismissively. "They were over water." Quellin turned to face Corey. "We felt it was important to demonstrate our concern and to show our capabilities to your military so there would be no doubt."

"Dr. Newton," Colonel Andrews added. "I have friends who are retired officers. One of them was stationed at the Minuteman III fields in Cheyenne, Wyoming, back in 1973. There were over two hundred missile silos there. He told me that they had frequent visits by UFOs and at least on one occasion a UFO hovered over a missile silo and erased the target tapes in the missile." Andrews turned to Quellin, "Believe me, Quellin, you have left no doubt in anyone's mind about your capabilities."

"We loath intervening in human affairs. However, Dr. Newton, I think you can see that such demonstrations have been effective in convincing the various world powers to keep controls on nuclear weapons." Quellin's face took on a puzzled look. "However ... for some reason, humanity has been unable to recognize the destruction it is doing to the environment of this planet and to the human body with the massive amounts of chemicals being dumped into the environment. It seems that humans have the science but lack the political will to make a correction. It is unfortunate but this is why we must now step in."

Corey's eyes narrowed. "Why didn't you step in during our wars and our holocausts, when millions of people died?"

"Believe me ... that was *very* painful for us to watch. But, you must understand, we have a non-intervention policy throughout our galaxy. It is one of the rules of the Federation. As long as you do not threaten the planet or life beyond the planet, we cannot intercede. We had to let you settle your differences."

Corey looked at Colonel Andrews and then at Quellin. "So, you are saying there is a Federation rule that prohibits intervention with human activities by life forms beyond Earth?"

"Yes, unless the Earth itself is jeopardized by the humans."

"So, now *you* have determined that we are such a threat and *you* must intercede. What gives *you* that special right?" Corey demanded.

"Each sector of the galaxy is assigned a watcher to monitor and protect that sector," Quellin smiled at Corey. "We are your watchers, Dr. Newton."

Corey began to ponder this notion. He had no reply.

Quellin continued, "However, another Federation rule is that watchers must allow the planet and inhabitants to develop naturally. If we impose our will then we do not promote the diversity of life that is required in the universe. So, you see, that is why we must stand by and watch your violent attempts to settle your differences through wars. We try to be philosophical and view it as part of your development process. Hopefully, over time, you will learn to expel your hatred and become a more loving species. You are one of the most violent species we have ever encountered." There was a tone of disgust in Quellin's voice.

"What is this Federation you keep talking about?" Corey asked. He remembered Wendy using the same term when they were back at the base.

"This is a federation of planets within our region of the galaxy. There are other federations in the galaxy but because of the vast distances, each federation tends to act autonomously and operate in their own region. Our federation has several thousand member planets."

"Is that the number of habitable planets in our section of the galaxy?" Corey asked.

"Oh no," Quellin said, with a smile. "There are many more times that many planets capable of supporting life. Most of them have life forms that have not progressed sufficiently to participate. A few, unfortunately, have evolved into extremely aggressive life forms and have not been allowed to venture beyond their planet."

"How do you prevent them from going into space?" the colonel asked.

"We have ways of foiling their attempts without revealing our presence," Quellin said, his lips formed a faint smile. "We are hoping that someday soon, humankind will join our federation." He paused a long moment as he considered what he was about to say and then addressed Corey. "Dr. Newton, the unpleasant truth is that there are other members of the federation who do not abide by our rules. There are those who envy what you have here on this planet and would like to take it from you."

Corey's brow wrinkled. "Are you saying there are those who wish to harm us?"

"Yes, they will attempt to deceive you. However, you must not be deceived when they offer their technology on the pretense of helping humanity. You must be very careful. We are trying to protect you from being exploited by them but we are limited in our actions."

"So, do you keep other aliens from approaching our planet?" Corey asked.

"It would be nice if it were that easy. The Federation rules allow all members to visit and study any planet they choose as long as they do not interact. We even allow members of other federations to visit. However, other federations do not always abide by our rules, so we have to be on guard. Any overt aggression on their part would be legal cause for us to intercede and force them to leave. It is their subtle, non-aggressive interaction that *you* must guard against. Humanity's future will depend on your ability to do just that," Quellin turned and continued walking as the colonel and Corey filed quietly behind him. Both men became lost in thought as they considered what Quellin had just told them.

Chapter 6
There Is a God

Corey's attitude toward Quellin was beginning to soften. He was beginning to appreciate that Quellin had been open and honest with him. What he heard from him thus far made sense. *Colonel Andrews is not all that bad either,* Corey thought as he continued to follow Quellin down the long hall. He had to admit that many of Quellin's statements about humanity's handling of the environment were true. Also, his statement that the human race was violent was also true. *Why must we always live in conflict?* Corey thought to himself.

"Your conflicts are caused by hatred," Quellin responded forcefully without waiting for Corey to ask the question. "It was humankind's hatred toward each other that led to the holocausts and wars."

"So, what's the solution?" Corey asked.

"Unconditional love is the answer. It is the cure for all wars and is necessary if humanity wishes to avoid future holocausts. This is something humanity must learn. It is important for spiritual growth. Some have tried to show you the way, but you still have much to learn about spiritual development. If only your spiritual development had kept pace with your technological development, then perhaps we would not have to intercede."

"You just said that some have tried to show the way. Who are you referring to?" Corey asked.

"The one you called Immanuel is just one example. He came into your lives to show the way to The Light. Many others such as the one you call Buddha have tried to show you the way by demonstrating unconditional love toward humankind, but the message was lost."

"By Immanuel, do you mean Jesus?"

"Yes, he is also known by that name."

"He paid a terrible price for his efforts," Colonel Andrews said.

"It was *his* decision to enter your lives," Quellin replied. "He was fulfilling his destiny and perfecting his own spirit in the process. Many have received his message of love."

"When you say he was fulfilling his destiny are you saying he did not have free will?" Corey asked.

"No," Quellin looked at both men. "The Creator has granted every spirit free will. They are free to choose the path they follow."

"Then, what do you mean by destiny?"

"Perhaps I should have said that Immanuel was completing the mission he had set for himself," Quellin said.

"And that mission was . . . ?" Colonel Andrews asked.

"He felt that the religion in his time was on the wrong path. It had become a religion of fear. It taught people to worship a fearful God, one of hatred and revenge. It was a religion that used fear as a means of control in order to increase the wealth and power of its leaders. Immanuel wanted to show that God was a God of love and was to be loved. He taught that humans must learn to love one another and work toward developing a spirit of unconditional love. That is the only way to perfect one's spirit. That *is* the only way to The Light."

"So, is there such a thing as destiny?" Colonel Andrews asked.

"We believe the future is predictable. To some extent, you might call that destiny. However, even though the future is predictable, it is alterable. All living spirits can exercise their own free will to alter the probable future."

"I'm not sure I follow," the colonel said.

"Let me give you an example," Quellin said. "You humans are just now developing the technology to make accurate predictions in many areas. Forecasting your weather is one example in which you are improving your modeling capabilities. Imagine sometime in the future when your weather model is so precise that you can predict events with extremely high resolution and accuracy. For example, you might be able to predict the path of a cyclonic storm with great precision and you might predict that the storm will ravage a highly populated city."

"You mean like the hurricane that struck New Orleans in 2005?" the colonel asked.

"Yes," Quellin answered. "The response to that storm was to evacuate the city before it struck. In the future you will have the technology to alter the course and intensity of storms."

"What sort of technology can alter the course of a hurricane?"

"We believe that your scientists are close to developing a polymer that can be sprayed onto the ocean surface directly in the path of the storm. That will alter the course of the storm," Quellin answered.

"How will the polymer alter the storm's course?" the colonel asked.

"The polymer will prevent water from evaporating from the ocean's surface. That energy will not be available to feed the storm. The intensity will drop and the storm will change direction just as it does when it makes landfall. Thus you will be able to control its intensity and path," Quellin explained.

"But doesn't that create a pollution problem? I mean spraying a polymer on the ocean is like making a giant oil spill," the colonel observed.

Quellin smiled. "We believe that your scientists will develop a polymer that, after a few days, will be degraded by the sun's ultraviolet rays. It will then fall to the bottom of the sea where it could become a source of food for some species of marine animals."

"That sounds like an elegant solution," Corey added. "I hope they develop that soon."

"They will," Quellin assured Corey. "What I have told you is just one example of how *you* will have the ability to predict the probable future and *you* will exercise your free will to alter it. Likewise, we will exercise *our* free will to alter events."

"How so?" Corey asked.

"Our models predict that the probable future for the earth is global destruction of the environment by humans and that humans will not act to correct this situation. So, we must exercise *our* free will to intercede and make a correction for *you*."

Corey knew he could not refute this. It was time to move on to other subjects. He studied Quellin for a long moment. "Quellin, earlier you talked about The Creator. It sounds like you believe in God. Is that true?"

"Yes, but our belief in The Creator is not by faith as it is with you. We *know* The Creator exists."

"How do you *know* that?" Corey asked.

Quellin eyed Corey. "Dr. Newton, there are three possible models in regard to the universe. One possibility is that it has always existed and is static. Another is that it is expanding. A third model is that it is continually expanding and contracting in an oscillatory fashion. To which model do you subscribe?"

"There is very strong evidence that the universe is expanding at an accelerating rate."

"I would like to discuss your evidence for an *accelerating* expansion. But let us do that at a later time. Continue," Quellin said.

"Well," Corey continued, "The same evidence suggests that the universe will never collapse again. The rate of expansion reveals that there is not enough density to provide the gravity necessary for re-contraction."

"Okay, now, if the universe is expanding, that would imply that it had a beginning, does it not?"

"Yes, that's the Big Bang Theory. I subscribe to that."

"Yes, we know of your Big Bang Theory. I would like to propose an alternative theory for you to consider but, as I said, we can discuss that later. Continue your train of thought."

The idea of an alternative to the Big Bang theory intrigued Corey but he decided to wait for that explanation. He continued, "Well, from a thermodynamic point of view, the expanding universe is cooling and changing irreversibly toward disorder. This leads to two conclusions. One is that the universe will eventually die and the second is that it did not always exist. It had a beginning."

"Excellent! Whether it is what you call a Big Bang or some other model, it is immaterial," Quellin said. "We are of the same belief, the universe had a beginning. Now, Dr. Newton, I would submit to you that everything that has a beginning has a cause and since the universe had a beginning, it had a cause."

"Yes, that is logical but what was the cause?"

Quellin smiled. "Good question. I would expect that of you."

"Thank you," Corey said, with a smile.

Quellin continued down his path of instruction. "Well, it is logical when you think about it. The cause must have preceded the beginning. The cause existed when there was no physical universe. Therefore, the cause must be non-physical and reside outside of physical space and time. The cause must be an incorporeal and unchangeable entity with a personality."

"I'm not sure I follow. How can you conclude all of that?" Corey asked.

Quellin smiled. "Do you believe that events or material things pop into existence spontaneously?"

"No," Corey answered.

"Since the cause is outside of physical space and time, it need not have a cause because it never began to exist . . . it always was. Otherwise, there would be an infinite regression of causes, which, I think you would agree is impossible. The cause is independent of its creation. It is self-existent and not dependent upon creation for existence."

"Okay, I understand that but how can you conclude that the cause has a personality?"

"Would you not agree that it is the nature of a personality to cause an intended effect such as to create something out of nothing?"

"Well, yes," Corey agreed.

"It is this capability of making willing choices that is a property of a personality. Therefore, the cause is personal. It is logical, do you agree?"

"Yes." Corey said, half-heartedly.

"Dr. Newton, I think you would agree that to cause something as grand as our universe, there must have been a Creator who must be both extremely intelligent and extremely powerful."

"Yes, but it seems to me that your arguments are more philosophical than scientific," Corey replied.

Quellin considered Corey's statement for a moment. "As someone trained in the sciences of the universe, you must be aware of the intricate fine-tuning of the universe."

"Yes, I am and it does seem to point toward a designer. However, I do not consider it proof."

"Well, you *are* difficult to convince," Quellin said, with a smile. "Consider this. Over a half million years ago our scientists were able to prove the existence of The Creator."

"What was the proof?" Corey asked, insistently.

"The proof was mathematical. It was a question of probabilities."

"What do you mean?" Colonel Andrews asked. He had been standing on the sidelines of this conversation and was fascinated by the way Quellin had given a logical progression of information in order to not only answer Corey's question but also to lead him to make conclusions on his own.

"It was a mathematical proof showing that the finely tuned and balanced nature of the universe and the chance formation of life were statistically impossible, it had to be by design."

"I don't follow," Andrews said.

"As an example," Quellin explained, "consider the chance probability for the spontaneous appearance of DNA which is essential for *all* life. It was determined that the probability that such a complex molecule would spontaneously appear on any habitable planet in the universe over a four billion year time span was one in ten followed by over four hundred zeros."

"Yes, I agree. The spontaneous formation of such a complex molecule is extremely low," Corey said. "But, you have not convinced me that a Creator is required in order for that chance event to have occurred."

Quellin gave Corey a hard stare. "Dr. Newton, consider another piece of information. Perhaps *it* will convince you."

"Go ahead," Corey smiled. "I'm eager to hear your explanation."

"Over half a million years ago, our scientists proved that any event with a probability less than one in ten followed by one hundred and fifty zeros can only occur by an intelligent intent, or design. The proof of that is too elaborate for me to explain here. You will have to accept that as fact."

"Okay, I will accept that. Go on," Corey said.

"Since the chance of DNA spontaneously occurring is much, much lower than ten followed by one hundred and fifty zeros, it had to be by design. The last step in the logical progression is that design must have had a designer. We consider the designer to be The Creator."

Corey paused to consider Quellin's explanation. "Okay, what about evolution?" he asked.

"Evolution is simply part of The Creator's magnificent design. The universe is not static. It was designed to be dynamic. There is constant change. The design is so perfect that life can adjust to change. It can evolve, as you would say, to best survive in the changing environment. Life that does not adjust passes out of existence. Life that does adjust . . . thrives. You call that evolution. We call it part of the design."

Corey was impressed. Quellin had addressed his questions well. It was time to move on to another subject. "Quellin, from what I have read, your race is very careful not to harm humans. Why is that?"

"Yes, that is true. We are very respectful of human life. In fact, we are respectful of *all* life. First of all, we are your guardians. Secondly, we do not wish to harm any life form that has a spirit. We believe it is wrong to take such a life. Only The Creator can instill a spirit into a life form. Since we do not have that ability, we should not end that life. Only The Creator should do that. Also, we believe that it is wrong to take one's own life."

"Why is it wrong for someone to take their own life?" the colonel interrupted. "Aren't they just exercising their own free will?"

Quellin turned and eyed the colonel. "Yes, humans do have the free will to take their own life. However, that goes counter to the whole reason for existence. After all, all spiritual beings enter the physical world so that they can experience growth toward spiritual perfection. Each lifetime that one experiences, helps the spirit to grow. If one were to cut short that life then experiences of that life end."

"But what if that person is experiencing tremendous pain and suffering?" the colonel asked.

"That pain and suffering are also part of spiritual growth. Those who wish to end their life to escape pain and suffering are going to miss the spiritual growth that they would have had."

"What do you mean by spiritual perfection?" Corey asked. His mind was opening to take in more of Quellin's teachings.

Quellin turned to Corey. "Your spirit reaches perfection when you can give unconditional love. *That* is very difficult to do. I know that from own experience, Dr. Newton."

"I suppose I agree," Corey said, as he pondered Quellin's explanations. His eyes were drawn to the array of instruments hanging from the ceiling and his apprehension grew. "What do you plan to do with the colonel and me?"

Quellin smiled as he recognized Corey's fear. "Put your mind at ease, Dr. Newton, neither of you will be harmed. You will be released separately after we retrieve the communicator. Our scout ship should be returning soon and we can release you." Quellin hesitated for a long moment. "Forgive me gentlemen. I forgot that you need to take in nourishment several times each day. Are you getting hungry?"

"A little," the colonel answered, "but I can wait if I'm going to be released soon."

"Same with me," Corey said. "What about you?"

An apologetic smile appeared on Quellin's face. "Well . . . we do not eat. We take on nourishment in a different way. Come, I will show you." Quellin led the two down the hall and into a room that was perhaps twenty-four feet long and eight feet deep. The long wall made a smooth transition between the floor and the ceiling and had a gentle bulge outward. Corey surmised this wall was the outside wall of the ship.

Quellin studied Corey's reaction to the room. "You might call this our refueling station," he said as he pointed to the row of six large transparent cylinders equally spaced and about two feet from the back wall. They were about three feet in diameter, seven feet tall, and appeared to have been projected out of the floor. Quellin walked over to one of the cylinders and touched it. The cylinder immediately retracted into the floor, leaving behind a slightly raised surface. "We stand here," he said pointing down to the raised area by his feet. "Then the cylinder comes up around us and fills with nutrients for our body. We absorb the nutrients through our skin . . . much like you do with your trans-dermal medication. It is much less complicated and more efficient than your digestion process. There is no waste." He went over to a side wall and picked up a small vial from a shelf that extended from it. As he held it up, Corey could see that it was filled with a whitish gold-colored fluid. "This is the fluid we bathe in."

"What's in that fluid?" Corey asked. "It looks like gold."

"It does contain gold but not the gold you are familiar with. It is a suspension of white powdered gold," Quellin explained.

"How often do you have to immerse yourself in that?" Colonel Andrews asked.

"We do it about every four of your earth-days. It does not take long ... only about an hour and it is very refreshing and enjoyable. You might say it is invigorating."

Corey smiled. "It sounds boring to me."

"I would let you try it but I do not know if it would work for you."

Corey glanced at Andrews and then back to Quellin. "That's okay. I really enjoy the sensual aspects of eating food."

"Later, if you do get hungry," Quellin said, "we can synthesize some food for you to ingest through your mouths."

"Thank you," Corey said. After a pause he continued, "I've had a chance to examine one of your crashed scout ships and I noticed that it had no food or bathroom facilities on board."

"That is true because they are not needed. The duration of scout ship flights is only a few hours."

"What's the range of your scout ships?" Corey asked.

"Oh, their range is perhaps a million of your kilometers. Then they have to return to this ship to be recharged," Quellin eyed Corey for a long moment. "I see you are very curious about our ship technology. That is your profession, is it not?"

"Yes, and I *am* extremely interested in your technology but I don't want you to show me anything that will prevent me from being released."

"Dr. Newton, your memory of this experience will be blocked before we release you. I have no concern about answering *any* of your questions."

"Yes, Colonel Andrews warned me that you would block our memories of this visit. I understand," Corey said. "I just wanted to make sure," Corey smiled. "In that case, show me all that you wish."

"Well, you have just seen how we recharge our bodies. Next I will show you where we recharge and store the scout craft. Follow me please," Quellin said, as he led them to a lower level and down a long hall. They passed through an airlock and found themselves standing on a small balcony. Corey gazed down the huge tube-shaped tunnel that extended before them. It was about fifteen meters in diameter and nearly the length of a football field. It sloped downward toward the rear of the craft. Along the sides of the tube he could see what appeared to be a series of smaller tubes branching back into the craft. There appeared to be a rack tucked into each of these. On each rack was a scout ship like the one he and the colonel arrived in.

"How many ships do you carry?" Corey asked, as he began counting the branches. It was then that he noticed the same pungent citrus odor he smelled when he arrived.

"Several," Quellin answered. "It varies with each carrier ship, depending on the mission. This one can carry eight. However, we lost one due to a mishap. That was the one that carried the communicating device we are trying to retrieve." Quellin pointed toward the rear of the tunnel, "We dispatch and retrieve each scout ship through an airlock in the bottom-rear of the ship."

"What's that strange odor?" Corey asked.

"It is a form of disinfectant to cleanse the scout ships and crew when they return from a mission. We do not want to become contaminated by organisms that might exist on the planet that we are studying. Likewise, we do not want to contaminate the indigenous life forms."

"That makes sense. I take it there is more than one ship like this one," Corey said.

"Oh yes, many. Most are stationed at various places in and around this planet but some are on other planets and moons doing research. We also have underwater bases."

"Why?" Colonel Andrews asked.

"We place them underwater to remain hidden."

"Then I take it these ships are capable of operating under water?" Corey asked.

"Yes, of course."

"What's the power source for these ships?" Corey asked.

"It is the same energy that abounds in the universe. You have not developed it yet."

"Do you mean fusion?"

"No, fusion is possible but we found a better source…I will explain later."

Corey accepted that and decided to wait until Quellin was ready. "You know that I work for a company trying to develop advanced propulsion systems, specifically what I call gravity drive."

"I know . . . and you are on the right path, Dr. Newton. You will soon discover, as we did long ago, that gravitational fields can be created by manipulating electromagnetic fields. In fact, electromagnetic radiation is more effective in creating gravitational fields than is mass."

"Yes, I know," Corey replied.

"What does Quellin mean, Dr. Newton?" Andrews asked.

"In 1938 a scientist named Tollman stated in his book that a beam of light has a gravitational field around it. He showed mathematically that light is twice as effective as mass in generating a gravitational field."

"Yes, and with these gravitational fields we can provide the force required for our maneuvers."

"That's a question I have always had," said the colonel. I've heard that your craft can make hundred G accelerations and sharp turns at high speeds. How can you do that without harming the pilots?"

"I think I can answer that," Corey interrupted. "The best way to explain it is for you to imagine that you jump from a tall building on the planet Jupiter. Because of the huge mass of Jupiter, you would accelerate toward the surface at perhaps thirty Gs or thirty times the rate as on Earth. As you freefall toward the planet's surface you would feel weightless but in reality you are accelerating at thirty Gs. The aliens have the ability to project a gravitational field in any direction they wish. The ship and its occupants simply freefall toward or away from that field. If they point the field in a different direction, they change direction without any sensation of movement. Don't you remember, as we were aboard the scout ship we had no sensation of motion?"

The colonel thought for a moment. "Yes, I do remember, now that you mention it," Colonel Andrews said with a smile. "That's amazing."

"That is a good explanation, Dr. Newton," Quellin added.

"Okay, now for the hard part," Corey asked. How do you generate the gravitational field?"

"Well, for you it might seem hard, but we have understood the principles of gravity for longer than humankind has existed. To us it seems commonplace."

"So . . . how do you do it?" Corey repeated.

"We do it by manipulating electromagnetic radiation in such a way that the fields shed what you would call gravitons. We focus the gravitons to create the force we need. The shedding of gravitons is much the same as the shedding of photons during high acceleration of electrons."

"I am familiar with the shedding of photons by accelerating electrons but I am not familiar with the mechanism for shedding gravitons. Can you explain that?"

"The actual mechanisms we use are beyond my ability to explain. Perhaps sometime in the future we will meet again and I will give you a closer look at one of our scout ships. It will be much easier to explain the technology then."

"That would be most interesting," Corey smiled. "I think I am familiar with the fundamental principle you just described, but am having difficulty understanding the mechanism you use."

"Well, many things that seem difficult at first become simple once they are explained or you see them."

"I would like to know ... ," Corey was interrupted as the door behind him opened and a Gray appeared. Quellin turned toward the Gray and the two did what seemed to be an endless staring procedure. After the Gray left, Quellin turned back to the two men.

"Gentlemen, I am afraid you will have to stay with us a little longer than I had planned. It seems we have not been successful in recovering the communicator." He looked at Corey. "Dr. Newton, we have not been able to track down your friends yet and they seem to have the communicator."

"I'm sorry to hear that," Corey said sarcastically.

"It seems your stay will be extended, so I have ordered some food to be prepared for you both. We will go back to the conference room where we can talk some more after you two have had a meal."

Chapter 7
Meet Matthew

Corey and the colonel had barely seated themselves at the conference table when a Gray appeared at the door and brought in a tray of food and drinks. It set the tray on the table and promptly left.

"I think you both will find that quite enjoyable," Quellin said, pointing to the food tray. He stood up. "If you will excuse me, I have some administrative matters to take care of while you enjoy your nourishment. I should be back in about half an hour."

"Thank you," Corey said.

"Yes," the colonel echoed as Quellin left the room. There was a slight whish sound as the door closed behind him. Corey and the colonel both starred at each other and then the food.

"What is that?" Corey said with distain.

"I don't know. It doesn't look like anything I've ever seen before," the colonel said as he picked up a green cube of strange-looking substance off of the tray. "It reminds me of putrid green tofu." Corey watched as the colonel held it to his nose. "It smells like steak!"

"Go ahead, bite into it. I dare you," Corey said, with a smile.

"Here goes," the colonel said, as he bit the chunk in half. After a few chews, a smile appeared on his face. "This is really delicious. It even has the texture of beefsteak, a tender one at that." Colonel Andrews began to chew more vigorously. His appetite peaked as he realized the food was safe.

Corey watched the colonel as he ate, looking for any signs of distress. The colonel was thoroughly enjoying his meal. Corey's curiosity got the best of him. "Let me try one." He picked up a pinkish looking cube and held it to his nose. "This smells like chicken." He bit into it and chewed. "This is the best piece of chicken I've ever tasted!"

"It's a good thing the aliens don't open a restaurant or they'd put all of the other fast food guys out of business," the colonel joked. "Shall we try the drinks?"

"I'll go first this time," Corey said, as he picked up a container resembling a squeeze bottle ketchup dispenser. He squeezed some liquid into his mouth, swished it around, and smiled. "This tastes like a malted milk!"

For the next fifteen minutes both men enjoyed their meal, marveling over the variety of tastes and textures.

The colonel seems like a decent guy, Corey thought as he ate, *I wonder why he's working with the aliens.* It was not Corey's style to be shy and beat around the bush. He always got right down to the heart of matters. "Colonel, excuse me for being so blunt, but why have you betrayed humanity?"

Colonel Andrews nearly choked with surprise at Corey's comment and then swallowed, giving Corey a long stare. "I haven't *betrayed* humanity. I'm trying to *save* it. I've been a military man all of my life. I've always tried to serve my country. Now, I have a larger calling, to serve humanity. I know what the military will do if they get their hands on that communicator. It will be used to serve the defense industry—the war machine—not humanity. The aliens realize that and are desperate to get it back. The aliens have a plan to help humanity, but if that communicator is not retrieved it could jeopardize everything."

Corey eyed the colonel. "How did you get involved? For that matter, how did you even find out about the device and that we were working with it?"

"When you activated that device, the aliens detected it and activated me."

"What do you mean? How did they activate you?"

"I am what you might call a hybrid, a fifth generation hybrid. But I didn't know it . . . at least not until a few days ago."

"Please explain," Corey said with amazement.

"I was born of normal parents who had no idea I was not a normal child. Aside from excelling in my studies, my life was a normal one until a few days ago. Then, when I was off base visiting my wife in Vegas, I was abducted right out of my own bed. My wife had fallen asleep and I was dozing when a strange light appeared outside my window. Then, suddenly, four Grays drifted right through the window. I mean...through the glass! The window was shut!"

"Didn't that wake your wife?" Corey asked.

"No, she slept through the whole thing. They immobilized her. Then they took me right through the same closed window they entered through. The next thing I remember, I was looking down at the roof of our house as I drifted up toward their scout ship. After I was aboard their ship, they lifted the memory block they had placed on me years before. It was then that I remembered my past abductions that began as a young child and continued as I was growing up."

"So, they have been abducting you on a regular basis then?"

"Yes, during childhood. They would run me through training classes so that when the time came and they needed me, I would be ready. That was how I learned to use telepathy."

"What kind of training did they give you?"

"When I was very young, they spent time teaching me socialization and learning telepathy. Later, when I was perhaps eight, they would have me spend time at this machine that was like a flat screen TV but had a lot of knobs and buttons. Images would appear on the screen and I learned to use the knobs and buttons to manipulate the figures on the screen."

"It sounds like some sort of video game," Corey observed.

"Yes. At first the figures and symbols seemed confusing but eventually I learned to recognize them as their written language. As I grew older, during my training sometimes the screen would depict entire scenes. Sometimes they were frightening, even terrifying."

"How do you mean?"

"Sometimes the scenes were like movies showing mass destruction of whole cities. People who were emaciated would be lying dead or dying. Some would be on fire as the cities burned."

"Were these images of the future do you think?"

"Yes, I think they were showing me what our future will be if we don't change our ways. I think that's why I've always been environmentally conscious and deplored war. It's ironic that I should end up as a career officer in the military."

"Yes, it is," Corey agreed.

"Anyway, a few days ago, when they took me, they told me that a device that was extremely important to them had been activated and now they could find it. It had been hidden from them for decades. They told me where on the base it was located. My instructions were to take back the device and meet them at the location of the 1953 UFO crash site in the desert. And ... I did it."

"And you have no regrets?"

"No, absolutely not, none at all." He looked at Corey with pleading eyes. "You know, Dr. Newton, it really is imperative that the aliens get that device back, and quickly."

"You said that you were a fifth generation hybrid but didn't know it until they activated you. Didn't your parents suspect that you were different?"

"No, they just thought that I was a bright kid. They had no memory of their own abductions."

"So, your parents were abducted?'

"Yes. During their abduction, an egg was harvested from my mother and sperm from my father. The egg was genetically altered to include genetic material from a fourth generation hybrid. It was then fertilized by my father's sperm and then re-implanted back into my mother."

"So, then after nine months you were born and no one was the wiser."

"Yes," Colonel Andrews said.

"Correct me if I am wrong, but from what I understand, the previous generations of hybrids were not allowed to go full term and be born. Is that correct?"

"Yes. They would have difficulty surviving in our environment so their mother was abducted and the fetus removed after the first trimester. They are grown in special tanks aboard ship. The aliens have explained all of that to me. I've seen the growing tanks."

"You say they would have difficulty surviving in our environment. Do you mean our atmosphere is not right for them?"

"No. They can breath our atmosphere but they would need special food since their digestive system is not quite like ours. Also, when they are born, they look too much like the aliens to operate in our world un-noticed. They would not fit in and they would be outcasts. "

"Can they reproduce?" Corey asked.

"No. It seems sad, actually. They have to live their entire lives aboard the ship or in special underground military bases on Earth."

"Where are those special bases?"

"One is the underground base in Nevada that I ran. Another is in Dayton, Ohio, at Wright Patterson. I think one is in New Mexico and I know there are others but I am not sure where."

Corey studied Colonel Andrews for a moment. "Colonel, I just realized, I don't even know your first name. Mine is Corey, what's yours?"

"My close friends call me Matthew."

"Glad to meet you, Matthew," Corey said, as he smiled and shook his hand. "From what you said earlier, you believe that this whole process of creating hybrids such as yourself, fifth generation I mean, is to populate the Earth with our future leaders."

"Yes. We are more attuned to the mission and will be focused on what is the best path for humanity. We will govern for the good of many and not for our own selfish benefit."

There was a swishing sound as the door opened and a Gray returned to recover the empty tray. Within minutes, Quellin returned.

"How was your food?" he asked, as he took a seat across from the two men.

"Amazing!" the colonel responded.

"Yes, give our complements to the chef," Corey said.

"Wonderful, I am glad you both enjoyed it. What would you like to talk about next?"

Chapter 8
A New Universe

Corey looked at Quellin and smiled. "I have many questions, some are pretty fundamental, some go pretty deep."

"I will try to answer as best I can."

"Well, one fundamental question, for example, is the Big Bang Theory of creation correct? It seems to make sense to me but I have some issues with some of the basic laws of physics that it appears to violate. Are we on the right track with that theory?"

"Dr. Newton, why do you subscribe to what you call the Big Bang Theory of creation?"

"Because of the evidence," Corey answered. "I believe that the evidence points toward an expanding universe. In fact, it seems that objects farther out from us are accelerating. When scientists extrapolate backward, the universe seems to have begun as a point of nearly infinite energy. Suddenly it began expanding some 13.7 billion years ago. According to the theory, as the universe expanded, it cooled and matter formed out of the energy. Eventually stars and then galaxies formed as we see them today. That's it in a nutshell."

Quellin looked perplexed, his brow furrowed. "How can the universe begin in a nutshell?"

Corey laughed, "I am sorry, I shouldn't have used that phrase. The universe did not begin in a nutshell but my summary of the theory was small enough to fit into a nutshell."

Quellin still looked puzzled.

"Well…never mind the nutshell. Was my summary of the creation of the universe clear?"

"Yes, but, Dr. Newton, you mentioned that you believe the universe is expanding and galaxies are accelerating away from us. How does the evidence support that?" Quellin asked.

"Back in the early 1900's an astronomer by the name of V. M. Slipher showed that the light from distant nebulae is red shifted which meant it was traveling away from us. Later, Edwin Hubble used data gathered by Henrietta Leavitt to show that many of these nebulae were actually outside of our galaxy and in fact galaxies of their own. Slipher's data also showed that the farther away the galaxies, the greater the red shift. The interpretation of the data by Hubble was that galaxies are accelerating away from us."

"Interesting," Quellin said, with a smile. "I agree that red shift is a sign of a receding velocity and that the universe is expanding, but how does the evidence indicate galaxies are accelerating away from us? Would that not require some energy to produce the force of acceleration?"

"Yes it does and that has been a puzzle to me and to cosmologists. They have labeled that as dark energy and are searching to discover what it is."

"So, your scientists interpret a greater red shift at greater distances as a sign of acceleration?" Quellin thought for a moment. "Dr. Newton, is it possible that this observation is not being interpreted correctly?"

"Well, anything is possible but how else would you interpret it?" Corey asked.

"Would it be correct for me to say that the data indicates that objects closer to us are going slower than objects more distant?" Quellin asked.

"Yes," Corey said.

"Then could that fact not also be interpreted as a slowing down with time and would that not fit your data?" Quellin asked.

"What's the difference?" Matthew asked.

Corey chimed in with the answer as he realized Quellin's point. "It makes a significant difference because it means there is no need to create a mysterious dark energy to account for an acceleration process. It is much easier to explain a deceleration. That can be done with conventional physics and laws of thermodynamics." He looked at Quellin and considered Quellin's explanation for a moment. "Yes, Quellin, I agree, that *is* another way of interpreting the observations. In fact, I am surprised that interpretation has not been considered before." Corey was now intrigued. "So, what does your model of the universe look like?"

"Let me propose a model in which the whole original primordial universe is interconnected in a way similar to a three dimensional crystalline structure. This crystal extends out to infinity and existed before the known visible universe."

"When you say crystal, how is it constructed?" Corey asked.

"It is arranged it what you would call a hexahedron. At each node is what you might visualize as an energy hole. An electron and a positron are paired in this hole. They orbit each other in a stable orbit."

"We call that pair a positronium," Corey volunteered. "However, in our laboratories, the positronium has a very short life. It is less than a second before the electron and positron annihilate each other. When the electron and positron combine, their mass is converted into two very energetic photons and the positronium disappears." Corey looked at Quellin. "Now I am puzzled. If what you say is true, why didn't the whole matrix just disappear in an instant as a flash of light?"

"Remember, Dr. Newton," Quellin answered. "In deep space, the universe is at a very low temperature. All of the electrons and positrons orbit each other about their nodes in a synchronized fashion and are in a stable state of balance. The centrifugal force from their orbiting counteracts the electrical and gravitational attraction forces. In deep space they will remain in equilibrium indefinitely."

"All right then, we start with a universe that is a stable crystal of positronium. What's the scale of this crystal matrix of the universe? I mean, what's the separation between nodes?" Corey asked.

Quellin looked at Corey's hand. "They are separated by a distance similar to the length of your hand. As you can imagine, on a universal scale, there are a huge number of these positroniums, as you call them."

Corey's curiosity was now piqued. "Your explanation reminds me of the Dirac Sea."

"What's the Dirac Sea?" Matthew asked.

"It's a theoretical model of the vacuum of space as an infinite sea of holes or particles that possess negative energy," Corey explained. "It was formulated by a British physicist named Paul Dirac in 1928 to explain the anomalous negative-energy quantum states predicted by an equation he had developed. It led to the discovery in 1932 of the antimatter anti-electron known as the positron. Dirac won a Nobel Prize for his work."

"Then why isn't our current model of the universe a Dirac model?" Matthew asked.

"Dirac visualized the existence of the sea as implying an infinite negative electric charge filling all of space. In order to make any sense out of this, it was necessary to assume that the vacuum of space must also have an infinite positive charge which is exactly cancelled by the negative charge of the Dirac Sea. That was hard for cosmologists of his day to swallow."

"So I guess physicists went on to search for a better model," Matthew said.

"Yes. If only they had considered a positronium crystal lattice as described by Quellin, then Dirac's model might have won out," Corey explained.

"Why haven't astronomers detected this structure of positroniums?" Matthew asked.

"They are unable to detect them because, except for their mass, their properties cancel each other," Quellin explained. "Even though the mass of each is very small, on a universal scale, it amounts to a tremendous amount of mass. It is more mass than in all the stars and their planets."

"Well," Matthew thought for a moment, "why can't we detect the lattice through its huge mass?"

"Because it extends in every direction all around us and the gravitational effects cancel", Corey explained. "Perhaps that accounts for the dark matter which cosmologists are puzzled over," Corey mused.

"I am not familiar with this dark matter you talk about," Quellin continued,

Corey looked at Quellin. "So, you have explained that the universe began as a three dimensional matrix of positroniums. How did the universe get to be the way it is today with stars and everything?"

Quellin thought for a moment. "It is only when the matrix is disturbed that the electron and positron interact and combine. Long ago, there was an initial disturbance and the annihilation process began. The wave of photons expanded outward at nearly the speed of light and interacted with surrounding positroniums causing them to annihilate in turn releasing more photons. I believe you would call that process a chain reaction."

"What do you think caused that initial disturbance?" Matthew asked.

"We believe it was The Creator," Quellin answered. "In the beginning, the structure existed and it was undisturbed. Then The Creator caused the disturbance that caused the positroniums to collapse and annihilate each other, creating the chain reaction."

"What you just described reminds me of an explosion in which the flame front travels outward at sonic speed," Corey added.

"Yes, that is a good analogy," Quellin said. "As the energy from this wave passes other nodes, they also collapse, releasing more energy and the wave propagation continued. In fact, it continues today just beyond the edge of the visible universe."

"How does the matter we have today get created from this process?" Matthew asked.

"Some of the energy being released at the wave front is transmuted back into mass that eventually becomes simple atoms," Quellin answered.

"Yes," Corey added, "Remember, Matthew, matter consists of both mass and energy and it is conserved. Einstein showed the interchangeability of energy and mass through his famous equation, $E = mc^2$."

Quellin continued. "That is correct. Now, because of the near light speed of these atoms, their mass is very high and so gravitational attraction for each other dominates all other forces. They agglomerate into heavier particles. During this process of agglomeration, the collisions between particles result in a conversion of outward velocity into velocity in random directions. This results in a reduction in outward velocity."

"And thus the reduced red shift," Corey added.

"Yes, the agglomeration process continues as molecules, dust, and other particles grow even larger, forming stars. As a result of off-center collisions, linear velocity is converted into angular velocity, resulting in a further decrease of red shift with time. Meanwhile, the causation wave continues outward at near light speed."

"That answers a question of mine," Corey said. "Your model explains the origin of the massive amount of angular momentum in the universe."

"I don't understand," Matthew said. "How is all of this different from the Big Bang Theory? It sounds the same to me."

"If I understand what Quellin has just described," Corey said. "The difference is that the Big Bang Theory states that all matter, energy and mass, originated from a single point in the universe and started expanding outward about 13.7 billion years ago. In Quellin's theory, all matter already existed throughout the universe in the form of a positronium matrix."

"I'm not sure I follow," Matthew said.

"Let me give you an analogy," Corey said, "Consider a room filled with a mixture of natural gas and air. Those atoms are dispersed throughout the room. Someone lights a match and a flame front moves out away from the match at a tremendous speed. Ahead of the advancing flame front is the original gas mixture. At the flame front, which has some thickness, a chemical reaction is occurring and energy is being released. Behind the flame front are the products of combustion. So, the universe was already filled with matter but it was the deflagration process that changed it into the mass and energy we see today."

"That is correct and a very good analogy, Dr. Newton," Quellin added. "However, you put the age of the universe at 13.7 billion years. That is incorrect. The universe is older than you think since the deflagration began nearly forty billion years ago. Quellin studied both men. "Now, would you like to continue our tour?"

Corey glanced at Matthew and grinned. "Are you kidding me, let's go!"

Chapter 9
Let's Move

Thursday, May 15
7:52 AM

Pete woke with a start as a beam of light suddenly bore down on his closed eyes. Instinctively, he lunged out of its path. "Wendy, watch out!"

"What is it!" Wendy yelled, as Pete's movement pulled her out of her deep sleep.

"They found … usss," he suddenly realized the light was only a beam of sunlight. "Oh ahhh … Nothing," he said, groggily. The morning sun had burst over the mountains to the east and found a path through the boulders to Pete's face. It was not an alien craft searching them out as Pete had been dreaming. "I guess I'm just jumpy."

"What time is it?"

Pete looked at his watch. "I guess it's about 0800 hours."

"Have you decided whether we should head for Kingman or Hoover Dam?" Wendy asked, as she ventured out of their small cave. She gazed to her left and her eyes followed the dirt road below them as it went through the pass and intercepted a larger road in the distance. "That must be US Route 93 I see in the distance. It doesn't look to be very far," she hollered back. Pete was he exiting the cave, carrying the strange looking goggles.

"Yes it is, but the distance is deceptive in the desert. That road is actually about fifteen miles away. We can get there in about three hours. If we're lucky, we can get a lift into Kingman."

"So, you've decided on Kingman then?"

"Yes. I think there are more opportunities there. Also, if we go to Hoover Dam, there's more chance of being stopped in a security check for dam traffic. I don't think we'll need these goggles anymore. I'll leave them in the cave." Pete threw the goggles into the cave and began climbing down toward the dirt road west.

Wendy followed. "What do you think people will think when they see us; you in your flight suit and me in this blue jump suit? What shall we tell them?"

"I've always believed that honesty is the best policy. We should simply tell them we were on our way to a secret base when our helicopter was brought down by a UFO," Pete said, as he looked back at Wendy with a sheepish smile.

"You know, Pete, that just might work." After a few minutes, she yelled out to him, "Pete, I've been thinking. Telling that story is really a *bad* idea. I think we need something better, *far* better." Wendy thought for a moment. "How about this? I'm a cadet in some military school in Kingman and you were giving me an orientation flight on a light aircraft out of the Kingman airfield. We were forced to land in the hills when we had an engine problem."

"I like it!" he said as he stopped walking and turned around to face her. "You see, that's why you're the brains of this outfit. You can come up with brilliant ideas even on an empty stomach."

"Oh, don't remind me. I'm famished. How are we going to buy food? I don't have a cent on me. It's all at the base."

"Don't worry, I have my wallet with a credit card and about four hundred dollars in cash."

"What will we do when the cash runs out? It might be risky using your credit card. What if the aliens have spies who are monitoring credit card activity," Wendy said, half joking. "That artifact you're carrying is extremely important to them. They just might begin activating some of their sleeper cells."

"Good point. I think we have to assume the aliens are pulling out all the stops. After we get to Kingman and have some breakfast, we need to develop a plan that will generate income that can't be traced."

The two continued west down the dirt road until reaching Route 93. At eleven in the morning, there was only moderate car traffic heading north toward Hoover Dam. The sightseers headed out early to get a full day at the dam. Traffic moving south was sparse too. Wendy followed Pete across the highway to the west side. From there they headed south, walking backward. Pete held his right hand up, thumb high as any southbound cars approached. After the fourth attempt, a large twelve-passenger van passed. Brake lights came on and it slowed down, pulling over to the breakdown lane.

"We got one, Pete. Let's hope the driver isn't too inquisitive," Wendy said, as the two began running toward the van.

"We'll use your story," Pete fired back. He approached the vehicle on the passenger side and noticed the sign on the sliding door. It read **AL'S LIMO SERVICE.** Pete opened the passenger door and peered in.

"Need a lift?" the driver said, as he shot Pete a glance and then watched through his rear view mirror as Wendy, with her long flowing hair, followed in a fast run.

"Yes, thank you for stopping," Pete answered, panting for breath. "We do need a lift. Are you going into Kingman?"

"Yes I am. I'm on my way to work. I'll be glad to drop you two off in town if you want. Just climb in the back."

As Wendy climbed into the van, Pete noticed the man eyeing the uniform Wendy was wearing. He gave him the story Wendy had contrived. The man seemed satisfied.

"I guess you two are lucky to have escaped injury. You must have been doing some fancy flying to land in them foothills up there," the man said as he thumbed the direction over his left shoulder.

"Yes, we were lucky. We found a level spot a couple miles to the east of the highway," Pete lied.

"I have a pickup at ten thirty but I can drop you two downtown," the man said. "My pickups are at some motels on the Andy Devine Highway. I can drop you off in that area if that's okay."

"That's fine," Pete said. "Isn't that old Route 66 that runs by the airport?"

"Yep, there's a lot of motels in that area so I get a lot of business there."

"What do you do?" Wendy asked over his shoulder.

"I have my own limo service. By the way, I'm Al. My name is on the van," he said proudly. "In fact, I just came back from Hoover Dam where I dropped off some early-bird sightseers. They're there for the day. I have to pick them up at four this afternoon. Now I have to pick up a load for Laughlin. Gamble…that's what they wanna do. Lots o'folks like to cross over to Nevada to gamble and Laughlin is closer than Vegas. I run lotta groups to Laughlin from the motels along 66. Lotta their guests here on business wanna take a break and do some gambl'n over in Nevada. It's regulated there you know," the man said as he glanced over to Wendy with a smile. "You get better odds over there. I guess you probly knew that."

"That's what I heard," Pete said, with a nod.

The van made a left turn up the on-ramp onto I-40 East and headed into Kingman. Within fifteen minutes they crossed over the mountain and were at the exit for Andy

Devine. Al slowed from seventy-five to the exit speed. After turning south onto Andy Devine, he pulled into the parking lot of a restaurant. Several motels were in sight. "Is this okay? I figure you two must be pretty hungry after your ordeal."

"Yes, this is fine and you're right, we are hungry. Thank you very much. Can I give you something for your trouble?" Pete said as they exited the van.

"Nah, that's okay. Just remember to call AL's when you need a lift. Have a great day." He smiled and drove off.

Pete looked at Wendy and pointed toward the restaurant, "I think we need to keep our priorities straight. Let's have breakfast."

"I agree. Besides, we have some heavy thinking to do and need to feed our brains," Wendy said, with a smile as she followed Pete into the restaurant.

After being served, they began to discuss their plans for the day. Pete had an idea.

"Wendy, I've been thinking about what Al was telling us about gambling. If I was lucky, perhaps I could parlay four hundred dollars into a more substantial sum. As long as the winnings weren't too large, no one would ask any questions."

"What if you aren't lucky?"

Pete gave her a hard stare and smiled. "Think positive, Wendy. The last few times I left the base and went into Vegas, I returned at least a thousand dollars richer. I'm pretty good at blackjack. What do you think?"

"I think it's worth a try. We need to set limits though, so we can at least eat. What about our clothes? Shouldn't we get something less conspicuous?"

Pete looked across the street. "Yes, we should get some other clothes. I see a Shop-For-Less clothing store just a few doors down, across the street. We can get an inexpensive change of clothes there. That should do for now. Then we'll go to the motel down the street and get a room. After we shower and freshen up we'll see about getting on a shuttle to Laughlin."

"That sounds like a plan to me," Wendy said.

Chapter 10
The Holographic Universe
Mind Over Matter

As the three took their seats around the conference table, Corey felt compelled to speak. "Thank you, Quellin. I truly appreciate the tour and everything you have taught me. I only wish you would let me remember all of this when I return to Earth."

"Dr. Newton, I am sure you understand why we cannot allow you to remember all that you learn here," Quellin answered.

"Well, I'm unhappy with it but I understand." Corey's curiosity was getting the better of him. "Throughout our stay here we keep encountering Grays. Are those Grays alive?"

"Yes, they are alive just as a tree is alive," Quellin answered, "but they have no soul. We grow them. They are what you might call synthetic."

"How do you grow them?" Matthew asked.

"We grow them in a special container, much the same as we grow a fetus that we have extracted from a female human. In fact, the process is similar to the growth of the fetus in a female's womb. We stimulate a special seed and its cells start to divide and differentiate. Eventually the growth process for the Gray is complete and we can then start the programming process. An early step in their programming is to teach them to communicate telepathically."

"So they are living and thinking beings, then," Corey said.

"Yes, but they differ from us in that they have no soul, no spirit. We cannot make a soul or spirit for them. Only The Creator can make a spirit," Quellin said.

"Will you show me how you grow the Grays?" Corey asked.

"No, I am truly sorry. I cannot do that because they are made at the main base located in the asteroid belt. Perhaps someday you will have the opportunity to visit that base."

"What do you do if they break down?" Matthew asked.

"It is rare that they malfunction, but if they do then we send them out to the main base to be repaired. Normally, it is a programming issue, but occasionally it is a physical problem. For instance, occasionally they need to have their eyes replaced."

"Why do their eyes need replacing?" Corey asked.

"The Grays often work around our craft while it is operating. That exposes them to unusually high amounts of ultraviolet radiation which damages their eyes. After prolonged exposure, they need replacing."

"Where do you get replacement eyes?" Corey asked.

"We have developed a genetically altered sea animal similar to your lobster. Their eyes are a perfect match to those of the Grays. We simply remove one from the sea animal when we need it."

"Isn't that rather cruel?" Matthew asked.

"Not really, Colonel. We remove only one at a time. The remaining eye serves the animal while it grows a replacement."

"You said that you teach the Grays to use telepathy to communicate. I notice that Matthew can do the same. How do you do that?" Corey asked.

"That's something you can learn to do," Matthew chimed in. "You just have to set your mind to it."

"That is correct," Quellin agreed. "You can learn to do that. It is a matter of connecting to the universe and to each other through the use of psychic abilities. We all have these abilities. Ours is more developed than yours, but you can learn."

"I'm a nuts-n-bolts person. I'm afraid I don't buy into that psychic stuff. If it can't be explained in scientific terms then I'm a skeptic." Corey admitted.

"Dr. Newton, trust me, it *is* real," Quellin insisted. "At the present, your spirit is manifested in the physical world. We are in the physical realm. You detect your surroundings with various senses. You sense acoustic energy through your ears. You sense heat energy through sensors in your skin. You also sense pressure on your skin. You sense the presence of certain chemicals through sensors in your nose. And, we both sense light, which is electromagnetic energy in the shorter wavelength, through the sensors in our eyes."

"Yes, well I am familiar with those senses but you're talking about something different, something intangible," Corey responded.

"Well," Quellin continued, "telepathy is only intangible to you because you have not developed the sensor to receive it. Most living entities, including humans, have the ability to develop that sensor. What I am talking about is the ability of our brains to tune into the coherent quantum vibrations that permeate the universe. You know it as psychic ability. It allows communication without acoustic speech. You could tune into these vibrations by entering into a receptive, subconscious, non-sensual, non-thinking state of awareness. The process is optimized through practices of deep meditation, prayer, and other states of higher consciousness. This puts the brain into a highly synchronized and perfectly ordered spectral array of brain waves that form unique harmonic waves. The brain waves are now highly coherent and in this state generate the nonlocal holographic informational cortical field of consciousness that interconnects the brain and the holographic cosmos. Think of it as a frequency that resonates with the vibrations of the universe. During this state your brain operates at a lower frequency than when you are awake."

"I still don't buy it," Corey said.

"Is it the holographic nature of the mind that troubles you?" asked Quellin.

"Well, that's part of it. I'm not sure what you mean by that," Corey answered.

"I agree, I don't understand how the mind is like a hologram," Andrews said.

Quellin turned to Andrews. "Well, colonel Andrews, I believe that you are aware that your technology has progressed to where you have developed coherent light sources."

"Do you mean lasers?" Matthew asked.

"Yes, Colonel, I believe you call them that."

"Ahhh," Corey interrupted, as the significance of a holographic model set in. "Quellin, I think I can explain in terms the colonel will understand."

Quellin nodded. "Proceed."

"Matthew, you have seen photographs made by using laser light. You know them as holograms. They're quite amazing since they contain more information than a typical two-dimensional photograph," Corey explained.

Matthew nodded. "Yes, go ahead."

"Then you know that they contain a complete three-dimensional image, or record. That's because the hologram is made with coherent light and the extra information in the photo is captured through phase relationships that show up as interference patterns on the photographic film. When coherent light is shined through the film, a virtual three-dimensional image appears behind the film."

"Okay, I follow." The colonel acknowledged his understanding thus far.

"Well," Corey smiled, "did you know that a holographic film has a distributive property?"

"No, what is that?"

"By that, I mean if you cut it into as many pieces as you wish, each piece, when held up to coherent light would show the entire image, or record. It is slightly degraded, but each piece contains an image of the three-dimensional information of that scene."

Matthew looked amazed. "I didn't know that!"

"That is correct and an excellent analogy, Dr. Newton," Quellin said. "Now, do you know that every experience you have ever had is recorded in your brain and under the right conditions can be recalled?"

Both Andrews and Corey nodded. "Yes, I have read about that," Andrews said. "The human brain has always fascinated me. I recall reading that people, during a brain operation, have had various areas stimulated by a probe and suddenly have vivid recollections of events in their past."

"Yes, and is it not strange to you that such a tremendous amount of information can be stored in the small volume of your brain?" Quellin asked.

"It is indeed and I am not sure the medical professionals actually know how that works," Andrews responded. "I have read where neuroscientists have done probes of people's brains to find where a particular memory resided and it seems to be everywhere."

Quellin smiled at both men. "That is the distributive nature of the brain, much like the holographic film you talked about, Dr. Newton. It is the phase relationship of the signals sent out from each neuron that creates the holographic image of a memory that gets mapped over the entire brain."

"I think I understand," Corey said. "Just as a holographic plate contains a nearly infinite number of views, depending on the angle at which it is viewed, the same can be said of the brain. It can contain a nearly infinite number of memories, depending on how the information is accessed. Dr. Newton, your visit here will always be in your memory but we will try to block your view of that memory before you leave." Corey looked at Quellin. "Okay, what about this holographic universe you mentioned earlier and the coherent quantum vibrations that permeate the universe?"

"Well," Quellin answered, "what I am about to explain will be foreign to you so please bear with me."

"Go ahead, I'm listening," Corey said.

Quellin began. "Consider that each molecule has a complete history of itself and all other molecules in the universe. You might call this a holographic model of the universe or a quantum hologram."

"Why do you call it a holographic model?" Matthew interrupted.

"I think Quellin refers to the universe as a quantum hologram because it exhibits a distributive property in that each molecule contains the history of the universe. It's the same distributive property we discussed about the brain." Corey could see by Matthew's face that he was perplexed. "I know, it is hard to believe."

"That is an excellent explanation, Dr. Newton. Let me explain further," Quellin said. "On a macro scale, all matter in the universe vibrates as it makes quantum changes in energy levels. These changes radiate information in a coherent fashion."

"I still don't follow," Matthew said, still with a perplexed expression.

Corey decided to try another explanation. "Are you familiar with how MRI works?"

"Do you mean magnetic resonance imaging?"

"Yes," Corey said.

"I know of it but not how it works."

"MRI works by sending strong pulses of magnetic energy through your body," Corey explained. "The molecules in your body are magnetically aligned as the magnetic wave passes. With time, the molecules drop back to their original orientation, releasing energy that is detected by the machine. Each type of molecule is unique in the time it takes to drop back to its original state. Bone tissue takes a different time than muscle tissue. The computer sorts all of that out and produces the image that the technician sees on the computer screen."

Quellin looked at Corey. "Let me expand on that. In the model I am proposing, not only molecules but the entire matrix of the universe vibrates in a phase-conjugate-adaptive-resonance manner."

Matthew's brow furrowed as he glanced at Corey. "What did he say?"

"He means it's like a standing wave. A standing wave is a form of phase conjugate resonate wave," Corey explained.

"I hate to act dumb but what do you mean by a standing wave?" Matthew asked, apologetically.

"A good example of a standing wave is the vibrating string on a guitar. It's fixed at both ends. These are called nodes. These nodes are stationary but the string can be seen to vibrate from side to side. The wave does not move along the string and thus appears to be stationary or standing." Corey explained.

Matthew's face lit up. "I see, and waves on a lake are not standing waves because they move along the surface until striking the shore."

"Exactly," Corey said.

Quellin continued. "Yes, and in the universe, information is carried in the phase relations of the standing waves as the universe vibrates. Again, think about a hologram. In the universe, these relations can change and be transmitted faster than electromagnetic energy. It can be almost instantaneous."

"Okay . . . so far," Corey said, as he was beginning to buy into Quellin's explanation.

Quellin looked at both men. "The model I am proposing has interesting properties. One of these is that the history of all matter is continuously emitted and broadcast throughout the universe and is received by and interacts with other matter through a process of quantum information exchange. Consider our discussion about how information is mapped onto the brain in a method similar to holography. The information in a quantum hologram encodes the complete event history of the object with respect to its three-dimensional environment."

"So this process occurs only at the sub-atomic level then?" Corey questioned.

"No, not just at the sub-atomic level. This holographic information exchange occurs also in the larger macro-scale world. However, at a macro scale level, these quantum effects cannot exist in more than three dimensions."

"Are you saying that the universe consists of only three dimensions and not the eleven I keep hearing about?" Matthew asked.

"Yes, at the macro-scale," Quellin answered.

"How is this so?" Corey asked.

"Let me explain. Particles do not move or behave independently when involved as a group in the same process or in energy transfers. They unite as an enduring discrete three-dimensional assembly of particles with compatible spin and polarization characteristics."

"Much as a swarm of bees or birds acst as a single unit." Corey added.

"Yes, that is a good analogy," Quellin responded. "The process may include the exchanges of energy, matter, or even information and consciousness...including thought. The swarm of bees you mentioned appears to have a consciousness as a group."

"So, it's like patterns of energy to which we give meaning." Corey added.

"Yes, precisely," Quellin said.

"Does this information propagate at the speed of light?" Corey asked.

"No," Quellin answered. "The propagation speed is a second property of the model. Because the universe acts as a whole, through the medium of quantum correlation, any event that occurs anywhere in the universe is immediately available anywhere else as information."

What do you mean?" Corey asked.

"That is, each portion of space instantaneously contains information about all others."

"That blows my mind!" Matthew exclaimed.

"Yes it does," Corey agreed. "Are you talking about action at a distance?"

"Yes, I suppose you could think of it that way," Quellin answered.

"That sounds like Bell's Theorem," Corey said.

"What's that?" Matthew asked.

"In 1935 Einstein had published a paper that showed that under certain circumstances, quantum mechanics predicted a breakdown in locality. Einstein referred to this as spooky action at a distance and refused to believe his own results," Corey explained.

"What do you mean by locality?" Matthew asked.

"Locality means that if an event occurs somewhere in the universe, we will not know of it or feel its effects instantly. We will have to wait for light or other energy forms to travel through space and reach us. That takes time. With nonlocality, if a star a billion light years away blew up, we would know about it instantly.

In the 1960s, a physicist at CERN by the name of J.S. Bell proposed a theorem that overthrows the notion of locality and establishes nonlocality. No one has ever been able to disprove Bell's Theorem." Corey thought for a moment. "It seems that the whole universe is integrated into a single, thinking entity. I guess, given that, I would place information on the same level of importance as energy."

Quellin gave Corey a reassuring smile. "Very perceptive, that is right except that information is more important."

"How does this happen?" Corey asked.

"It happens through wave-like resonance. Space and time are not a factor. The universe is unified and joined together holistically, through a process of non-local resonance."

"Well, you've lost me again," Matthew said, as he rolled his eyes.

"I agree with the colonel," Corey said. "This is very difficult to understand. When you say resonance; resonance of what?"

"It is the vibrations of the matrix, or aether as you call it, which transfers energy and information. It occurs within the underlying zero-point field that connects all matter, energy, and information in the universe. You see, information does not obey the same inverse square law for space-time as energy propagation." Quellin looked at both men for signs of understanding. "In the simplest terms," he continued, "the transfer of information occurs within the fabric of the universe. It is time independent and cannot be shielded by electromagnetic shielding."

"So, I assume that this information that permeates the universe is recoverable," Corey observed.

"Yes, under proper conditions."

Matthew smiled as a wave of brilliance came over him. "So, because the information is time independent, that allows people to look back in time and visit past lives. Am I right?"

"You are precisely correct," Quellin said with a smile.

Corey looked at Quellin. "If I understand what Matthew and you just said, it means that all information, past, and present is permeating the universe. If we learn to tap into *it* then we *can* look into the past." He was beginning to grasp what Quellin was saying and a smile of understanding began to appear.

"Yes, you can view events in the past and at any three dimensional coordinates," Quellin said.

"Isn't that how remote viewing works?" Matthew asked.

"Yes."

"What's remote viewing?" Corey asked.

Matthew looked at Corey and smiled. "Well it's nice to know that I may know something you don't. For over twenty years we have used it in the military for spying. I'm surprised you weren't aware of it."

"No, I'm afraid I haven't heard of it. Please explain."

"Remote viewing refers to our psychic ability to experience and describe activities at distant places *and* times that are blocked from ordinary perception."

"How does it work?" Corey asked.

"The military intelligence ran a secret facility where a team of trained viewers were given assignments to view.

They were in the form of coordinates given in a sealed envelope."

"By coordinates do you mean longitude, latitude, and time?"

"No, not necessarily. The coordinates could simply be in the form of a photograph or a written question. One protocol is for the viewer and the monitor to take the sealed envelope into a room. After getting into the proper relaxed state of mind, the viewer would begin talking about things that would come into his mind. The monitor would record this and later the monitor and viewer would discuss their session with a controller who would know what was in the envelope and what the coordinates meant."

"What sort of information did they get from these sessions?" Corey asked.

"Well, for example, the coordinates might be the location of a secret enemy defense installation. After several sessions, it might be possible to view into some of the buildings and see what was being done. The information gathered by the remote viewing teams was often remarkably accurate."

"You said that this can be used to look at distant times. What do you mean?"

"On occasion, the coordinates would involve viewing into a different time. For example, one viewer recorded a session which took him back to the time of the Great Pyramid and he was able to describe how the pyramid was built."

"What about the future?" Corey asked.

"Yes, that too. But you have to understand, they view only the probable future. Since the future has not actually happened yet, the actual future can be altered by our actions. Quellin has already explained that," said Matthew.

"Yes," Quellin added. "I think you can see how this whole discussion reveals quite clearly the connection that exists between our minds and the universe."

"Quellin, you said earlier that we can recover this information under proper conditions. Can you explain?" Corey asked.

"I would be glad to," Quellin answered. "Information is recoverable by establishing resonance between your brain and the universe. It simply remains for you to develop the connection. The brain can act as a phase gate and decipher the information. Our brains store and manage information not in digital format, but rather in analog format using non-local properties of the quantum hologram."

"How do I make the connection?" Corey asked.

"By training," Quellin answered. "The human brain has these capabilities at birth but they suppress them by cultural conditioning during childhood. Subsequently, through lack of practice, this natural ability for conscious, intuitive perception atrophies. It takes training to recover this ability."

"Yes, it is that sort of training that remote viewers have to go through." Matthew added. "Corey, you see, it's like a psychic Internet and in order to make a mind-to-mind connection, all you have to do is log on. That's how we do mental telepathy." Matthew had the smile a professor might give to a student after giving a simple explanation for a complicated concept.

A broad smile appeared on Quellin's face. "Very good, that is a great analogy. Colonel, while you may not remember it, as you were developing, we would periodically abduct you for training in the psychic area."

"Yes, now I do remember," Matthew said.

"Good. Perhaps you would explain the process to Dr. Newton."

"I'd be glad to." He turned to Corey. "What really happens is that you learn to get your mind into a very relaxed state and operating at a low frequency so it can tune into the stream of information. You let your mind drift without trying to direct or focus your thoughts. Soon, you will begin to receive information in the form of thoughts."

"That is correct," Quellin added and turned to face Corey. "And, Dr. Newton, I would encourage you to develop this psychic aspect. It will give an expansive dimension to your life. It will evoke a greater sense of purpose and inspire you to reach for your higher potential as a conscious being."

"Yes, it is what we call the sixth sense," Matthew added. "Quellin, this thing you call the quantum hologram seems to me to be the mind of God. I remember an ancient Sanskrit proverb that goes something like, 'God sleeps in the minerals, awakens in the plants, walks in the animals, and thinks in man.'"

"Excellent! You are so correct! It *is* an intelligence that permeates the entire universe and we are all connected through it. It *is* a collective consciousness," Quellin agreed.

"I think I understand now," Corey said. "What you're saying is that information is radiating throughout the universe, much like the radio waves we broadcast. It simply remains for us to get into a relaxed state so that our brain resonates with these information waves. It's much like tuning a radio."

"Yes, that is an excellent summary," Quellin said.

A thought occurred to Corey. "Quellin, we have been discussing many things that involve matter. By that I mean energy and mass. I am wondering now just what our spirit is. Apparently, when our bodies die, the spirit does not and moves on to another life. What is the spirit?"

"I was wondering when you might ask that," Quellin said. "The spirit is another form of energy. Our spirits are made of energy. Our scientists believe that the energy content of the spirit that inhabits our bodies is far less than the energy content of the mass of our body. They have concluded that only The Creator has the ability to transmute energy into a spirit. They do not know how it is done."

"How do our spirits enter our bodies?" Matthew asked.

Quellin turned toward Matthew. "A few days after conception, the mass of the fetus has grown large enough so that it can begin its own vibrations. At that point a spirit can enter the body by getting into resonance. The body and spirit are then joined for life."

"When two people are in love is that a sign that their spirits resonate in harmony?" Corey asked.

Quellin gave Corey a broad smile. "That is precisely what love is, the harmony of our spirits." He gave Corey and intent look. "Dr. Newton, I suspect your spirit is in harmony with Dr. Ahearn's." Corey blushed.

"What happens when we die?" Matthew asked.

"When a body dies, its natural vibrations end and the spirit separates and moves on," Quellin answered.

"Where does our spirit go?" Corey asked.

Quellin studied Corey for a moment. "Dr. Newton, if you were given the answers to all your questions I think much of life's excitements would vanish. You *must* have the ability to experience self-discovery."

Corey nodded and gave a smile of appreciation. "I agree. I remember a quote from Albert Einstein in which he said: 'The most beautiful experience we can have is the mysterious. It is the fundamental emotion that stands at the cradle of true art and true science. Whoever does not know it and can no longer wonder, no longer marvel, is as good as dead, and his eyes are dimmed.'"

"I am impressed, Dr. Newton. That is very profound," Quellin said.

Chapter 11
A New World Order

"Quellin looked at both men. "Perhaps you have more questions? Dr. Newton, you may be glad to know that you will be allowed to recall some of what you experience here when the time is right and when it will benefit our mission."

"Oh. What is your mission?" Corey asked. He was finally going to find out what the aliens were up to, he thought.

"Our mission is to prevent the destruction of humankind and Earth's environment. We have determined that it will be necessary to overtly influence the decisions humans are making in government affairs. To do that, we must first get our people into place."

"What do you mean by *your* people?" Corey asked.

"Dr. Newton, you are aware that we have been making genetic adjustments to the human species for several generations now."

"Are you talking about the hybrids?" Corey asked.

"Yes. They will be the future leaders during the transition."

Corey glanced at Matthew and then back to Quellin. "Colonel Andrews has told me he is a hybrid. Is he one of our future transition leaders?"

"Perhaps he will be. They are going to be our liaisons to assist in the communications between humans and us."

"What skills do they have that make them suitable for that?" Corey asked.

"They have been genetically altered to enhance their psychic sensitivity and also to remove some of their self-centeredness. We want them to be in positions of leadership but to lead for the good of humanity and the world and not for personal gains or ego enhancement as your leaders do today. Also, you are a very emotional species. They will govern through reason and not by emotion."

"Are these hybrids all aware of their mission?" Corey asked.

"Very few of the altered ones know they are special or what their mission will be but they will be awakened at the proper time."

Corey probed further. "When will that be?"

"It will be soon, in just a few years. We must wait until humanity is conditioned to accept us without fear. We do not want to bring about chaos in your economic or religious systems."

"What will happen when the hybrids are awakened?" Corey asked.

"They will work to bring about the proper social reform."

Corey eyed Quellin. "And what would that be?"

"We wish to modify your system of government and create one world government. In that way we hope to reduce the probability of conflicts among your kind."

"What type of world government?" Corey asked, with concern.

"It will be patterned much like the government of the United States as it was originally intended by the writers of your constitution. We were very pleased by the form of government they envisioned but are very disappointed to see how it has been corrupted into the form you have today. Your present government consists of people who are making a career out of governing. We feel that your founding fathers intended for your government officials to be more representative of their constituents and not be professional politicians. We want to correct that. Your elected officials will serve only one term. That way they can focus on the issues at hand."

Corey was incredulous. "So, even those leaders who do a really good job will not be able to get re-elected then?"

"That is correct. No one can get re-elected. Dr. Newton, there are always plenty of good people available to serve in the government. Having the ability to be re-elected causes a distraction from the real job that has to be done ... running the government."

Matthew jumped into the conversation. "Come on, Dr. Newton, you know that our representatives in congress spend only ten percent of their time running the government and the rest of the time raising money for the next election. Do you think that with 300 million people in this country there are only 100 people qualified to be senators and 435 people who can do a good job as representatives?"

"No, but who would want the job if it's only for a single term?" Corey fired back.

"I think there would be plenty." Matthew responded as he turned to Quellin. "How will the new government be organized?"

"As with your present government, there will be three branches: the legislative branch in the form of a House of Representatives and a Senate, the judicial branch in the form of a Supreme World Court, and a World President."

"So, since you said there would be only one world government, there will be no separate countries. Is that true?" Corey questioned.

"There will be no need for separate countries. Throughout the world, congressional districts will be drawn up with 500,000 residents in each district."

"What about language differences?" Corey asked.

"Local languages will be preserved but there will be a common world language that all people will be required to learn. It will be the language used in all important research papers and in all business and governmental transactions," Quellin explained.

"So, how will the election process work?" Matthew asked.

"Each citizen of the world will have to register in his or her home district at the age of twenty five," Quellin said. "From that age until the age of the average life span, each person's name will be in a pool from which they may be drafted to stand election. The representative for each district will serve only a single four-year term. During the election year for a district, and four months before election day, ten names will be drawn at random from the pool. Each of the ten persons will have two months in which to appeal and explain why it would be a hardship for them to serve in congress."

"Why would it be a hardship to serve in congress?" Matthew asked.

"Perhaps, for example, they might be ill or they might have a business that will suffer if they leave. There are a variety of legitimate reasons to be excused. After the appeal process, four of the remaining candidates will be drafted at random and will be given one month in which to prepare their campaign. The candidate cannot spend more than what is provided from public funds."

"How much will their salary be?" Corey asked.

"Their salary will be equal to the average income of that district. While serving, all their debts and assets will be frozen. When they have completed their term in office, they will return to the job they left."

"So, when their term begins, they have to pack up and move to Washington." Matthew said.

"No, they will stay in their district."

"How will the representatives keep in touch with their constituents and each other?" Matthew asked.

"The representatives will be required to have regular office hours and to schedule at least one televised public meeting each week in which current issues and proposed new bills will be discussed. To interact with fellow representatives, each week they will participate in a teleconference with all of the other members from around the world. At these meetings, new bills will be presented, debated, and voted on."

"What about the senate?" Corey asked.

"A state will consist of one hundred adjoining congressional districts. One senator will be elected for each and will serve only a single five year term. To serve in the senate, one must have served in the house of representatives but not within the past four years."

"Why make them wait four years?" Corey asked.

"They must wait four years so that there are no ties to any serving representative. That will prevent the building of a power base. Each senator's salary will be four times the average salary for his or her state. The operation of the senate will be similar to the representatives."

"It sounds like members of congress will not need to travel to Washington. Is that true?" Corey asked.

Quellin smiled, "The central government may not be in Washington. It will be in the most convenient place on the planet. Travel there will not be required unless a special meeting is needed as determined by a simple majority of the members. That keeps them at home with their constituents. Also, it reduces the risk of terrorist actions."

Matthew glanced at Corey and smiled. "It's sort of like not keeping all your eggs in one basket."

Quellin looked puzzled. "Eggs? What eggs?"

"That's sort of a private joke," Matthew smiled.

"Well, if the representatives and the senators don't have to spend time at the central government, that doesn't leave much to be done there." Corey commented.

"Actually, there will be much work done there." Quellin said. "The World Supreme Court, the World

President and all of the various administration offices will have to be located there."

"How long will the President serve?"

"The World President will serve a single six year term. To become President, requires having served in the Senate, but not within the past five years."

Of all candidates who want to run for President, only four will be chosen to run based on luck of the draw. The candidate receiving the largest popular vote will be President and the one receiving the next largest vote will serve as Vice President. Their salary will be eight times the average salary for the state from which each comes."

"That makes sense," said Corey. "What about the Supreme Court?"

"There will be fifteen members of the World Supreme Court who will each serve a maximum of fifteen years. Each year the term of one member of the court will expire and the President will appoint the replacement with the approval of the Senate. To be considered, the member must have served a full term in the Senate, not served in the Senate for at least five years, and must have practiced law. Once appointed, the member will earn a salary equal to the average of the Senators' salary."

Corey was beginning to think that this new world order was making a lot of sense. "Quellin, why haven't you implemented this new world order a long time ago?"

"Your communication and transportation technology was not good enough to support such a system until very recently," Quellin answered. "Such a world order is now possible."

"What about our economic system. How will that be?" Corey asked.

"It will be a free enterprise system similar to what you have now but with the appropriate amount of regulation to thwart greed. We have determined that such a system is the most productive for humans."

"Quellin, I just had a thought," Andrews observed. "If there are no countries then there will be no need for the military."

"Because of the nature of humans, it will be necessary to maintain a police force," Quellin answered. "There will be a military, but it will only be required to protect the planet from outsiders."

"What outsiders?" Corey asked.

"As I told you earlier, there are those who are envious of your planet and wish to enslave you. You *must* be on guard."

Corey gave Matthew a questioning glance. As he did, the door swished open and a Gray appeared. It gave Quellin a long stare and left. For a long moment Quellin seemed frozen in place. He then turned to Corey. "Dr. Newton, it is time to prepare you for your return to Earth. We will meet again in the future."

Chapter 12
L is for Luck

Thursday, May 15
3:38 PM
Laughlin, Nevada

As AL'S LIMO pulled away, Pete and Wendy walked into XXX casino. Pete paused in the lobby and turned to Wendy holding his finger to his mouth indicating they needed to talk softly. He leaned close to her ear.

"Wendy, I am going to play some blackjack and you can watch if you wish. Have you ever played?"

"No, how is it played?"

"Well, it's a card game where several people play against a dealer. The dealer will deal each player two cards, one facing up and the other down. The played takes a peak at his down card in a way the dealer cannot see. The dealer then goes to each player and asks if they want another card. The object is to get a total count of 21. If you go over, you loose. If you are too far under 21 then the dealer, who is also playing, may beat your score and again you loose. If you get 21 and so does the dealer, then you may win or loose depending on the table rules. If the dealer goes over 21 then everyone wins."

"It sounds like the dealer has the advantage," Wendy observed.

"Yes, but if you are careful and watch the cards you can shift the odds to your favor by a couple of percentage points."

"How can you be careful?" Wendy asked.

"If you have a good memory and observe carefully, you can have a pretty good idea of what your third card will be, based on the odds."

"Is that what they call card counting?"

Pete smiled and whispered, "Yes, and the casinos do not like it but they can't do much about it if you don't make it obvious. We certainly do not want to announce what we're doing. That's why I'm talking softly. You probably know that Cory got his doctorate from MIT. It's interesting that a group of student from MIT made history by card counting."

"How so?"

"They joined an organization that trained them in card counting techniques. Then a group of a dozen or so students and their trainer would go to a casino and play blackjack. They were clever. They had several members of the group who were designated as 'big players'. They would lay back and only go to tables designated as 'hot' by their team members who had been card counting as they played. Since the odds at these tables were in favor of the player, the 'big players' would bet heavy. Over a year or so the team net over a million dollars. Eventually they got caught."

"What did they do to them?" Wendy asked with concern.

"They were roughed up and blackballed from all of the casinos. I'm not proposing that we try their system because we do not have the training. I want to keep it simple. I have my own system. Come and observe," He said as he led her into the casino hall. The noise from the slot machines was almost deafening. "Notice that ninety percent of the floor space is occupied by these noisy slots. This is where the casinos make their money. The odds are

definitely against the slot player." He led her over to the
blackjack tables and began to play.

***

Wendy was impressed. In just two hours Pete had
managed to parlay two hundred dollars into over nine
hundred. She stood behind Pete as he continued with his
game. Eventuall she became bored, leaned forward and
spoke into his ear. "Pete, I've never gambled but I've
always wanted to try playing the slot machines. Do you
suppose I could have some of your winnings so I could try
my luck?"

Pete smiled, "Sure, here's a twenty. Try the penny
machines near the front door. They say the ones near the
entrance have the highest payoff. I have to warn you, most
people loose their money on slots sooner or later."

"Thanks, Pete, maybe I'll be lucky." Wendy took the
twenty-dollar bill and headed over to the slot machines.

Pete went back to playing and continued to
demonstrate skill and luck at blackjack.

* * *

Within twenty minutes, Wendy was back.

"That's why they call them one-armed-bandits," Pete
said with a smile as he turned to her, expecting to see a
frown. Instead, Wendy looked like the Cheshire cat in
Alice in Wonderland, she was beaming. "Why are you
smiling?" He asked.

"I won!" she laughed. "I was playing those penny
machines and got one up to six dollars. I then went to the
quarter machines like you said. I got thirty-six dollars and
then began to loose so I cashed out."

"Smart move, so how much did you win?"

"Well, I still felt lucky so I took the thirty dollars from the quarter machine and decided to play the dollar machines."

"Oh . . . that's not good," Pete said.

"Yes it was! At first I was loosing but then all of a sudden, bells began going off and lights began flashing. The attendant came over and told me I had just won nine hundred dollars! I cashed out. Look!" Wendy held out a fist full of twenty dollar bills.

"That's wonderful! You *are* lucky."

"Do you think we should leave now?" Wendy was anxious to leave before they lost what they had gained. "There's a shuttle going back to Kingman at five."

"Yes, let's go, I'm up seven hundred. We have enough to get us through a couple of weeks. We should leave while we're ahead."

* * *

When they returned to the hotel in Kingman, Pete upgraded their room to a two-bedroom suite. The small efficiency kitchen would allow them to save money on meals and they would have a common area in which to work.

That evening, the two went shopping for another change of clothes and basic food supplies. When they returned, they had their supper and began to discuss the project. There was much more to be done. Wendy still had more work to do in order to decipher the artifact. Once that was done, they had to connect to the alien main computer, if they could. The problem remained; how to activate the device without alerting the aliens. Wendy and Pete continued to ponder that problem as they had desert.

The TV was playing in the background and the seven o'clock local news was just starting. The anchorwoman was giving a synopsis of the news they would cover during the next half hour. " ... and after the weather," she said, "we have this late breaking story that occurred late this afternoon out at the airport. Authorities found a stranger, dressed in strange clothes, wandering down the tarmac in a secure area. He appeared dazed and disoriented as he was apprehended."

Wendy glanced at the TV just as the screen cut to a long shot taken through the airport's security fence. In the scene, two armed men were holding a man in a blue jump suit. As they began to escort him into the terminal, the camera zoomed in for a tight shot of the man in blue.

"That's Corey!" Wendy screamed, as she jumped up and ran closer to the set.

"What do you mean?" Pete hadn't been watching.

"They just showed Corey being taken into the Kingman Airport terminal by two armed police. They say he's dazed and disoriented." Wendy turned up the volume on the TV.

The anchorwoman continued speaking, "We will have more on that story after the local weather. Howard, what's your five-day forecast?"

Wendy turned the volume back down as the weatherman spoke. "Pete, this is wonderful! They've released Corey. We have to rent a car and go out there."

"Hold on, Wendy. That is great news but we have to be careful. They may have let him go as bait to draw us out of hiding. We have to give this some careful thought. Let's see what else the news has to report." He motioned for her to turn the volume back up.

". . . and that's the story from the weather department, Katie."

"Thanks, Howard, and now back to the unfolding story out at the airport. Sid, our roving reporter, is on the scene. What can you tell us, Sid?"

The screen switched to a scene inside the terminal where Sid was on camera with an airport official. "Well, Katie, I have Mr. Rathburn, the airport manager, here with me." Sid faced the official-looking man standing next to him. "Mr. Rathburn, what can you tell us about this stranger?"

"Well," Mr. Rathburn said, "at about five this evening, several workmen out on the flight line were replacing bulbs and noticed a strange flash of light at the end of runway two-one. At first they thought it was some type of incendiary device that had exploded. There was no sound. Whatever the cause, it just disappeared without even so much as a puff of smoke. A few minutes later, they saw this stranger in the distance, staggering toward them on the runway. He was coming from the location of the explosion. They thought that maybe he had been injured in the explosion and they ran to help him. When they reached him, they said he seemed unharmed but was incoherent and in a state of shock."

"What was the man doing on the runway? Did he say?" Sid asked.

"The man seemed unable to speak. As I said, he seemed to be in a state of shock," Mr. Rathburn answered.

"Where did they take him?" Sid asked.

"They took him to Kingman Memorial Hospital for observation," Mr. Rathburn responded back to the camera.

The camera panned back to Sid. "Well, that's it from here. Back to you at NEWS 76, Katie."

"Thanks, Sid, let's hope the young man is all right." The camera cut back to Katie at the studio. "We'll do a follow-up on this strange case and report back on tomorrow's evening news. Now on to other news . . ."

Wendy switched off the set and turned to Pete. "What do you think, Pete?"

"We need to find out where the hospital is and develop a plan to get Corey out of there," he said, as he rubbed the back of his neck.

"Do you think he'll be watched?"

"You bet. I think we have to assume the aliens released him to serve as bait to draw us out. We'll have to be clever about this. Let's take a taxi to the hospital and check things out," Pete said, as he looked at his watch.

* * *

No one paid attention to the man and woman sitting near the window in the restaurant located across the street from the hospital. The couple appeared to be having a casual conversation. He was having a coffee and she a hot tea. Occasionally, they would glance out the window and over toward the hospital's emergency entrance.

"I think they probably brought Corey in through that entrance," Pete said as he pointed out the window and toward a canopied entrance to the hospital.

"Yes, I agree," Wendy said, as she watched an ambulance turn up the drive and then back up to the emergency door. She watched intently through the twilight as the ambulance paramedics pulled a gurney out of the rear doors of the vehicle. The canopy lights silhouetted a woman in a half sitting position on the gurney. Judging by her extended belly, Wendy guessed that the woman was about to give birth. Twenty minutes after taking the woman inside, the paramedics and their ambulance departed.

Pete rubbed his chin. "Even if we can get inside and break Corey loose, we have no good way of escape. We can't rent a car because the aliens may have a way to track my credit card. Car rentals won't take cash." Pete looked at Wendy, "Do you have any ideas?"

Wendy gazed out the window. "Yes, a kernel of an idea is beginning to develop. Let's go back to the motel."

Chapter 13
The Rescue

Thursday, May 15
9:38 PM
Third floor, Kingman Memorial Hospital

"You haven't touched your food. I left it here longer
than I'm supposed to. I was hoping you'd gain an appetite.
Are you beginning to feel better?" The young nurse asked
with concern. Corey starred blankly up at her from his bed,
trying to comprehend his situation. Everything in the room
was a fuzzy white blur.

"Aside from my ears ringing, a splitting headache, and
feeling like my nose was jammed into my brain, I feel all
right. Where am I? Why am I here? Is this a hospital or
something?"

"Yes, this is a hospital. Don't you remember, they
brought you here a few hours ago. You were in some kind
of explosion or something at the airport." The nurse gave
Corey a sorrowful look. "You don't remember?"

"No. All I can remember is some sort of crash."

"I don't know what happened. They just said you were
in a state of shock from some kind of explosion or accident

at the airport this afternoon. Some workers out on the runway found you wandering around in a daze after they saw a big flash of light."

"Flash of light? Yes, I do remember a flash of light. I was running after someone and then there was a blinding light or something ... and ... and ... I was floating, I think ... I was floating ... Oh ... I don't remember."

"Do you remember your name?"

"My name? Of course ... my name is ... my name is." Corey's face contorted in an expression of panic. Tears welled up in his eyes as he stared at the nurse. "I can't remember!"

"Now then, don't be too concerned," she said as she grabbed his hand softly. "Amnesia is a common symptom after experiencing a traumatic experience. It's your body's self defense mechanism at work." She patted his hand. "Give it time. Just relax," she assured him with soft stroking to his arm. Then she noticed blood oozing from his nose. She grabbed a washcloth and held it up to his nose. "Sit up and put your head slightly forward," she said tersely. There was an urgent tone in her voice that Corey recognized instinctively and he sat upright in his bed. "Your nose is bleeding," she said. "Hold this while I get you an ice pack." Corey held the cloth to his nose.

"But how can I forget my own name?" Corey insisted loudly as the nurse left the room. He could begin to taste the blood that was dripping down the back of his throat. In less than a minute she returned and applied an ice pack to his nose.

"Here, hold this to your nose for at least ten minutes and don't remove it until I tell you. Try not to swallow any blood as that may make you nauseous."

"Okay. But ... I don't understand ... how come I can't remember my name?"

"Don't worry about it. You're getting yourself worked up over nothing," she said.

"Nothing! I can't remember my name! I don't think that's nothing."

"It'll come back to you after you settle down and have some rest," she said. "Are you sure you can't eat just a little bit?" She moved his food tray closer and stirred some food around on the plate. Corey showed no interest in the food. She held his water cup up to his mouth. "Here, at least have a drink of water. You need to stay hydrated." Corey put the straw in his mouth with his free hand and took a long draw of water.

"Can you leave the food tray a little longer? I'll try to chip away at it. I promise," Corey said.

"Okay, but I'll have to take it at ten. Remember, keep that cold compress on your nose until I tell you to remove it," she said, as she backed away and left the room.

* * *

State College, Pennsylvania
11:58 PM EST

Dr. Robert Greenwith had fallen asleep in his favorite chair as he read one of his many journals. The ringing of the phone on the wall startled him. He pulled himself out of his chair and spun around to answer the phone. "I've got it, Lisa," he hollered up to his wife as he picked up the phone.

"Hello, Dr. Greenwith here."

"Hi Bob! It's Wendy!" The voice on the other end answered.

"Wendy! How are you?" Bob glanced down at his phone to see the phone number on his caller ID display. "How's your project coming? I see you're still out of town…928 area code. I'll have to check that out," Bob said jokingly.

"Don't bother, Bob, I'm in Kingman, Arizona. I'm taking a break from the project. Things are going great," Wendy lied, "but I need your help."

"Just name it. How can I help?"

"I want to rent a car but we can't use our personal credit cards because it might jeopardize the security of the project. I was wondering if we could use your personal card. We'll keep our charges under a thousand and I'll pay you back when I get back to State College."

"Sounds like cloak-n-dagger stuff . . . but sure, you can use my card. Let me get it out of my wallet. Do you have pencil and paper?"

"Yes, I'm ready."

"Okay, here's the info," Bob said as he read off the card information.

"Got it! Thanks, Bob!"

"Can you fill me in on what you're up to or is it still hush hush?"

"I can't tell you anything yet. It's still super-confidential. In fact, please keep our conversation tonight confidential."

"You got it. My lips are sealed."

"Give Lisa my love and tell Tigger I miss him. I'll try to call you again when I can, Bob. Keep well. Bye for now."

"I will. Take care, Wendy. Bye," Bob said as he hung up. Wendy's call brought back memories of the visit by Mr. Allison, the recruiter from Washington. He had been sent to recruit Wendy for the summer, or longer. The project was so secret, Mr. Allison would only say the project was of high national security and the President of the United States was involved. In fact, it was the involvement of the President that convinced Wendy to sign up. They wouldn't tell her what the project was. They wouldn't even tell her where she was going for the project. *Kingman. I guess it's near Kingman, Arizona.* Bob thought to himself.

Wendy turned to Pete as she hung up the phone. "That problem is solved. We now have a credit card we can use. You'll have to pose as my boss, Dr Robert Greenwith. I think you might be close to Bob's age. You even look like a college professor," Wendy said as she examined Pete's graying temples. "Let's hope they don't ask for photo ID."

"Car rentals usually do. I'll have to do some fast talking."

"Tomorrow morning I'll call the car rental and pose as your secretary. I'll tell them that before you left town for your trip to Arizona, you gave me your credit card and asked me to make car reservations. I forgot to reserve you a car and give you your card back. On top of not having a reserved car, now you're traveling without your credit card. I'm sure you are really pissed at me and I am afraid my job is on the line for such a stupid mistake. I'll say, 'Please help me.'"

Pete smiled. "That should work. I'll give the agent the fast shuffle on my ID. We'll need to get some kind of disguise before we go into the hospital tomorrow."

Wendy thought for a moment. "I noticed a sign for a costume shop on our way to Laughlin this afternoon. After we get a car we can run over there and see what they have."

"Good, we'll take care of that first thing tomorrow and then head back to the hospital to get Corey."

***

Thursday, May 16
2:42 PM
Third floor, Kingman Memorial Hospital

Corey was dozing after finishing a light lunch when he was awakened by a light touch on his shoulder. He opened his eyes and stared into two large black eyes. He flinched and pulled back. It was the nurse. He recoiled as though her eyes held some unpleasant memory.

"I'm sorry, I didn't mean to startle you. You have a visitor, a man from Homeland Security. He wants to ask you some questions about yesterday. I told him you were still suffering from amnesia but he insisted. Do you feel up to it?"

"Yes ... I feel up to it, but I'm afraid I can't help him much. I still don't remember my name and what happened." Corey hesitated. "Okay, go ahead and bring him in."

Within a few minutes the nurse led in a tall man with long but neatly kept gray hair and a beard. He was carrying a briefcase. Corey's face was expressionless as he sat up in the bed and raised his hand to greet the stranger.

"Hi, I'm Mr. Osborne from Homeland Security."

"Hello Mr. Osborne," Corey answered back with a quirky smile. "I'm afraid I don't know who I am."

"Yes, the nurse told me. Amnesia is a funny thing. One minute your mind is blank and the next minute something triggers a memory and you can begin to remember. Perhaps if we can chat for a while I can help you recover some of your lost memory."

"I would like that. You don't realize how terrifying it is not to know your own name."

"That's what I've been told," Mr. Osborne said as he turned to the nurse standing behind him. "Nurse, I wonder if I can have some time alone with this man. Some of the things I want to discuss have confidential elements of airport security. I'm sure you understand."

"Oh yes, I'll leave you two alone so you can talk. Just push the buzzer if you need me," she said, pointing to the cord wrapped around the bed rail. "I hope you can help him. He's been so worried about not knowing his name." She left the room and closed the door behind her.

Mr. Osborne turned to Corey. "Do you remember how you ended up at the Kingman Airport?"

"No. I just remember seeing a blinding light and found myself lying on the runway. I picked myself up and looked around. That's when I saw the terminal and started walking, no—staggering—toward it. Then these two guys come running up to me and start asking all kinds of questions. I started to collapse and they grabbed me and helped me into the terminal. From there, they brought me here. That's all I can remember," Corey said.

"You don't remember anything before the bright light?"

"No. As I said, I don't even know my name."

"Maybe I can help you remember your name. Let me go down a list of names and perhaps one of them will trigger a memory."

"Sure, I'll try anything if you think it will work," Corey said.

"I'll go alphabetically." Mr. Osborne thought for a moment. "How about Adam?" Corey starred at him blankly. "Okay," he said, "How about Andrew?" Still no response. "How about if I just start calling off names and you raise your hand when one sounds familiar."

"Okay, that sounds reasonable," Corey said.

"All right then. Bob ... Bill ... Corey," Mr. Osborne hesitated as Corey's expression changed. "Does Corey sound familiar?"

"Yes, for some reason I feel comfortable with that."

"Good. For now, I will call you Corey. Now I want to ask you how you happen to be in a restricted area of the airport yesterday?"

"I still don't remember. I just remember a flash of light and ... and ... strange ... I remember floating up as I'm holding onto someone. Then the next thing ... I'm here ... in the hospital."

"This person you were holding onto, was it a man or woman?"

"Ah . . . a man . . . I think. Yes. It was a man." Corey's face began to light up as he realized that he could remember.

"Good! We're making progress. Again, what do you remember about being at the airport?"

"Nothing, other than what I already told you."

"Okay, let's change subjects for a while. Do you remember if you have a wife or girlfriend?"

"No."

"Let me try a few names and see if they evoke a memory. How about Ann?"

"No."

"Betty?"

"No."

"Wendy?"

"Wendy?" Corey's face lit up. "That sounds familiar. I think I know a Wendy."

"Good! Now how about if I pair Wendy with a name like Pete?"

"Yes! I know them both!" Corey's face broke out into a broad smile. He could see Wendy's sweet face framed by her auburn hair flowing over her shoulders. "I can visualize her face. I remember now! I was in a helicopter crash! That's what happened. That's why I was at the airport. Pete and Wendy were with me!" Corey suddenly looked alarmed. "Are they all right? Were they brought here to this hospital?"

"Corey, that crash was not at the airport. It was out in the desert and everyone survived. They're fine."

"How do you know that?"

Mr. Osborne leaned closer to Corey. "Think Corey, do you also remember what Pete looked like?"

"Yes, he was tall with graying temples."

"Try to imagine me without this long hair and beard." Corey studied the man. A smile appeared on the man's face.

"Yes! You are him!" Corey blurted out, loudly.

"Shhhhh," Pete said as he put his finger to his lips. They might be listening."

"Who?"

"Don't you remember the project?" Pete said in a whisper.

Corey looked into Pete's eyes and thought for a moment. "Yes, I remember now. Why am I here in the hospital?"

"Keep your voice down to a soft whisper. What's the last thing you remember about the project?"

Corey thought for a long moment. "I remember being aboard a helicopter that crash landed and then a man took off running ... and Wendy yelling for me to get him. He was a colonel, I think. Yes, he was in the Air Force. He took something. The last thing I remember is running after the colonel and tackling him. Then . . . there was this blinding light and we both began to float upward in a spiral. Then I woke up on the runway. What happened?"

"You both were abducted by the craft that caused us to crash land. Do you remember going aboard that craft?"

"No, I don't remember any of that. How long ago was all of that? How long have I been here?"

"The crash was two days ago. You were held aboard the alien craft for over twenty hours. They released you last night at the airport. You don't remember that?"

"No, not at all. What alien craft? Where's Wendy?"

"I can't tell you now but she is safe and waiting for us. I'll fill you in on the alien stuff later. Do you feel well enough to walk ... or run if required?"

"Yes, I feel fine now, especially since I know who I am. I'm Dr. Corey Newton," Corey said proudly to Pete.

"That's right. Right on," Pete said as he smiled and opened the briefcase he was carrying. "We got you some clothes. You have a blue jump suit in your closet but you'd look conspicuous running around in that. Go into the bathroom and change out of your jonnie and into these," Pete said, as he handed Corey underwear, a light blue denim shirt, blue jeans, and a belt. "Grab your shoes from the closet and hand me your jump suit. I'll put it in the briefcase."

After Corey finished dressing, Pete glanced at his watch and peered out of the small window in the door. "I think they just finished with a shift change. That's lucky for us. Put on this fake mustache and wear this baseball cap. When no one is in the hall, we'll sneak down to the elevator. Act casual."

Within three minutes, the two men were casually crossing the street in front of the hospital and heading toward the restaurant facing the street. Wendy watched anxiously through the restaurant window as Pete and Corey crossed the street. She ran out to meet them in the parking lot as they neared their rented car. Corey rushed to her side. Wendy did a double take at Corey's fake mustache and then they embraced.

"Okay you two, save that for later. We have to get out of here," Pete said as he slid into the driver's seat. "Corey, we have a small suite rented a few miles from here. It's only temporary though. Now that we have you back, my plan is to move closer to the base."

"Oh ... where's that?" Wendy asked.

"Las Vegas," he answered.

* * *

During the ride back from the hospital, Wendy and Corey rode in the back seat. They held each other as though the other were trying to make an escape. Pete refreshed Corey on the project, the aliens, and the chase to recover the artifact from the colonel. Wendy filled Corey in on how she and Pete escaped from the helicopter and the pursuing alien craft.

"How have you been paying for everything? I'm sure you can't chance using credit cards," Corey said.

"You're right," Wendy said. "Fortunately, as it turns out, Pete's somewhat of a card shark at blackjack."

Pete glanced back at Wendy and smiled. "That's not quite correct, Corey. I'm not a card shark. I just happen to be good at blackjack."

"That's an understatement," Wendy said. "Pete parlayed three hundred dollars into a thousand in less than three hours of playing. He definitely *is* good."

"I'm nervous," Pete said with concern. "I have to tell you both about a concern that has been nagging me."

"What is that?" Wendy asked.

"Well, doesn't it strike you both as odd that we were able to get Corey out of that hospital so easily. Something's wrong. I feel it in my bones."

"Perhaps, but we're back together now no matter what happens," Wendy said, as she turned to Corey. "I was so excited when I saw you on television." She stared into Corey's eyes. "I was afraid I had lost you. Are you sure you're all right?"

"I'm okay now but yesterday I felt like I had been run through a meat grinder. Seeing you, makes me forget all of that." Corey cringed and rubbed his left ear.

"What's wrong, Corey?" Wendy said, with concern.

"My left ear feels strange … it feels like a bug is crawling around in there." Corey kept putting his little finger into his ear to ease the discomfort. "Maybe you can check it out when we get to the motel."

* * *

After they returned to the motel suite, Corey plopped down in the overstuffed chair and relaxed as Wendy went to the refrigerator to get refreshments.

"What would you two like to drink? We have soda, milk, or water. I could make you some tea if you'd like," Wendy said as she stared into the refrigerator.

"I'll just have some water," Pete said.

"Nothing for me, thanks," Corey said. "My ear is bug'n the dickens out of me. Could you check it out when you have a chance? I swear there's something crawling around in there," Corey complained.

"Sure, sit up and let me look at it," Wendy said as she handed Pete a glass of water. Corey cocked his head to give Wendy a clear view. She peered into his left ear. Her eyes suddenly widened and she jumped back. "Pete! Corey's right. There *is* something moving around in there. Come look!"

Pete examined Corey's ear. A concerned expression washed across his face. "Wendy, get me my flight jacket, please," he said, calmly, so as not to alarm Corey. Wendy handed him his jacket and Pete extracted a small wire pick from the small pocket on its upper arm. He held Corey's head cocked to the right and took a closer look into his ear.

"Corey, I want you to hold *very* still. I think I can work that thing out of your ear. Wendy, get a washcloth and hold it under Corey's ear." Wendy returned with the cloth. "Don't ... move, Corey," Pete said, as he carefully inserted the probe into Corey's ear. "Hold it ... hold it ... got it!" Pete said as he flicked what looked like a small rectangular piece of earwax onto the towel Wendy was holding.

Wendy looked at it and screamed, "It's moving along the washcloth, Pete!"

Pete bent over to get a closer look. It was too small to see much detail. "Wendy, in the top vest pocket of my flight jacket is a small survival kit. Open it and give me the magnifying glass, please." She handed him the glass and he bent closer, peering at the strange crawling thing on the cloth. What he saw was a small rectangle about an eighth of an inch long and a sixteenth wide. He flicked it over with his pick. Running along the entire length of the bottom were several rows of tiny hair-like filaments flailing in the air. Pete stared in amazement as the device flailed about on the cloth. "My God! What is that thing?"

"Let me see," Corey demanded as he turned his head to view the bizarre substance.

"Corey!" Wendy screamed as she saw blood starting to flow from his nose. "You're bleeding! Let me get another cloth and some ice."

"Again?" Corey said. "This happened yesterday in the hospital and the nurse had to put a cold compress on my nose."

"It happened yesterday, too?" Pete asked as his face became pale. "Wendy, get a large bath towel quickly. I think we're going to have a lot of blood here." Pete studied Corey with concern. "Corey, you said you felt as though your nose had been jammed into your brain yesterday. I think I know what's happening here and why it was so easy to get you out of the hospital."

"What are you thinking, Pete?" Wendy said as she gave Corey a large bathroom towel to hold under his nose.

"I think you have an implant in your nose, Corey." Pete answered. "I think that thing from your ear is one, too. They're probably tracking devices. We have to get that thing out of your nose right away!"

"How?" Corey moaned.

"I read about these implants in my UFO research. Some abductees were able to expel them by blowing their nose hard. Bend over and blow hard into the towel."

Corey obeyed and blew as hard as he could. Dark red blood began soaking the towel. Suddenly within the gush of blood a small cubed-shaped object about the size of a BB appeared on the towel.

"That's it!" Pete cried. "Good work, Corey!"

"The pain in my nose is gone too," Corey said, as he took the cold compress from Wendy and held it to his nose.

"Good! Now we have to clear out of here, fast! I don't know how long it will be before they track us down. Wendy, flush those implants down the toilet. Everyone grab as much stuff as you can and throw it into the car. Corey, keep that cold compress on. We're going to move on to our next base of operations. Let's go!" Pete barked, in his command voice.

Chapter 14
Base Camp

Thursday, May 16
6:46 PM
Las Vegas, Nevada

"You'll see why I picked The Regal Tropicana Hotel here in Las Vegas and requested this particular suite as soon as you look out of the window," Pete said to Corey and Wendy, as he unlocked the door to the seventh floor suite.

As she followed the two men in, Wendy scanned the room. Directly ahead was the south wall. It was covered by floor to ceiling drapes covering a wall of windows. To the right of the door, the suite had a small kitchen area with a bar-type counter that faced the south wall and the living area. Beyond the counter and to the right was a door leading into one of the two bedrooms. Between that door and the south wall was a large sleeper sofa that folded out into a queen size bed. A long coffee table was positioned in front of the sofa. Along the wall opposite the sofa were two arm chairs on either side of a TV. To the left of the chairs was another door leading into the second bedroom.

Wendy and Corey followed Pete as he led them over to the south wall. "Look," he said as, he pulled back the drapes. He pointed left to the view below their window. Lit by the setting sun was an airport. "That's McCarran International Airport. And that complex of buildings directly in front of us is a government owned charter service. It's known as Janet Airlines."

"What sort of charter service?" Wendy could see a single small terminal surrounded on three sides by a dozen planes. Six of them looked like Boeing 737's. "I don't see any markings on those planes sitting on the tarmac around that small building. There's just a red stripe running along the fuselage," Wendy observed.

"That's right, except for tail numbers, they're unmarked because many of those planes are contracted to the government to fly workers back and forth to a secret base."

"Yes," Corey chimed in with a smile. "And that would be Area 51."

"You got that right!" Pete confirmed.

"How is that going to help us?" Wendy asked.

"I don't know yet but I know I can hop a ride back to the base when I need to. That terminal is only four blocks from here so I can walk over. It will allow us access to Area 51 without detection in case Wendy needs to visit the UFO again." Pete rubbed the back of his neck. "We all have to put on our thinking caps and develop a plan. We need to come up with a way to activate the device without being detected."

"That's a tall order," Wendy said as she studied the aircraft below. As she watched, occasionally one of the planes would move out to the runway. She turned toward Corey and smiled. "The good news is that we're surrounded by casinos. Pete's in his domain here. With his luck at cards, we'll never run out of money."

"Yes, so you told me in the car," Corey answered. By the way, speaking of car, how long can we keep the car before the rental agency gets nervous?"

"I told them I was going to be in Vegas a few weeks after completing my business in Kingman and would turn the car in here at the airport," Pete explained.

Corey stared out of the window toward the unmarked aircraft casting long shadows on the tarmac below as the sun was low and to his right. His stare became blank as his mind went into gear to solve the problems at hand. Suddenly, a grin began to spread over his broad chin. Wendy looked up at him and began to smile.

"Okay, genius," Wendy said. "What are you thinking about? I sense a plan hatching."

"Yes, not a plan, a Faraday cage," he responded with a smile, as he looked first at Wendy and then Pete.

"What's a Faraday cage?" Wendy asked.

"An ideal Faraday cage would be a metal sphere but I think we can probably come close by using copper tubing covered by chicken wire."

"I'm still lost, what are you talking about?"

"He's talking about a way to shield the outside world from any signals that might be generated by the device when you turn it on," Pete explained.

"Exactly!" Corey said. "Wendy, the physics behind it are probably more than you want to know, but to put it simply, the electromagnetic radiation from anything inside that sphere is trapped on the surface of the sphere and is not broadcast out of it."

"But, how do you know that the device radiates electromagnetic waves?" Wendy asked.

"I don't know. Not for sure, but I don't know of any other form of radiation that can travel through the mountain we were in at the base, reach the moon, and return at the speed of light."

Pete stroked the back of his neck. "I remember being shown what they called a Faraday cage when I was visiting the Army intelligence facility at Fort Huachuca in Arizona. They were developing technology to shield communication devices so they would not broadcast sensitive information to those who might be trying to spy on their operations. Corey, I think you might have the answer." Pete reached over and gave Corey a pat on the back.

"So what is it? What does it look like?" Wendy asked.

"What I have in mind is to construct a large spherical cage out of copper tubing covered with chicken wire," Corey explained.

"How large a sphere?"

"Large enough for you to sit in it with a small table and the device. It will be about six or seven feet in diameter," Corey answered.

"Why do you have to cover it with chicken wire?" Wendy asked.

Corey stroked his chin as he came up with a good analogy to help explain. He pointed to the microwave in the kitchen area. "Wendy, that microwave over there generates radiation that has a wavelength of about a third of an inch. You can watch the heating process by looking through the window in the door of the microwave, right?"

"Yes, but the window is covered by a metal mesh," Wendy observed.

"That's correct, and the openings in the mesh must be smaller than a third of an inch or else the microwave radiation would leak out. That would be bad. Usually, the openings in the grid are less than an eighth of an inch to insure no radiation escapes."

Wendy considered what Corey had explained. A puzzled expression appeared on her face. "But, Corey, the openings in chicken wire are larger than a third of an inch. Won't that let radiation from the device leak out?"

"I'm gambling that the radiation from the device has much longer wavelengths," Corey answered, "It's probably closer to radio waves. That's how it can pass through a mountain."

"I think Corey is probably right," Pete said. "But we will need to test it."

How will we do that?" Wendy asked.

There was silence in the room as they each began to consider a plan. Corey stroked his chin. Pete stroked his temples and rubbed the back of his neck. Wendy walked over to the armchair facing the window, sat down and stared at the floor.

After a few minutes passed, Wendy suddenly jumped up from her chair. "I have an idea!"

"What is it?" Pete asked.

"Well, remember, when we were back at the base and, Pete, you took us to the room with the crashed UFO?"

"Yes," Pete and Corey answered in unison.

"We climbed into the craft with the device to try to learn more about what symbols might be common between the device and the craft. Corey got the control panel in the craft to work. I turned on the device and was working with it. Suddenly, as Corey was playing with the instruments on the craft's control panel, the device seemed to respond to what he was keying into the control panel."

"That's right!" Corey said, as he got the connection. "That's when I determined that the control panel was transmitting a signal. It was being relayed back from another device and picked up by Wendy's device. Based on the time delay, I calculated the distance to be about two hundred and forty thousand miles away. That's the same distance as the moon."

"I don't follow," Pete said, with a puzzled expression.

"We can use the craft as a receiver to detect any signals that might escape the Faraday cage!" Corey exclaimed. He looked at Wendy. "You never cease to amaze me."

"So, what are you proposing, Corey?" Pete asked.

"I'm proposing that we build a Faraday cage. Then you and I return to the base and I board the UFO and activate it at a prescribed time. Wendy will stay here and at the prescribed time will climb into the cage and activate the device for one minute. I'll watch the instruments on the craft to see if they are receiving any signal. If no signal is detected, then the Faraday cage is blocking Wendy's signal and we have our solution."

"And ... if you detect a signal?" Pete asked.

"Then we're back to square one and Wendy better clear out, fast," Corey said as he glanced over to Wendy.

"I hate to put a damper on all of this," Pete said, "but if the Faraday cage works then we will only be able to recover the information contained within the device. We won't be able to tap into the alien's main computer."

"That's true," Corey said. "But at least we can get a step closer to knowing what the aliens are up to. Sometimes problems have to be solved a step at a time. We can figure out the next step later."

Wendy taped Corey on the shoulder and gave him a sheepish smile. "I think I know the next step."

"What!" Corey said with a surprised expression.

"Yes," Wendy said with a smile that said she was king. "I know how we can tap into the alien's computer."

"Why am I not surprised?" Corey said with his broad grin.

"What's your idea, Wendy?" Pete asked.

"Well, back at campus we have a computer program installed on each laptop that allows us to get onto the Internet and quickly download our email. We can then get off line and read our mail later, at our leisure. Perhaps we can do the same with this device."

"Yes," Pete said, "When we're ready, I'll fly us back to Kingman. Wendy can quickly do a download and then we get the hell out of there and fly back here."

"Pete," Wendy said. "Don't be too hasty. Even if the device does let us download, I am not proficient enough at running it to try downloading just yet. I need more time to sort things out."

"Okay, I understand, for now we'll take the first step and see if this cage works. Let's follow Corey's plan and check the cage. I'll call that phase one. Phase two will be to recover information within the device. Phase three will be to connect to the alien mainframe." Both Wendy and Corey nodded in agreement. Pete gave Wendy a concerned look. "Wendy, if we detect the signal, I'll call you from my office phone and you get out of here as fast as you can. We need to have all of our clothes and stuff already loaded into the car so you can make a fast getaway."

"Where will we meet?" Wendy asked.

"We'll meet you in the gift store in the LUXOR."

"Where's that?" Wendy asked.

"That's the large pyramid building just down the street. You can't miss it." Pete walked over to the window and looked down. "Corey, you and Wendy get the materials you need for the cage. Meanwhile, I'll go down and take the shuttle plane back to base, get my plane, and return here. That way, we can fly to the base anytime we wish with the minimum amount of notice. Also, we can fly to some other site when we are ready for phase three." Pete looked at them both and smiled, "I think we have a good plan. Now let's get to work."

* * *

The sun was low as Pete walked the final distance down Haven Street to the guard shack at the entrance to the terminal parking lot. After showing his ID, he walked the remaining four hundred yards to the terminal. As he entered the charter terminal, he retrieved his identity badge from the vest pocket of his flight jacket and held it up for the security guard at the door. With a nod, the guard waved him in. Pete walked casually over to the check-in counter. The man behind the counter looked up from a clipboard he had been studying and gave Pete the suspicious eye, a prerequisite for the job.

"Hello, I'm Colonel Mitchell," Pete said as he slid his ID card over to the man. I know I'm not on your passenger list but I've been recalled to the base for an urgent meeting. I'd like to take the next flight out."

The man studied Pete and then his ID card. He knew not to ask any questions that relate to base activities. Pete's ID looked okay but he needed to check with someone higher up. "Yes sir, but I need to call the base first," he said as he picked up a green phone under the counter. Immediately, there was a voice on the other end.

"Dispatch here," the voice said.

"Sir, I have a Colonel Mitchell here who says he needs a special passage to the base. Will you authorize?"

"What's his ID number," the voice said. The man behind the desk read off Pete's ID number and waited. He starred at Pete suspiciously for what seemed an eternity. Finally, the voice came back on the line and the man nodded. "I see," he said into the phone, "I'll take care of it. Thank you." He put down the receiver and eyed Pete again. Pete's heart was pounding and he could feel the blood coursing through the veins in his neck as he looked for the nearest exit and prepared to bolt.

"Colonel Mitchell," the man said sternly, "you must be pretty important. They told me to welcome you back and give you the red carpet treatment. They said to send you out immediately, even if the plane is empty. The base commander wants you to report to him as soon as you get to the base."

* * *

The acting base commander, Colonel Weir, was waiting at the bottom of the stairs as Pete disembarked from the unmarked Beech King Air B200C. He was the only passenger. "Colonel Mitchell, welcome back!" he said as he shook his hand. "Follow me, we need to talk." The two boarded a waiting Humvee and within minutes, they were in his office at base headquarters. "Sit down, Colonel," Weir said. "Would you like something to drink?"

"No, thank you," Pete said politely.

"Colonel, I need to find out what happened out there in the desert after you recovered Colonel Andrews. Your pilot, Captain Herber, radioed in two nights ago that you had made an extremely hard landing due to power failure. He said his chopper was flyable but wanted a copilot to help him fly back. He said that you and your party had run into the desert. We sent a rescue chopper but when they got there, everyone was gone except for the pilot ... and he was incoherent. The rescue pilot said your pilot was just sitting there staring out the windscreen in a state of shock."

"Is he okay?" Pete asked, with concern.

"Yes, physically. But," Weir shrugged, "he has no memory of even calling in for backup. The last thing he remembers is taking off from Kingman after getting repairs. Where are Colonel Andrews and your two scientists?"

"The two scientists are in a safe place but I don't know where Colonel Andrews is." Technically, that was the truth.

"You don't know?" Weir was incredulous.

"No, the two scientists followed me into the desert after the crash. The colonel was injured so he stayed with the craft. There was no moon, perhaps he wandered off and got lost in the darkness," Pete lied.

"Why did you leave the craft after it went down?"

Pete hesitated as he pretended to have a memory lapse. He looked at Colonel Weir. Do you know why the pilot has no memory of that night?"

"No. I'm hoping you can shed some light on that."

Pete studied the colonel and then decided to dole out a little more truth. "What I'm going to tell you may sound far fetched but you know the weird things that go on at *this* base. Some people would say the base itself is far fetched."

"I'm used to high strangeness, so tell me what happened."

"Well," Pete continued, "the reason our chopper crashed was because it was forced down by an alien craft as we were returning from Kingman. We suddenly lost all electrical systems. The engine was still running but none of the flight instruments were working. There was no moon and the terrain was dark, so when the pilot tried to set down, he misjudged our height and made a hard landing."

"So ... you still haven't said why you abandoned the ship and ran into the desert," Colonel Weir queried. "Did you panic?"

"No." Pete looked back at the colonel with disgust. "I'm afraid I can't tell you all of the details. Details of our project are EYES ONLY. Let me just say that because of the nature of our project here, I had good reason to believe that my scientists and I were the target of the attack on our craft. It was my judgment that the three of us should put as much distance between us and the chopper as we could. We hid in the darkness of a cave in the hopes they would not track us down."

"And Colonel Andrews chose not to go with you?" Colonel Weir asked.

"Colonel Andrews was wounded and could not have kept up with us so he elected to stay with the craft," Pete lied again. "It is entirely possible that the aliens came back and took him. I don't know."

"Well, if the aliens downed your craft, why did they leave and then come back?"

"I don't know. You know, I have enough difficulty reading human minds and find it impossible to read alien minds." Pete responded, sarcastically.

Colonel Weir eyed Pete for a long moment and then took on a more relaxed pose as he accepted Pete's story. "Okay. We have done a thorough search of the area in which the chopper came down and found no signs of the colonel. I have to assume you are right and the colonel was taken. Let's hope they release him unharmed."

"Yes," Pete agreed.

"So, what can I do to help you?"

"I came back to make my report to the President and to get my plane so I can periodically return to base with one or more of my scientists, as the need arises. I would ask that my comings and goings be kept low profile. I don't want to file flight plans that allow agents of the aliens to track me down and perhaps intercept my flights or discover where I have the scientists."

"Do you think there might be alien agents working on this base?" Colonel Weir asked. He already knew the answer.

"Yes, I have been told that. I can't say who told me but it was someone extremely high up the command chain."

Colonel Weir understood and did not press the issue further. "I will arrange whatever you need," Colonel Weir agreed. "Whenever you decide to return to base, just trigger your IFF transponder when you enter our restricted airspace. My men will be instructed to let you land."

"Thank you. That should work fine," Pete said.

"Good. I'm glad to help. Well, I'll let you be on your way. I'm sure you have much to do."

"Thank you, Colonel. By the way, if you make contact with Colonel Andrews would you call my office phone and leave a message. I'll check that periodically."

"Sure," Colonel Weir said.

"Thanks again," Pete said, as he left the base commander's office and headed over to his office to make his report to the President and to sign out his plane.

Chapter 15
The Proof of the Pudding Is In the Testing

By the time Pete returned to the suite it was past 11:00 PM. As he entered the room he was surprised to find Corey and Wendy laboring over a large structure that resembled a bowl about seven feet in diameter. It was an assembly of equilateral triangles made of copper tubing soldered at each of the joints. Pete could see that it was taking the shape of a seven-foot geodesic sphere. Wendy was cutting equal lengths of tubing and soldering them into triangles as Corey soldered each triangle into place in the sphere. There was a haze in the room and the air smelled of hot copper and solder.

"What do you think, Pete?" Corey asked. "When it's finished, it will have over two hundred and forty triangles in it."

Pete smiled, "It's a work of art."

Wendy laughed. "That's what I told him but he thinks I'm kidding."

"Well, it is quite impressive," Pete said. "What can I do to help?"

Why don't you help Wendy by cutting the copper tubing," Corey suggested.

"Sure, I'll be glad to," Pete said, as he took a length of tubing from the floor and set the tube cutter at the length Wendy showed him.

"Corey's a genius," Wendy said, smiling at Pete. "He sat down and actually calculated how long the tubes had to be so that the sphere would be large enough for me to climb into but still fit in the room without touching the ceiling."

Pete shot a glance toward Corey. "That's impressive, Corey."

"Thank you." Corey smiled back. "Wendy didn't think I could figure it out but I guess she is a believer now."

"Well, everything is all set at the base," Pete said. "We can come and go as we wish and the path will be cleared for us." He surveyed the structure and the pile of materials on the floor. "How much more do you have to do on this thing?"

Corey pointed toward a roll of chicken wire next to the south window. "After we finish the sphere then we just have to attach that chicken wire and we're good." Corey held up some paper clips. "I'm going to use these as tie-wraps and then solder the chicken wire into place to give it a good electrical connection."

Within two hours the three had finished the construction of the sphere and were ready to apply the chicken wire.

"What would you like me to do?" Pete asked.

"Just start tie-wrapping the chicken wire in place and I'll start soldering," Corey said.

"Pete, look what I bought," Wendy said, proudly, as she held up a box of disposable latex gloves.

"What are those for?"

"Well, you know how my fingers get all sticky when I use honey to work the device."

"Yes," Pete responded. He remembered how, in order to get the devise working, Wendy discovered serendipitously that it was necessary at times to pull up on the depressions in the device. Eight depressions were located where buttons would normally be. The aliens had suction cups on the tips of the four fingers on each hand

and it was natural and easy for them. "How do the gloves allow you to pull up?"

"I found these bug trapping sheets that have sticky stuff on them. I just put on these gloves and then touch the sticky sheet to transfer the sticky to the tips of my fingers. Much neater, don't you think?" Wendy beamed.

"Much neater," Pete agreed.

"I keep telling her she's a genus," Corey said, jokingly.

By three in the morning, the Faraday cage was finished. Corey looked at Wendy. "Well . . . that's it. Let's see how easily you can get in and out."

"Get in?" Wendy observed. "We forgot to make a door."

"What do you mean by *we*," Corey said. "*I* did not forget. It's over here." Corey pointed toward the section by his knees. "You just swing this piece of chicken wire aside and climb in. After you climb in, you *must* remember to wrap the piece of bare copper wire around the tubing and through each of the hoops in the chicken wire and pull it very tight. That's *very* important."

"Why?" Wendy asked.

"Because if you don't have a good electrical connection, the cage may leak some of the signal," Corey explained.

"Okay, I get it. Let me see how easy it is to get in," she said, as she wriggled through the opening in the tubing. "That's not too bad. Do I have to sit on the floor?"

"No," Corey said. "That's why I bought this stool with an attachable table. Here, you'll have to attach the table support and table top in there," Corey said as he passed the stool and table support through the opening. "First bolt the table support on and then the table." He passed the table top, screws, and screw driver through to Wendy. "Here's the rest of what you'll need."

"Great, now I have a table to set the device on and a place for a writing tablet to take notes. I can tell you worked hard to make me feel at home," Wendy laughed.

Pete looked at his watch. "It's after 0300 hours. Let's get some sleep and pick this up in the morning."

"Okay," Wendy yawned in agreement.

"Corey, you and I will share that bedroom. It has two queens," Pete said, pointing to the room on the left side of the window. "Wendy you get the other room all by yourself." Pete looked at Corey. "All by herself. Is that okay with you?"

"Ahhh . . . sure," Corey said, as he glanced toward Wendy for her reaction.

* * *

The shaft of light inched its way up Corey's arm then his shoulder and onto his face as he slept facing the south window in the bedroom. Beads of sweat began to appear on his forehead. He began to mumble in his sleep. "No! . . . Don't ... I don't want you to do that! ... Not my nose! ... It huuurts." Corey shot up into a sitting position, facing the shaft of light. It bore into him as he blinked and held up his hand to block the light from his eyes. *Ohhh . . . Christ . . . it's just the sun,* he thought as he realized where he was.

He climbed out of bed and slid on his blue jeans and shirt and made his way to the living room. He stood in the doorway a long moment as he marveled over the structure they had assembled the night before. Working his way around the Faraday cage, he took a seat by the south window and stared out at the airfield below him. Even as the sun was just beginning to peek over the mountains on the left side of the field, he marveled at the number of planes lined up for takeoff.

"Did you sleep well?" a soft voice said from behind. He had not seen Wendy in the kitchen area making tea.

"Oh, yes, thank you," he said as he turned to look at her.

"Would you like a cup of tea?" she said.

"Sure, I'd love one. How long have you been up?"

"Not long. I usually rise with the sun," she walked over and gave Corey his cup of tea. "Well, your work of art looks just as good today as it did last night, don't you think?"

Corey smiled. "Yes, it sure does."

Wendy looked toward Corey and Pete's bedroom. "I guess Pete's still sleeping."

"Yes, he's sleeping like a baby. I had some sort of bad dream. That's what woke me up," Corey said.

"What was your bad dream about?" she asked as she stroked his forehead and felt his sweat.

"I can't remember exactly. I just remember something about someone trying to put something up my nose."

"You must have been remembering the implants," Wendy said.

"Yes, I guess so."

"Do you remember anything about your time with the aliens?"

"Every now and then I get flashes of memory but not enough to make sense. I wish I could remember more. I'm sure I must have seen some fantastic technology."

"I'm sure you were like a kid in a candy store," Wendy said with a smile.

"You two are early risers," a voice from the back of the room said.

"Oh, hi, Pete. Good morning!" Wendy said. "I hope our talking didn't wake you?

"No, you didn't wake me. I'm also an early riser."

"Would you like me to make you a cup of tea?" Wendy asked.

"No, thank you," Pete said. "Coffee's my cup of tea. I need to have some injected into my veins to get me back with the living in the morning. What do you say we all go downstairs and get breakfast. I'm famished."

"That sounds good to me. I'm starved too. Let me finish dressing," Corey said as he went back into the bedroom.

"I'm not that hungry," Wendy said, "but I suppose I should eat something before we start to work. How are you for money, Pete?"

"I still have a few hundred left. We can hit the casino downstairs tonight to restock," he said.

"Okay," Wendy said. "It'll only take me a minute to finish dressing."

* * *

They took a booth in a remote corner of the cafeteria after filling their trays from the buffet. It was early and the room was nearly empty. Pete wanted to start planning their day but talked softly to avoid being heard by other patrons.

"I have a plan," he said, in a low voice, "but before I forget, I want you two to know that last night I put the device in the hotel safe. So, if anything should happen to me, either of you can retrieve it by using your first name and showing your hotel key. To test that out, Wendy, I want you to get the device out of the safe this morning when we go back to the room."

"Okay," she said, "but what's your plan for today?" She took a sip of the orange juice.

Pete finished chewing the bacon he was eating. "You," he said, pointing to Wendy with his fork, "will go into the cage with the device and with your gloves and stuff. We will synchronize our watches before we leave." He pointed his fork toward Corey. "Corey, you and I will fly back to the base and get aboard the craft. At exactly eleven twenty-five, you will activate the craft and Wendy, at *exactly* eleven thirty you will activate the device. Leave it on for *exactly* two minutes and then shut it off. We'll hope we don't detect anything."

"Sounds good," Wendy said.

"And remember, Wendy, if I call you then get the hell out of that room." Pete looked at his watch. "Okay, let's synchronize our watches. I have 08:15. let's set our watches to 08:16 on my hack." Wendy and Corey both adjusted their watches and waited for Pete. "Hack," he said as his second hand passed twelve.

"My second hand was ten seconds after twelve when you said hack," Wendy said. "Is that okay?"

"Yes, just remember not to activate the device until your second hand is ten past twelve," Pete said. "okay, lets finish eating."

***

Pete wiped his mouth. "If everyone is finished with their breakfast, let's get moving," Pete ordered. "Wendy, we'll follow you to the front desk to make sure you get the device."

Wendy and Corey followed Pete out of the cafeteria. They hadn't noticed that they were being watched. A man in a dark suit was sitting alone in a booth in the opposite corner of the room.

* * *

By ten thirty-six Pete and Corey were back at the base and in Pete's office.

"Have a seat, Corey. I have to call operations and get clearance into the crash room to view the UFO." Pete picked up his phone and dialed. "This is Colonel Mitchell. May I speak with Colonel Weir, please," he said into the phone. Within seconds the colonel was on the phone. "Colonel, I need to have access to ART C from eleven to eleven forty-five." There was a pause. "I know this is short notice but they will have to leave. Check my orders, Colonel, and you will see a Presidential stamp on them." Another pause. "Thank you, Colonel, I'm sure they will understand. Tell them we will not touch a thing and will be out of there at eleven forty-five, sharp. Thanks again," Pete said and hung up.

"I guess your project *is* top priority," Corey said with a smile.

"Yes. We have ten minutes before we need to head over. Sit tight. I want to check my phone messages." Pete picked up the phone again and listened to his messages. He was particularly interested to see if they had made contact with Colonel Andrews. No contact. "Good," Pete said as he hung up. He looked at his watch. "Let's head over."

By eleven ten the two were in the crash room where the UFO was stored, suspended by cables from the ceiling.

It was in a special sling that held it four feet above the floor. At thirty feet in diameter and eleven feet thick at the center, it was impressive to look at. The floodlights in the floor shined against the craft's skin that looked like dull brushed aluminum. The lights lit the craft with an eerie glow. "Someone has changed the angle so that it's tipped," Corey observed.

"Yes, but I'm not surprised. Other groups are working on this thing too."

Corey worked himself around to the side of the craft that had a large nine-foot wide gash. It was through this gash that Corey and Pete were able to work their way up

into the UFO and onto the flight deck. The maximum headroom at the center was only about five feet, so neither man could stand. To Corey, everything seemed to be in two-thirds scale.

"Nothing's changed," Corey said as he crouched over the control panel in the tight space. Each man was much too large and together they filled the space designed for crew members who were only four feet tall. Corey reviewed the instruments to remember how to power up. "What time is it, Pete?"

"Eleven seventeen," Pete answered. "Go ahead and fire it up."

Corey looked down at the controls. "Oh shit!"

"What?'

"I forgot to bring the sticky stuff. I need to push on some of these depressions and pull on others to start this thing," Corey said as he pointed to the depressions on the control surface.

Pete smiled. "I'm glad that one member of this team can function in the morning. Here, use this." He pulled a packet of honey from his pocket. "I snagged it from the cafeteria this morning."

"Great!" Corey gave a sigh of relief as he applied the honey to his fingers.

Pete looked at his watch. "We're running late, Corey. It's eleven twenty-six, get this thing going."

Corey ran his fingers over the control surface, alternately pushing some depressions and pulling up on others. "I'm sure this is how I got it started last time."

Pete looked at his watch. "Eleven twenty-eight, you really need to get this thing going!" Just as he spoke, the panel lit up. "You know how to get my blood pumping, Corey. Now what do we watch for?"

"Wendy told me she was going to key in the string of symbols that make these three lights go on" Corey said, as he pointed to three triangular shaped figures on the control panel. Pete glanced at the controls and then at his watch. "Eleven twenty-nine and forty seconds," Pete counted off. "fifty seconds, fifty-five, eleven thirty!" They both watched the controls for what seemed an eternity . . . nothing. Pete checked his watch. "The two minute mark is coming up in five more seconds . . . that's it! No signal after two minutes!"

Corey broke into his distinctive broad smile. "Wonderful! Let's get back and tell Wendy," he said as he shut down the craft.

"That is truly remarkable. Good job, Corey." Pete was ecstatic. He looked at his watch. "Let's get out of here. It's almost eleven forty-five."

Wendy had placed the device on the cutting board so she could use both hands to finger the controls in order to turn it on. Now that she had it on, she was intent on watching the time to make sure she turned the device off at exactly eleven thirty-two. She did not notice the man in a dark suit who had just entered the apartment.

Chapter 16
What's Going On Here?

"Exactly what is going on here, young lady?" the man said.

Wendy dropped the device and nearly fell off the chair when she heard the unexpected sound. She turned toward the man as she retrieved the device from the floor and hid it behind her, frantically shutting it off.

"Who are you and how did you get in here?" she demanded.

"I'm the house detective and I got in here with a pass key. I'm authorized to enter a room if I think something quirky's going on. Judging by that contraption you're sitting in, I would say something very strange is going on. Please explain."

* * *

Pete and Corey were jubilant as they returned to the hotel room. Pete led the way in. Corey nearly plowed into Pete as he stopped dead in his tracks. The room was empty.

"Wendy?" Corey called out. "Are you here?"

Pete checked both bedrooms. "She's not here. Maybe she went down to play the slots."

"I don't think she would do that without us, Pete,"
Corey said. The room phone began to ring. "Maybe that's
her." He picked up the phone. "Hello."

A voice on the phone said. "I have your young lady
downstairs in my office. I suggest you come down, too. I
want to talk to you, both of you."

"Who are you?" Corey demanded.

"I'm the house detective and you have some
explaining to do. Come to the front desk and ask for me."
The man hung up.

"Oh shit, Pete," Corey said. "We're busted. They have
Wendy."

"Who has her?"

"The house detective, he wants to talk to us. We better
think fast. How do we explain all of this?"

* * *

"Are you all right?" Corey said as he saw Wendy
sitting in the office they had been led into. Wendy jumped
up and ran over to Corey and gave him a hug. As she did
she whispered into his ear. "I told him nothing, not even
my name but he has the device." Corey glanced over at
Pete and shook his head subtly. Pete understood the
message.

"What right do you have to invade our privacy?" Pete
demanded of the man in the dark suit.

"Sir, you are guests in our hotel and it is my job to
make sure *all* of our guests are safe and have a good stay. I
git paid to keep an eye on things. It's my job to check
people out, especially when they start act'n suspicious. And
you three fit that bill. You surely do." The man did not give
Pete a chance to retort. "First, you check in and pay cash,
no credit card. Second," he points to Wendy and Corey, "I
watch these two as they get on the elevator last night with
their arms filled with yards of copper tubing, bundles of
chicken wire and who knows what else. This morning I

watch you whisper'n at your breakfast table as though you're planning sump'n clandestine. So, after you leave I decide ta check things out, see. I felt I had probable cause to enter your room. And what do I find?" he points toward Wendy. "This young lady sit'n in a gigantic cage covered with chicken wire and playing with some type of electronic gadget I never seen before." He picked up the device from the desk and held it in front of Pete. "Don't you find all that just a bit strange? I sure do. Can *you* explain what's go'n on here?"

"Sir, have we done any harm here?" Pete asked.

"I don't know. How do I know that the contraption in your room ain't some sort of listen'n device that helps you mysteriously tap inta our gamming room activity? Or, perhaps that device somehow takes control of the roulette tables. I don't know. You explain to me what that contraption is."

"Sir," Pete said, as he got up close to the man, "what I am about to tell is a matter of national security and if you repeat it to anyone you are liable for a ten thousand dollar fine and up to ten years imprisonment. Do you want me to continue?"

"Mister, I'm a retired security police from the Air Force and when I was on active status I held a top secret clearance. There ain't much I haven't heard nor seen." The man's eyes narrowed as he stared at Pete. "Go ahead."

Pete pulled out his military ID and showed it to the man. "I am Colonel Mitchell. You no doubt know what goes on in that charter building at the airport behind this hotel."

"I've heard rumors," the man said as he pulled back from his attack.

"Good. Then you know that the charter service operating there is hired by the government to ferry workers out to a top secret facility."

"Yes, I've heard that too. Some say it's Area 51."

"Well, you said that, I didn't. I'm not at liberty to say. Officially, Area 51 does not exist. Let's be clear about this, you mentioned it, not me. But, I have been charged with an investigation into the goings on at that charter terminal. These two are scientists working with me on that project. You do not have a need to know their names. That device upstairs, crude as it may seem, is actually a very sophisticated listening device." Pete pointed toward the device in the man's hand. "That gadget, as you called it, cost the government, no, the taxpayer, over one million dollars. It is a very special receiver and must be used inside that cage—contraption you call it—in order to detect the frequency we are monitoring. Sir, what you may have just done by arresting us and calling attention to us is blown our cover. If any of the workers here even casually mention this to someone who works at that terminal, it's over, our cover is blown." Corey and Wendy stood in awe.

"But ... well ... you aren't really under arrest." The man began to stumble over himself. "How was I ta know? I was just do'n my ... you would have ... you know. There's no need for anyone to know. No reason to get upset. I don't think you looked too conspicuous ... coming to my office, I mean. No one will know." He looked at Pete with pleading eyes. "How can I help?"

Pete thought for a moment. "You did say you held a top secret security clearance?"

"Yes."

"Good. Then I have not violated my oath by giving you the details that I have." Pete eyed the man. "Do you really think you could help us without being conspicuous?"

"I will sure try."

"Assuming our cover is not blown, we plan to be here another week or so. I would rest a lot easier if I knew you were making sure no one enters our room. I mean, no one ... not even the cleaning staff ... especially the cleaning staff. They may have friends at the shuttle service and blab about seeing a strange contraption in our room."

"I can do that, but I'll have to bring the manager in on this."

"Can he be trusted?" Pete asked seriously.

"He's my brother-in-law."

"Well, okay then. Let him see our room. That will put his mind at ease. But instruct him to keep his mouth shut. Do you understand?"

"If he tells me he'll keep his mouth shut, he will," the man assured Pete.

"Okay then, we'll return to our room and I'll forget this whole thing happened."

"Thank you," the man said. He looked at Wendy, "I'm really sorry I startled you, ma'am. I was just doing my job."

"I understand, no harm done," Wendy said as she followed Pete and Corey out of his office.

* * *

"That was one big scare," Wendy said as they returned to the apartment.

"I thought we had had it," Corey admitted. "Pete, you never cease to amaze me. You were soooo cool down there."

"That was just part of my survival training. We're taught to keep cool and think calmly under stress if captured," Pete said modestly.

"Well, you did that," Wendy said. The suspense was killing her. "I've been dying to know, did you detect any signal while you were at the base? I was able to transmit for the whole two minutes before the detective barged in."

"No! We received no signal!" Corey beamed.

"Then I guess I can get back to work and start using the device," Wendy said.

"Yes you can," Pete agreed. He checked his watch and smiled. "It's 1600 hours."

"What does that mean?" Wendy asked.

"Happy hour. After all we've just been through today, I think we deserve a break. Come on, I'll treat you two to a drink at the bar. And if we see the hotel dick, I'll invite him, too.

* * *

"What would you all like to drink?" the barmaid asked, as the three settled into a booth overlooking the casino.

"You wouldn't happen to have Weissbier would you?" Pete asked.

"You're in luck, we do, but only in one liters," she said.

"Great! I'll take one," Pete answered.

"That does sound good," Corey said, as he looked at Wendy. "Have you ever had that?"

"I think I have. I think it was when I was visiting The German Museum in Munich."

"What did you think of it?" Corey asked.

"What, the museum or the beer?"

"The beer, silly," Corey shot back.

"I can't remember," Wendy said, turning to the waitress, "but I'll try one too."

In no time the waitress returned carrying a tray with three one-liter glasses of beer and a bowl of pretzels. After she left, Pete handed Wendy and Corey their glasses and held his high.

"Let's toast to a successful mission," he said. They all raised their glasses and clanked them together.

They decided to have supper at the bar and discuss the plan for the next day. It was agreed that Wendy would spend the day in the cage working with the device and getting as much information as she could. Pete and Corey would be on standby if she needed assistance.

"Well, now that we have that settled," Wendy said, "I'm going to go back to the room and work with the device a little tonight."

"Do you need some help?" Corey asked.

"No. I think you two might just be a distraction with all of your gibbering." She winked. "Corey, why don't you help Pete at the blackjack tables? We could use a new infusion of money."

"I agree," Pete said, "Corey, you probably would be a distraction and more money would be useful. So, what do you say? Let's go to work. How are your skills at blackjack?"

"Very basic, so I don't want to miss an opportunity to study under a master. Let's go." They all headed off to the tasks that lay ahead.

Chapter 17
Phase One

Wendy returned to the room, closed the drapes, and turned on some soothing classical music as she prepared to enter the cage. They were playing Debussy music on a local radio station and that suited her mood perfectly. She grabbed the notebook she had purchased the night before and crawled, with the device and her other paraphernalia, into the cage. After securing the small opening, she began her task. Within seconds, she had the device activated and began deftly moving her delicate pianist's fingers over the keypad, alternately pushing and pulling on the depressions. As symbols appeared on the screen, she recorded them in her notebook, noting which combination of keys produced each symbol. Recalling that the aliens only had four fingers, she assigned the left four keys with the symbol L1 through L4 and the right four keys the symbol R1 through R4. Then she used a notation system with a plus in front of a key she had pushed and a minus if she had pulled.

Three hours had passed and she had over twenty-five pages of notes. Her back was beginning to ache and her mouth was getting dry.

"Time for a break," she said to herself as she shut down the device. She was climbing out of the cage when the door to the apartment opened and Pete and Corey bounded in.

"Hi guys," she said. "Perfect timing, I was just taking a break." She climbed up off of the floor and sat in the armchair. "How did you make out at the tables?"

"Oh, not too bad," Corey beamed as he held a wad of twenties in front of Wendy.

"How much?" she asked.

"Oh, only about seventeen hundred dollars!" He fanned the bills out. "Pete won over a thousand and I won nearly seven hundred."

"Not bad for three hour's work. Corey's a fast learner and did well," Pete said.

"I guess he did," Wendy agreed.

There was a knock on the door. Corey quickly hid the money under a couch cushion.

Pete went to the door and put his eye to the peephole. He turned back to Corey. "It's the private detective and another man," he whispered.

"We won that money fair and square," Corey said.

Pete turned back and opened the door. "Good evening, detective." The detective barged into the room followed by a tall and lanky man.

"Good evening, Colonel, sorry ta intrude so late in the evening. This is Mr. Balboa. He's the manager of the hotel. He wants ta see what you have here and make sure it's not go'n to jeopardize hotel operations." Pete gave a sigh of relief. The detective pointed toward the cage. "I assured him that that thing was a tool you're using ta investigate the airport operations. Top secret stuff I told him."

Mr. Balboa walked over to the cage and examined it closely. "Colonel, I'm not a technical person, but I don't see how this thing can cause any problem for us. I will honor your request for secrecy and instruct the head of housekeeping to keep his staff out of this room. Is that acceptable?"

"Yes, thank you," Pete agreed. "And you understand that you must not mention anything about our operations to anyone. That means *no one*."

"Yes, I do and you have my word I will keep this confidential."

Mr. Balboa turned to the detective and motioned for him to follow as he went out the door. There was a positive click as the door shut behind them. Wendy sank into the armchair as the tension left her body. Corey turned to Pete and gave a broad grin. "Beautiful," he said.

Pete turned to Wendy. "How did you make out while Cory and I were slaving over a hot blackjack table?"

"I took twenty-five pages of notes," Wendy said, holding up her notebook. "I have a lot of data that relates symbols on the screen to combinations of key strokes. Now I have to organize my notes and try to understand the symbols. Already, I am beginning to see some patterns."

"Great! Can I see your notes?" Pete asked.

"Certainly," Wendy said as she laid the book on the coffee table and paged through.

Corey came over to see what she had. "I remember seeing many of those symbols when you and I were exploring the controls in the crashed UFO."

"Yes," Wendy said. "And, I think these are their numbers." She leafed through the pages pointing out the symbols. "I am convinced now that they are using the octal numbering system. These symbols appear only when I press down on only one depression at a time and there are only eight buttons."

"It makes sense that they would develop an octal system since they have only eight fingers," Pete added.

"Yes," Wendy agreed.

"So, how do you plan to organize all of this?" Pete asked, as he scanned through the pages of notes.

"I'm not sure yet. After you two go to bed, I want to work on this while I have some quiet time. I work best late at night when I have nothing to distract me but my music."

"Thanks a lot. So, I'm a distraction," Corey said, as he smiled at Wendy.

"You are a nice distraction but nonetheless, a distraction," she smiled back.

"Well, I can take a hint," Pete said, as he glanced at his watch. "It's 2200 hours. I'm going to bed." He looked at Corey and winked. "Don't distract Wendy too long. Good night," he said as he closed the bedroom door behind him.

"Wendy, are you sure I can't help you organize this stuff?"

"No. I really would like to do it myself in quiet time. That's the way I work. But, we can sit and talk for a while and listen to some music. Let me make some tea for us."

"Well, surely I can help with that," Corey said as he followed her into the kitchen area. She had just set the teapot on the stove when Corey came up next to her and wrapped his arms around her waist. Wendy turned and their eyes met. The two locked in an embrace and kissed each other tenderly.

"I was so afraid I had lost you," Wendy whispered.

"Even aliens can't keep me from you for long," he said, as he kissed her again.

The scream of the teapot startled Corey and he released Wendy as she turned to make the tea.

"Let's sit on the couch and listen to some music while we drink our tea." She led Corey into the living room.

Debussy's music played on as the two relaxed together on the couch.

"This *is* soothing," Corey said, as he sank deeper into the soft couch. He stared at the Faraday cage in front of them. "I wish I could remember more about my time with the aliens."

"Give it time. It will come back, I'm sure."

"Yes, I think you're right. I can remember a little more each day. You know, I've met several people at the UFO conventions who were hypnotherapists. They gave papers on how they helped many people who have had abduction experiences."

"How did they help them?"

"They got them into a deeply relaxed state so they could remember their experience and get a better understanding of what was going on in their lives. They could then at least try to deal with it. I think after this is all over, I'll look up one of those therapists. I know there's a very good one in the Ozarks—Eureka Springs, Arkansas, I think."

"In a way, I envy you for your experience. How much can you remember now?"

"I remember chasing after Colonel Andrews after the helicopter crashed and just when I caught him, we were both somehow beamed into a strange ship. I remember we were both on the floor in a white room when we woke up. We chatted for a while and then a Gray came into the room and stared at the colonel for a moment and then left. Later, the colonel said that the Gray told him we were on a scout ship bound for the mother ship which was on the moon."

"The Gray didn't talk to the colonel?" Wendy asked, with a puzzled look.

"No. The two communicated by some type of mental telepathy. I didn't used to believe in all that psychic mumbo jumbo but now I do. My whole understanding of psychic phenomena has changed since my abduction."

For the next hour, Corey went on to explain to Wendy his new understanding of the universe.

"That's really impressive, Corey. You should write some sort of paper on that when we return to normal life."

"Yes, that would make a great paper but I'll need to develop a more rigorous mathematical proof before the scientific establishment will believe me."

"Yes, that's probably true. The establishment doesn't like to be proven wrong. My father always used to say, 'Bucking mainstream science was a risky proposition and could be a career breaker.'"

"I think that is true," Corey agreed. "You know, I'm becoming more and more convinced that the really creative thinkers in history were influenced by the aliens. I believe that such innovative people as Leonardo DeVinci, Newton, Einstein, Tesla, H.G. Wells, Jules Verne, and even Gene Roddenberry, the creator of *Star Trek*, were somehow fed information by the aliens, perhaps to kick start humanity into a more and more advanced technology."

"You know, Corey, one week ago I would have laughed at that idea. Today, I agree. Corey, as a result of your abduction, do you think you've gained any better insight as to what the aliens are up to?"

"Yes." Corey paused. "I believe they don't mean us any harm." He stroked his chin in thought. "And, you know, I think Colonel Andrews believes that too. In fact, I think he earnestly believes he was helping humanity by trying to return the device to the aliens."

"How can he think that?" Wendy asked.

"He believes, and I think he's right, that when we can tap into the alien's computer, the military will take over and use the technology for military purposes. That could dramatically upset the balance of power and, in the wrong hands, could be a disaster for humanity."

"What do you mean?"

"I'm talking about the military complex, those at the top, those who make fortunes supplying weapons. Even President Eisenhower, who was the Supreme Allied Commander during World War II, was concerned about them. He said so in his farewell address to the nation. I believe there are those who operate behind the scenes and pull the strings. They're the power brokers, they make the decisions but remain in the shadows. Some people think they even control presidents and rulers of many of the world's countries. People refer to these people in the shadows as the Illuminati."

Wendy thought for a moment. "How does Pete fit into this?"

Corey gave Wendy a long look and answered in a whisper. "Pete's a great guy but also a loyal military man. He follows orders. That's been his life's training. Pete's working for the President, his commander-in-chief. He reports directly to him on our progress. What do you think the President will do when we give him an ability to tap into alien technology?"

"He's supposed to use it to protect us from an alien invasion," Wendy whispered back.

"You know, if the President had a mind to, or if directed to by the Illuminati, the information we discover could be passed to the military complex, you know, the ones who get rich making weapons. That could completely destroy any balance of power we might have today." Pete thought for a moment. "Plus, I'm not convinced that the aliens *are* planning to invade. At least not in the traditional sense."

"Why do you believe that?"

"I don't know. It's just a feeling I have. Maybe I learned something aboard the alien craft that makes me believe that. Perhaps, with time, my memory will come back."

Wendy gave him a long look. "So, are you saying we should not try to accomplish our mission?" she whispered.

"No," Corey said in a whisper. "I'm not saying that, not yet anyway, but we should be very careful how we handle any information we uncover and what we tell Pete."

Chapter 18
Phase Two

Saturday, May 18th
7:22 AM

Corey and Pete staggered out of the bedroom to the high-pitched whistle of a steaming teapot. Wendy was preparing the water for the morning round of drinks and already up and dressed. "Good morning, gentlemen! I'll have our drinks ready in two minutes. Have a seat."

"You seem chipper this morning. What time did you go to bed last night?" Corey asked, as he took a seat at the breakfast bar.

"About three."

"Three!" Pete exclaimed. How can you be so . . . so normal after only four hours of sleep?"

"I don't know. My mind was too active to try to sleep any longer so I got up."

"Did you get much done last night or was Corey too much of a distraction?" Pete winked at Corey.

"I was in bed by eleven thirty, honest," Corey said as his cheeks became red.

"That's right, Pete, by eleven thirty he was in bed and then I put in some OT. You owe me big-time. My mind was racing so fast that I couldn't go to bed. I had to get my data organized and figure out how to operate the device efficiently."

"Well, did you?" Pete said, with a smile. He knew she had, Wendy would not quit until the job was done.

"You bet," she said with a smile. "But since I put in so much overtime, I thought you'd take Corey and me out to breakfast as soon as we finish our tea. I'm famished and can't concentrate enough to be able to explain what I accomplished last night."

"Okay, okay, you've convinced me. I owe *you* big-time or at least a breakfast. But why do I owe Corey?"

"Because, he was my inspiration," Wendy said.

"Oh?" Pete looked at Corey, rolled his eyes, and smiled.

Corey shot a glance at Wendy and then back to Pete. "I think it must have been something I said last night." He began to blush.

"Why are you blushing, Corey?"

"Pete, why are you grinning?" Wendy said. "Oh, I get it. No. Nothing happened last night. It's like Corey said, he inspired me with something he said last night."

"Well," Pete said, "you have my curiosity aroused. What did he say that inspired you?"

"Last night Corey was telling me about his experience aboard the alien craft after he was abducted. He mentioned that a Gray communicated with Colonel Andrews by mental telepathy. That got me thinking. They don't think linearly!"

"What's the significance of that?" Corey asked.

"They think in blocks of ideas. Their writing is non-linear. Many of the characters are logographic in nature and they use a glyph for every morpheme."

"I love it when you talk technical to me," Corey said, with a smirk. "What did you just say?"

"A morpheme is a linguistic unit, such as the word *dog*. A single glyph can represent a single word or thought. It's much like the Chinese or Mayan writing. Our western form of writing is linear in the sense that we write a string of characters from an alphabet to represent a word. The aliens use a single glyph where we have to use a string of characters for a word. Their writing is much more efficient," Wendy explained.

"Doesn't that make for a lot of characters or glyphs, as you call them?" Pete asked, with concern. He could see the project becoming hopeless.

"Yes. There may be thousands required to communicate intelligently. In China, for example, a well-educated person will know well in excess of 4,000 to 5,000 characters or glyphs."

"How is the alien writing organized?" Corey asked.

"It is arranged similar to the old Chinese who wrote in columns. The first column started on the left and worked across the page to the right."

"Everything I just said doesn't apply to numeric values. The aliens seem to use a string of symbols for those."

"So, have you figured out what all of those symbols are that you recorded in your notebook?" Pete asked.

"Don't ask me how, but yes, I have. As I studied them last night and kept writing them over and over, they began to make sense. I don't know how or why, but they make sense to me now."

"Can you show me?" Pete asked. He was not surprised that Wendy was able to understand the writing. He knew this was part of her extraordinary gift. That's why he picked her for the team.

"Sure, here are a few examples," Wendy said as she opened her notebook. She ran through several pages of notes she had transcribed from her raw data collected the night before. As she pointed at each symbol, she explained the thought she felt it conveyed and the required keystrokes to get that symbol.

"That's great, Wendy," Pete said. "You're now at the point where you can read and write on that device.

Assuming it is capable, do you know how to save and open files on it yet?"

"No. I have to work on that. I'm still taking baby steps here." She smiled at Pete. "Can we eat now? I'm famished."

"Certainly. Just give Corey and me a chance to finish dressing and I'll treat you both to breakfast.

* * *

The hotel cafeteria was nearly empty so Pete led them over to the same secluded booth they had used before. The hotel manager waved to them as they entered. He was in the opposite corner booth reading the morning news and drinking coffee.

"Wendy, I am amazed at the progress you're making. When do you think you will determine if files can be saved or opened?" Pete began pressing, as he studied the menu. Before she could answer, the waitress came to their booth.

"Good morning, would you like to order from the menu or try our buffet?"

"Do you have vegetarian food in your buffet?" Wendy asked.

"Yes, ma'am, we do."

"Then I'll take your buffet."

"Me too," Corey said.

"I guess I will too," Pete said, as he put the menu back and looked up at the waitress. "They both drink tea and I drink coffee if you want to bring that."

"Certainly. Help yourself to the buffet and I'll get your drinks. Just pay at the cashier when you leave," she said, as she filled out the check and left.

The three sat quietly as they ate. Corey occasionally glanced over to see how Wendy was doing. She was deep in thought and picking at her food. Finally, he interrupted her thoughts. "Wendy, take a break. Eat your breakfast.

You can work on that problem when you get back to the room."

"Oh, I know. I can't help it. I can't get that device out of my head. I keep seeing symbols drifting by in my head and want to reach out and grab some and construct a message."

"Sometimes answers come easier after you give it a rest," Corey said. "That's been my experience when I've had to solve some tough problems."

"I know. You're right."

"Okay," Pete said. "After we eat, I want to go over to the airport and check on my plane. It needs some service. Do you want to come, Corey?" Pete asked.

"Sure, it'll get me out of Wendy's hair so she can concentrate better. Is that all right with you, Wendy?" Corey gave Wendy a questioning smile.

"Sure, I'll be fine and you're right, I will be able to concentrate better," Wendy said, with a wink and a smile.

Pete grabbed the check and motioned for Corey to follow as he got up from his seat. "See you later. Enjoy your peace and quiet while we're gone."

As soon as the two were out of sight, the hotel manager came over to Wendy's booth. "Mind if I join you?" he said. "I'm Mr. Balboa, the hotel manager. Remember, we met last night."

Wendy was caught by surprise. "Oh, hello. Sure, I remember you. Please, have a seat," she said, nervously as she motioned for him to sit.

"I don't mean to bother you or interfere with the work you're do'n."

"Oh, don't worry about that. You are not a bother."

"I hope my brother-in-law didn't come on too strong last night. It's his job to be suspicious, you know."

"Oh, I understand. We're not upset. We appreciate your help."

"Well, I just wanted to tell you that I think you're do'n important work. It's important that someone monitors what's go'n on. In the shadows I mean," he said softly.

"We try," Wendy said politely.

"Speaking of shadows, have you ever heard of the Illuminati?"

"I know a little." *Interesting*, Wendy thought, *Corey mentioned the same thing last night.* She thought for a moment. "Illuminati translates to 'enlightened ones' in Latin. I think the name was adopted by those who believed that the illuminating light of God came, not by church dogma, but from within oneself as the result of enlightenment." Wendy remembered reading about it when she was visiting The German Museum in Munich. "I believe it was a Bavarian professor in the late seventeen hundreds who spread the ideas of the Enlightenment through his secretive society. It became known as the Order of the Illuminati."

"I knew y'd know," Mr. Balboa said, with a smile. "That was a very intellectual answer. I could tell from the first time I met you that you were well educated."

"Well, thank you. I have studied a lot of history, and I did spend some time in Germany." Wendy said.

"I'm sure my education doesn't match yours but I read a lot, and lately, I've been read'n about the Illuminati. Just as you said, they were against the Church dogma. Needless to say, the Church wasn't happy."

"That's true," Wendy agreed. "By the end of the eighteenth century, the Church pressured the Bavarian government to ban all secret societies. I believe it was due to the Freemasonry's inadvertent involvement with the Illuminati that legends of the Illuminati persist even to today."

"That's true," he said. "Just look at the Great Seal of the United States and you can see the Illuminati's ever-present watchful eye over us Americans."

"I know that back in the 1700s, the original goal of the Illuminati was the overthrow of the church and the government. What do you think its goal is today?" Wendy asked.

"From what I read, it hasn't changed much. The Illuminati is bent on world domination. Their goal is to form a world government to have complete control over the entire world. It's also their goal to destroy all religions and governments in the process. You know, they operate on a very long-range basis, years or even centuries. They've dedicated their descendants to keep the plot going until their goal is achieved. And you know, they're do'n it all in secret. They use front groups to spread their influence."

Wendy listened politely but this was beginning to sound like a rehash of the conversation she had last night with Corey. "What do you mean by front groups?" she asked.

"Look at the United Nations," he said. "The Illuminati had hopes that the United Nations would be the one world government. Fortunately, that idea was scuttled by the United States."

"How did we do that?"

"From what I read, the United States' Senate was reluctant to approve the UN. The only reason it was approved was largely because the State Department assured the Senate that the UN would not become a World Government and would not interfere with the sovereignty of the United States. Can you imagine what the world would be like today if the UN had sovereignty over the United States?"

"I'm not sure what you mean," Wendy said.

"Think about it. America was founded on the idea that men are born totally free and choose to give up specified freedoms to a limited government. Under the American concept of rights, the individual possesses God-given rights that the state must protect. Our Constitution says that freedom is the natural condition of man and the protection of freedom is government's first responsibility."

Wendy was becoming impressed with the man's knowledge of civic affairs. "How does the UN's philosophy differ?" Wendy asked, as she exposed her own ignorance on the subject.

Mr. Balboa looked at her in amazement. "Differ? The philosophy of the UN is that government is sovereign and may control freedoms and privileges in order to manage its citizens. They say it's to achieve peace and prosperity for all. Did you know that the UN has a document called the Covenant on Human Rights. It's like the Bill of Rights in the U.S. Constitution. One article of the UN Covenant says that religious freedoms and beliefs are subject to limitations of their laws. By contrast, our Bill of Rights says that Congress shall make *no* law about the establishment of religion or prohibiting the free exercise of religion."

Wendy was impressed. "That's scary," she said.

"You bet it is! Hey, I'm ex-military, just like my brother-in-law. Before I got my degree in hotel management, I gave four years of my life defending the American way of life. I don't want that to go down the tubes. We have to stay vigilant."

"I agree," Wendy said.

"Another article of the UN Covenant says that freedom of speech and of the press can be limited by laws. Our Bill of Rights says that Congress shall make *no* law that takes away the freedom of speech, or of the press. That's it, period."

"It seems that the UN assumes that freedom is the government's to give," Wendy observed.

"That's right. Not only that, but according to the UN philosophy, the citizen has a duty to the State to help the State promote socialization. Could that really mean communization?"

"That brings to mind images of George Orwell's book, *1984*," Wendy said.

"Yeah, I read that book too. That's what put me on guard." The man paused as he collected his thoughts. "Did you know that within the UN, UNESCO was created to construct a world-wide education program to prepare the world for a global government. You probably heard of the philosopher, Bertrand Russell."

"Yes, I know of him," Wendy said.

"Did you know he was an advisor to UNESCO and he said that every government that has been in control of education for only one generation will be able to control its subjects without the need of armies or policemen?"

"No, I did not know that," Wendy answered.

"Yes, and from the beginning, UNESCO has designed programs to capture children at the earliest possible age to begin the educational process."

"I've always been in favor of the UN," Wendy confessed. "I thought it offered hope for the world by providing a forum for countries to air and resolve their differences. Now, you've got me concerned."

"We all should be. That's why I'm glad you're keep'n an eye on those folks here at our airport." He looked at his watch. "Well, I gotta get back to work. It's been nice chatt'n with you."

"Thanks, it was a good talk," Wendy said, as the man got up to leave.

That man is certainly a conspiracy theorist, Wendy thought to herself.

* * *

It was after 1:00 PM when Pete and Corey returned to the room. Wendy was asleep on the couch.

"Slacker...look at her," Pete said jokingly to Corey.

"She must be making up for last night. I'll make some tea. The teapot will wake her."

He was right. Within five minutes the teapot began its scream. "Whaa ... who," Wendy said as she sat up and rubbed her eyes. "What time is it?" she was disoriented. "Why is the teapot going?"

"Corey's making you some tea and it's 1300 hours," Pete said.

"Thirteen what? What's that in English?" Wendy said.

"It's after one in the afternoon," Corey said.

"Oh. I got tired at about noon and decided to take a nap."

"That's okay," Pete said. "You deserve it."

"Wendy smiled at Pete. "We're ready to start phase two. I now know how to save and retrieve files."

"Here, drink your tea," Corey said, as he handed her a cup. "Then you can show us how it's done."

Wendy sipped on her tea. "It really is quite simple. You press L1, L4, R1, and R4 simultaneously to save a file. You lift up on them to retrieve a file. After you do that, you enter an eight digit number for the file you want to save or retrieve."

"Have you opened any files yet?" Pete asked, excitedly.

"I opened a couple, just to see if it worked. Then I decided to take a nap."

"Can you show me one?" Pete asked, anxiously.

"Pete, give her a chance to finish her tea. You act like a kid on Christmas morning," Corey said, with a smile.

"Oh, that's all right. I can tell you what they were. They seemed to be simple destination orders for the ship. Message one was for the ship to proceed to what appears to be coordinates. I don't know what they mean or where it is. It just gave three numbers. I assume they are x, y, and z coordinates."

"That sounds reasonable," Pete said. "Maybe we can figure out the location based on the other messages. What was file number two?"

"That one told them to observe some test. They were to sample and record radiation and report their results."

"Wendy, did you find any sort of directory to the files?" Pete asked. "I'm curious to see if they have some sort of time stamp on the files."

"I'm not sure how to do that yet."

"What was the third file?" Pete asked.

"I only opened two. I started with number one and started working my way up. I can open more now that you two are here to help give them meaning," Wendy said as she finished her tea and prepared to enter the cage. Within minutes she was sealed in the cage and had the device turned on.

"I'd sure like to know what powers that thing," Corey said, as the technology of the device continued to amaze him.

"Yes, that's all we need is to have the battery go dead," Pete added.

"Okay, I'm ready now," Wendy said. "I'll bring up file number three." She pressed on the four required depressions to recall a file and then pressed the fourth depression on the right three times. Corey was watching.

"Why did you press that depression?" he asked. "Why didn't you press the third from the left?"

"Their numbers go from right to left, just as ours," she answered. "The first depression on the right seems to increment by one. The system makes sense if you think about it. In our number system, the least significant number is on the right." She continued working the keys and taking notes as she went along. Eventually, she filled two more pages in her notebook. "Well, do you want to see what I have so far?"

"Yes," Pete answered. "Read it back to us."

"Well, I went back to the first two files to see if there was a time stamp."

"What did you find?" Pete asked.

"At the end of each message are three eight digit numbers, one above the other. The top two numbers are the same but the bottom is slightly different for the first two messages. Let me look at the third message. Yes, it's different also. What do you think they mean?"

"Maybe the top numbers are identification of the sender and receiver and the third number is some sort of date or time stamp," Pete guessed. "Can you bring up a much later file?"

"Let me try the largest file number I can, just for the heck of it." She pressed all eight depressions consecutively from right to left. "There is no file there. Let me try a smaller number." She pressed the first key on the left. "None there either. I'll try eight," and she pressed the second depression from the right. "Yes! There is a file there." She then tried pressing both the first and second depression from the right. "Nothing, I guess the last entry is eight."

"Are there numbers at the end?" Pete asked.

"Yes there are. The top two numbers are the same and the bottom number is larger. Let me write the numbers down." She wrote 37173423 for the top number, 0000006 for the second, and 05134731 for the bottom number. Corey studied the numbers.

"Wendy, what were the bottom numbers for the first and second files?"

"They're the same except for the last five digits. The first file had one-two-six-three-two and the second had two-zero-zero-zero-seven."

Corey stroked his chin several times. "If these numbers represent time then the last two digits might be similar to minutes since I don't see why they would have to make log entries with a finer resolution than that. That means the next two digits to the left might represent time similar in length to our hours and the fifth would be on the order of days. So that would mean that the second entry would be about a day after the first and the eighth file would be about two days after the first."

"What was the third file?" Pete asked.

"It was time stamped two-zero-six-three-six."

"That would be a few hours later according to Corey's reckoning. What was the message?"

Wendy studied her notes. "It said they were to monitor radiation within a length that is given by four eight digit numbers."

"What are they?" Corey asked.

"The first eight digit number has four digits on the left side, three dots and then one digit on the right."

"What were the numbers?" Corey asked.

"One-three-seven-five on the left and the number six on the right side," Wendy answered. "The second eight digit number has a one and zero on the left and zero on the right side." Wendy looked at Corey, "I don't understand that."

Corey jotted down the numbers and studied them for a few moments. "I think if they're talking about radiation, then they probably use the radius of the hydrogen atom as a basic unit of measure. That's similar to one angstrom, which we use in measuring wavelength. If I assume they use scientific notation in large numbers then they are saying the wavelength for the first set is one-three-seven-five followed by six zeros."

"That would be an octal number," Wendy reminded Corey.

"That's right." Corey grabbed a pencil and paper and began calculating. "When I convert octal to decimal . . . let me see ... that comes to about two hundred million angstroms. That's about two centimeters." Corey thought for a moment. "That makes the wavelength similar to microwave radiation. The wavelength for the second set comes to eight angstroms. That's similar to x-rays." Corey paused for a moment. "That's pretty much the whole spectrum!"

Pete stroked the back of his head. "I think these entries were probably made in 1953, just before they crashed. The craft was discovered on May twentieth but the crash may have occurred a day earlier. That would make the crash date the nineteenth of May." Pete's thoughts raced through the history he could remember from the early 1950's era. Then it dawned on him, "Of course, Upshot-Knothole!"

"What's that?" Wendy asked.

"That was a series of atomic bomb tests conducted in Nevada in the spring of 1953. To be more precise, it was May. I remember reading that some tests were even televised.

Wendy looked at Pete, "So, you think the UFO was at the Nevada test site monitoring the atom bomb test?"

"Yes," Pete said. "Check the entries after number three."

Wendy opened file number four. "Pete, I have file four opened what do you want me to check?"

"What was the time stamp on that?" Pete asked. Wendy scanned the screen.

"That had the last five digits of three-four-six-zero-seven," Wendy said.

"That was about one or two days after the third entry," Corey said.

"What does the log entry say?" Pete asked.

Wendy returned to the device screen to read the entry. "It says something to the effect of 'On station and awaiting test'."

"Okay, now go to the fifth entry," Pete said.

Wendy anticipated Pete's order and was already looking at the entry. "It's time stamped three-four-seven-one-six and says 'Something must be wrong. It is much later than previous tests and nothing has happened. There must be a failure of the mechanism.' That is the end of the message."

"That time stamp is about an hour later than the previous," Corey said.

"Okay, go to the sixth," Pete said.

"That one is time stamped three-four-seven-two-one and the message reads 'Going in closer to mechanism to perform scan and determine cause of failure'."

"Now do the seventh," Pete ordered.

"That is time stamped three-four-seven-two five." Wendy read the entry and gasped, "Oh my god! The message says the mechanism detonated causing their craft serious damage."

"What does the last message say?" Pete asked.

"That one is time stamped only a few minutes later and says they are heading in the direction of the sun and searching for a suitable area for an emergency landing."

"Heading toward the sun," Pete mused. "Those tests were all conducted in the morning so if they headed toward the sun, they headed east, toward Kingman. They were probably trying to reach Red Lake."

"Do you mean the dry lake where Colonel Andrews crash landed?" Corey asked.

"Yes. They probably were looking for a level spot in a desolated area so Red Lake would be a logical choice. They were having control and crashed in the foothills, about ten miles northwest of the Kingman Airport. That's the spot were we intercepted Colonel Andrews. It all makes sense, now," Pete said. He looked at Wendy. "Wendy, after lunch, would you record all of the entries on a separate sheet of paper. I'd like to review them with you both and then make a report to the President." He gave her a smile. "By the way … great job!"

"Thank you. It will take only a few minutes for me to transcribe my notes," she said as she turned the device off and climbed out of the Faraday cage. The threesome headed down to the cafeteria for lunch.

Chapter 19
Phase Three

Hotel room
4:33 PM

After lunch, Wendy finished transcribing the log entries and gave them to Pete for review. He studied them intently for twenty minutes. "I see nothing clandestine in any of this," Pete said, as he finished. He walked over to the window and stared out.

"I agree," Wendy said, "it seems they were just doing scientific studies into our nuclear testing program. So, what's the next step?"

Pete turned toward Wendy and smiled, "Phase three, we need to tap into their main computer."

"I'm not sure how to do that," Wendy said. "I think you need to bring in a computer wiz kid who's good at hacking."

"Wendy, I have every confidence in the world that you and Corey can figure it out. While you are doing that, I have to fly back to the base and make my report to the President. I'll tell him what we have so far and that you're preparing for the next phase. I should be back by twenty hundred hours. You can give me a progress report when I return."

"But . . . but I am really concerned about how we're going to hack in. We won't have much time to screw around. I think you're too confident in our abilities. We shouldn't rush. You understand my concerns don't you?" Wendy pleaded.

"Sure, but don't worry, things will work out. They always do. We have to keep this project moving forward." He turned to leave, "Well, I'm off now. Work hard while I'm gone." With that, Pete disappeared behind the apartment door as it closed behind him.

"When is twenty hundred hours?" Wendy asked with a puzzled expression. "I wish Pete would speak English when it comes to time."

Corey smiled. "That's eight o'clock tonight. He'll be back in about three hours."

"So we have only three hours in which to perform a miracle," Wendy said, as she climbed back into the cage carrying the device and her notebook. She was up and running within five minutes and briskly flexing her fingers over the depressions. She looked up from the screen and over toward Corey. "Do you think I will need some sort of user name and password to log on?"

"Well, if one was required, I'm sure the aliens have blocked that one by now," Corey answered. "The user name might be the same though, if we could figure out what that might be. Look at their first few entries. You said the top two numbers were the same on every entry. What were they?"

Wendy showed Corey her notes through the cage. The top two numbers were 000037173 and 0000006. "What if the bottom number were the ID number of the scout ship that crashed and the top number the ID of the mother ship on the moon," Wendy observed.

"Yes, the mother ships can carry up to eight scout ships, so there could be a number six," Corey agreed.

"How do you know all of that?"

"What?"

"That the mother ship can carry up to eight scout ships."

Corey rubbed his chin in thought. "I don't know. It must be in my latent memory of my abduction," he said with a puzzled expression.

"That's interesting. Perhaps your memory is coming back." She returned to the task at hand. "Okay, if the user name is the number six then perhaps all I have to do is try to access the mother ship using the same method I use to access a file. I mean, there aren't many buttons on this thing so it can't be too complicated."

"You might be right. I guess all we can do is to give it a try," Corey said.

"When we get to Kingman, we'll turn it on, log on and get what we need." Wendy said. "Then we'll get out of there, fast."

"Okay, assuming you are successful at logging on, how will we know what to download?"

"Well, for our first attempt, I'll just key in a variety of large file numbers in sequence. When we get back here, I'll go into the cage and see what we got."

"That sounds reasonable, but you'll have to act quickly." Corey stroked his chin. "Perhaps you should get out of the cage and we should plan everything now and write down the keystrokes. Then you should go back into the cage and practice on some dry runs. That should minimize the time you're on the air in Kingman."

"That sounds like a good plan," Wendy agreed as she turned off the device and prepared to exit the cage.

* * *

The sun had set by the time Pete returned to the apartment. Wendy and Corey were sitting on the couch listening to music and chatting. Wendy looked up and smiled as Pete entered the room. "Welcome back," she said. "How'd the President receive your report?"

"He was extremely pleased with our progress and said to give you both a note of thanks for your diligence. He's anxious to know how we make out in phase three," Pete answered. "How are you making out on that?"

Corey smiled. "We're ready."

"You figured out how to tap into the alien computer?" Pete asked, with a smile.

"Perhaps," Wendy answered. "At least we have a plan." She explained to Pete what they had in mind and that she had been practicing the keystrokes.

"How long do you expect to be online?" Pete asked.

"With practice, I've been able to get down to fifty-six seconds," Wendy said.

"That's great," Pete said.

"Where do you think we ought to do it?" Corey asked.

"I've been giving that some thought. We certainly don't want to do it here in Vegas. I think the last place the aliens knew where we were was in Kingman. They probably have their agents on high alert there so that may not be the best place. I'm thinking Phoenix. There are a number of small airports around there. Scottsdale has one we could go into."

"Isn't Luke Air Force Base near Phoenix? Why not fly into Luke?" Corey asked.

"We'd have a higher profile there because I'd have to file a flight plan to get in. In fact, that's why we're going to wait until tomorrow morning to do this."

"What do you mean?" Wendy asked.

"If we fly anywhere tonight, I'll have to file a flight plan and fly IFR. If we wait until daylight tomorrow, I can fly into Scottsdale by VFR and if I fly low enough, I can stay out of controlled air space."

"What's IFR and VFR?" Wendy asked.

"IFR means I have to fly by Instrument Flight Rules and file a flight plan. VFR means I can fly by Visual Flight Rules and as long as I stay out of controlled air space I can pretty much do as I please with minimum contact with the

FAA and the airport controllers. We should be able to fly into Scottsdale unnoticed."

"I'm for that," Corey said. Wendy nodded in agreement.

"Okay then, that's our plan," Pete said.

* * *

Scottsdale, Arizona
Monday, May 19th
10:23 AM

Pete approached the Scottsdale airport from the north heading due south. Five miles out, he began making his descent. Glancing toward Corey, who was in the seat to his right, he pointed ahead. "We have to parallel those mountains." He pointed to his left. "Then we make a dogleg to the right to line up on final. Those mountains have taken their toll on pilots who were less than careful." Just as he finished saying that, he remembered Wendy's fear of flying. She was in the rear seat with her eyes tightly closed. With her right hand, she was tightening her seat belt. With her left, she was gripping the armrest so tightly that her knuckles were white. Skillfully, Pete turned the plane and aligned with runway two-one. His landing was flawless. Five minutes later he brought the small plane into a parked position in the transient section of the tarmac outside the small aviation terminal. Wendy issued a sigh of relief as Pete stopped the engines.

"See, Wendy, that wasn't so bad," Pete said, as he shot Corey a glancing smile. "I'll tie the plane down but we need to be ready for a hasty departure," he said, as they exited the plane.

Wendy was carrying the small duffle bag containing the device and her note pad. "Where are we going to do this?" she asked.

"There's a small restaurant and coffee shop in the terminal. We'll do it there," Pete answered as he attached the last tie-down to the plane. "I'm going to do my preflight check now so we can leave quickly."

* * *

The restaurant was empty, so the trio took a booth near a window overlooking the flight line. The booth was in a far corner away from traffic. Within a minute a waitress was at the table with three menus.

"We all just want something to drink," Pete told her. "I want a black coffee and they want tea," he explained as he pointed toward Corey and Wendy. "I'd like to pay you as soon as you bring the drinks. We have to leave right away." The waitress nodded and left to fill the order. "Okay, Wendy, as soon as we finish our drinks, you activate the device. One minute after that we're out of here. All agreed?"

"Yes," Wendy and Corey answered, in unison.

Wendy was too nervous to drink her tea and anxiously waited as the other two finished their drinks. She was ready to get started and had been mentally rehearsing her keystrokes as they drank. Pete and Corey were finishing their drinks as Wendy retrieved the device from the duffle bag and donned her gloves. She was about to apply the sticky substance and activate the device when the waitress returned. Wendy was so startled she nearly dropped the device on the floor. Her heart was pounding.

"Excuse me," the waitress apologized, as she pointed toward the uniformed man standing next to the reception station behind her. "The airport manager asked me to find out if you own the plane that just tied down outside?"

"I do," Pete answered. "Is there a problem?"

"I'm sorry, but perhaps you should talk to him. I'll tell him to come to your table," she said, and to motion him over to the table. The man nodded, came over and addressed Pete.

"I'm sorry to disturb you, sir," the man said. "We have a tie-down fee here."

"Oh, I'm sorry," Pete said apologetically. "I'm used to landing at military bases. I forgot. We're only here for a short time while we take a coffee break."

"There's a tie-down fee whether you are military or not and no matter how long you're here. It's only twenty dollars a day but I have to enforce it, I'm sorry. If you don't mind I'll need you to come upstairs to the flight office and fill out some paperwork."

"Sure, no problem, I'll be there in a moment," Pete said to the man.

"That's no problem. I'll wait for you in the flight office. Just take the elevator to the right, after you leave the restaurant," he said as he turned and left the restaurant.

Pete looked at Wendy and in a soft voice said, "Hold off until I get back. If I don't return in ten minutes, get a cab to the nearest hotel. I'll find you." He looked at the clock over the door. "It's ten-forty one. Give me until ten fifty-one and then take off as fast as you can."

"Okay," Wendy said, nervously as she replaced the device into the duffle bag. She and Corey watched as Pete left the restaurant. The minutes seem to drag by as she kept looking at the clock. The minute hand clicked to ten fifty and Wendy nudged Corey who was sitting at the other side of the booth. "Do you think we should leave? It's been almost ten minutes and Pete said to leave if he's not back by then."

"Let's give him another minute," Corey answered, as he focused on the wall clock. The minute hand clicked to ten fifty-one. He turned to Wendy. "Okay, let's pack up." Wendy closed the bag and followed Corey as he started toward the door. Just then, Pete appeared.

"It's okay, you can sit back down," Pete said, as he motioned for them to return to the booth. "I have everything taken care of. They have their money so they're happy."

"Good. Shall we start now?" Wendy asked as she slid back onto the booth seat.

"Let's do it," Pete said.

With that, Wendy took out the device, put the gloves back on and applied the sticky substance. Her fingers played over the surface of the device and suddenly it was activated. She then performed the keystrokes she had been practicing since last night. After waiting a few seconds, she shut the device off, peeled off her gloves, and returned the device to the duffle bag. "I'm done. Let's go," she said anxiously.

"Good. We're out of here," Pete said, as they all left the restaurant as casually as they could.

Chapter 20
The Message

Base Camp II
Las Vegas
1:33 PM

Wendy eased herself into the cage, taking her duffle bag and notebook with her. Within minutes she had the device activated and began retrieving the information she had downloaded earlier. She wrote feverishly as information poured onto the tiny screen. Occasionally her face became contorted with disbelief at what she was reading and she would stop writing and push back.

Pete was watching anxiously. Finally, his curiosity got the best of him. "What does it say, Wendy?" he said in a commanding voice.

"Let me finish," she snapped back. Pete backed down. Within ten minutes, Wendy finished and was climbing out of the cage. Her face was pale and she looked exhausted.

Corey helped her out. "Are you all right?"

"Yes, just tired. That was draining. Can I have some tea before going over my notes with you? I'd like some of that tension relief tea."

"Sure," Pete said. "Corey, why don't you make some tea for you both? Wendy, sit and take a rest."

As Corey prepared the tea, Wendy went over her notes to make sure they made sense.

Corey brought the tea over to the couch where Pete and Wendy were sitting. "Here, Wendy, drink this. It's ginkgo tea, good for your brain."

"Thanks, Corey. That's not calming but I probably need something for my brain more than I need calming." She smiled at Corey as she took the tea and began to drink. Pointing down to her note pad, and shaking her head in disbelief, she said. "Pete, we have some amazing stuff here. It almost seems like they were waiting for us to tap into their computer. I found much of it hard to believe. Listen to this." She began reading:

Welcome. You may enter freely this one time. Our message to you is clear. Share it with all humanity. You must carry this message forward. We say: Beware those who offer much but deliver little. They will deceive you to achieve their ends. You must question carefully. Do not despair. There are those who love humanity and are ready to assist.

Wendy looked up at Corey. "Does that sound familiar?"

He stared in amazement. "Yes. That's very similar to the Crabwood message."

Pete looked at Corey and then Wendy. "What message are you talking about . . . Crabwood?"

Corey retrieved a folded piece of paper from his wallet. "I've been carrying this in my wallet for years. I don't know why. For some reason it intrigued me. This message was laid down in a crop design that appeared in a field near Crabwood, England, in 2002. The message was in a spiral pattern that turned out to be binary coded ASCII." Corey looked at Pete. "You know, English! Don't you find *that* amazing?"

"Yes, that is amazing and a bit suspicious to me. Go ahead and read it." Pete listened intently as Corey read the message.

Beware the bearers of false gifts and their broken promises. There will be much pain but still time. Believe. There is good out there. We oppose deception.

After Corey had finished, Pete thought for a moment as he mulled over what Wendy had read. "Amazing, the content of the message *is* virtually the same. Wendy, continue reading what you have."

Wendy looked at Corey, her eyes questioning whether she should continue. Corey made a subtle nod for her to continue. She began to read again:

Your isolation in our galaxy is coming to an end. For several of your generations, you have begun to encounter others from the galaxy. They are technologically more advanced than you, but they are poor in spirit. They seek the biological and mineral wealth your planet offers.

"I guess this confirms our fears," Pete said, glancing at Corey and then Wendy. "We are being invaded, but it sounds like it's from another group of aliens, not the ones who own the device and who abducted you, Corey. Wendy, continue reading."

Wendy glanced at Corey and then began to read again.

The Federation prohibits forceful invasions but beware, there will be a silent invasion if you allow it. The invader's goal is to gain control of your world and its inhabitants. They do not regard you as their equals. They loathe you and believe that you are destructive and that you are ruining the planet, a planet they want to have for themselves.

"Hold up, Wendy," Pete interrupted. "You mentioned the Federation when we were at the base. Do you have any further thoughts as to what it is?"

"I think that's the Galactic Federation," Corey answered for Wendy.

"How do you know that?" Pete asked.

Corey's face became contorted as he pondered Pete's question. *How do I know that?* He thought. "I don't know how I know it, Pete, but I *do* know it."

"He's right, Pete," Wendy chimed in. "It is the Galactic Federation. I know that too but I don't know why."

"Just what is the Galactic Federation?"

Wendy gave Pete a strange look. "I just know that our galaxy is partitioned into many zones. Each zone is overseen by a race of beings that resides in that zone. I don't know how or why I know that." Indeed, Wendy was as perplexed as both Pete and Corey about her knowledge of the aliens. She did not recall the mind meld with her aide, Sandra, back at the base. Much about the aliens was revealed during that session but only to her subconscious mind.

Pete gave both a bewildered look. "Corey, do you agree?"

"Yes."

Pete looked at Wendy. "Continue reading."

She began again.

The intruders are not multi-dimensional beings. They are physical beings like you. They are few in number but they will use the weapon of deceit. You will think they are here to help humanity. They will use technology and deception to engender belief, even reverence, in them. Humanity will be deceived into thinking the intruders' superior technology will benefit humankind greatly.

You must be on guard. Your freedom and well-being is at stake. The invaders seek to take away your freedom. First will come your freedom of the mind and second the freedom of your soul. Without freedom, there will be little personal satisfaction and happiness. Your spirit will fade and you will become as a hive.

Wendy hesitated as a chill ran down her spine. She searched her notes and then finished.

End of message.

She looked up at Pete. "That's it, that's the end of the message," her voice trembled as she lied. "What do you think?"

Pete thought over all he had heard. "To summarize, it seems that there are physical entities from elsewhere in our galaxy and they intend to take over our planet without force in some covert manner. Their method will be to deceive us into thinking it would be a good deal for us to work with them in exchange for their technology. Apparently, they have been here for decades and interacting with us in some way that has gained our trust. It appears that these aliens are not the owners of this device and are not the ones who abducted you, Corey. Do you agree?"

"Yes, but I am confused. Many abductees, under hypnosis, have reported that the aliens told them they are about to make their presence known. The aliens who abducted me told me they are about to make their presence known. Is it possible that the 'bad' aliens are also abducting people and telling them the same thing?"

"Yes, I agree, it is confusing," Pete admitted. "It was the abduction reports that alarmed the general who found the device and triggered our project, but now we may be talking about two different groups of aliens. I think I need to return to the base and update the President and to warn him. When I return, I would like to do another download." He looked at Wendy. "Do you think that would be possible?"

"I don't know. We can try," she responded, as she glanced over toward Corey for his reaction.

"Good," Pete said. "Tomorrow we'll select a new destination where we can go and do another download. For now, Wendy, you get some rest." He looked at his watch. "It's 14:20 hours. I won't get back much before eighteen hundred so why don't you two go to supper without me."

They both nodded in agreement as they watched Pete leave the apartment. After he was gone, Wendy turned and stared at Corey. "There's more," she said in a soft voice.

"What do you mean?" Corey asked, with a puzzled expression.

"I left out some of the message." Wendy gave Corey a strange stare. "Pete did not hear it all."

"Why not?"

"I think you need to hear the rest before I explain." Wendy led Corey over to the couch and reopened her notebook. Listen to this."

Your military and civic leaders will perceive that an alliance with the invaders will be best for their own political gain and will acquiesce. You must hold your political leaders to task. Beware of your military establishment.

"Pete *is* military and reports to the most powerful political leader on this planet. That worries me. That's why I didn't read that part to Pete," Wendy looked at Corey questioningly. "Are we to believe this message will ever reach the general public if we leave it in Pete's hands?"

"I think not," Corey agreed. "Pete will do his duty and give this to the President and that will end it." Corey looked at Wendy with a questioning gaze. "Have you ever heard about secret underground bases where a race of aliens is working with our military to share technology in exchange for a foothold on this planet?"

"No."

Corey shook his head. "I've heard of several. One is near Los Alamos in New Mexico. That's one of our most secret weapons development facilities. From what I've heard, these aliens are reptilian in form and are not very nice."

"I've never heard of such a thing. That's creepy." She stared blankly at the floor momentarily as a fleeting memory of a reptilian form crossed her mind. She turned to Corey. "How do you know about all of this?"

"That's the lore in ufology circles. Most people don't believe it. Frankly, I was skeptical myself, but given all that has happened and especially this message, I'm now a believer. Those may be the aliens mentioned in the message."

Wendy shook her head in disbelief. "There is more to the message. Listen to this." She began to read from her notes again.

The invaders are few in numbers and cannot use force. For them to succeed, you must acquiesce of your own free will. If you choose not to, then they will be forced to withdraw. Your best weapon is for all humanity to be aware of the invaders and their real intent. You cannot fight them with your inferior technology.

Wendy looked up at Corey. "It seems that this information could be a threat to the invading aliens, the 'bad' aliens as you call them, if word got out to the general public." She gave Corey a hard look and repeated. "*If* word got out." She continued to read.

Take heart, you are not alone in your struggle to preserve your freedom. You have great allies in the galaxy who know freedom's cost. There are other physical beings such as us who seek to promote freedom throughout the galaxy.

Corey interrupted. "Somehow I feel that I've met these aliens."

"Me too," Wendy said. "Back at the base I had an experience with my aide, Lieutenant Gibbs."

"What sort of experience?"

"Well, I was in my room trying to translate the device. I took a break and was playing the piano when she came to my door."

"I thought our aides were not to enter our room except to clean."

"That's what she said she came for. She said that she heard me playing the piano and thought it would be okay for her to clean." Wendy looked at Corey intently. "Did you ever notice her eyes?"

"No, I can't say as I did. I never really saw her. Why?"

"Her eyes were the most piercing eyes I have ever seen. Somehow she convinced me to let her in. After she came into my room, she came right up to me. I mean … in my face. Suddenly I felt sleepy. The next thing I remember, I was having this strange dream."

"What sort of dream?"

Wendy looked at Corey with eyes that pleaded for understanding. She did not want him to think she was crazy. "I dreamt I was aboard an alien craft that was located in the asteroid belt. It was a gigantic ship." Wendy glanced at Corey and then at the floor. "It was over eight miles long and two miles in diameter."

"Yes, I remember, you told Pete and me about that back at the base but you said you didn't know how you learned all of that. You thought you learned it from the device. From what you just told me, your aide must have been doing a mind-meld."

"A what?"

"A mind-meld. Aliens have the ability to interact with us directly through our minds, like mental telepathy. You said she had strange eyes."

"Yes, very strange."

"Wendy, I think it is possible that she is either an alien or a hybrid planted at the base to watch for the device to surface."

Suddenly, Corey's eyes dropped as his face became pale.

"What's wrong, Corey?"

Corey looked into Wendy's eyes. "Your description of that alien craft brought back some memories of when I was abducted. I remember now. This alien who was aboard the craft, he looked like us. He seemed very wise and explained many things to me. He told me that their mother craft was several miles in size and was located in the asteroid belt." Corey hesitated. "No, come to think of it, I told him that. Somehow he knew everything I knew. Colonel Andrews was with me and Quellin had *me* explain all of this to the colonel. We were touring the ship we were on. As a matter of fact, when I was aboard the alien craft, Colonel Andrews told me that *he* was a hybrid. He said he didn't know it until they activated him. His activation happened just after you activated the device."

"Quellin? Is he the alien?"

Corey smiled. "Yes, that was his name. I'm starting to remember!" Wendy's relating her dream to Corey, jogged his memory. "What else do you remember about your dream?"

"Well, in this dream I was given a tour of the base." Wendy looked at Corey questioningly. "Did you know that they *grow* androids there like the gray one we saw on our tour at the base? And did you know they have to replace their eyes periodically because UV light damages them?"

"Yes, I know, that's another thing you told us at the base but actually the aliens call them synthetics, not androids," Corey corrected Wendy. "They grow them at the mother ship but I was not told how," Corey answered. "Also, I was told that they send them there for repairs. Just as you said, they have to replace their eyes periodically. They take the eyes from a sea animal that they farm."

Wendy was impressed. "You really are starting to recall a lot." She got up and turned on the radio, selecting a station that was playing classical music. The station was playing Brahms. "I hope you don't mind if I play some music. This whole conversation is rather stressful for me. I find music soothing."

"Not at all, I enjoy it, too," Corey said, with a smile.

Wendy continued with her story. "In my dream, I was taken into a large conference room. Corey, it was so beautiful. The walls were a pastel color and kept changing colors."

"Yes, the walls generate light and can be programmed for any color. I know that, too. What else did you dream?" Corey asked anxiously.

"While I was in the conference room, I was introduced to the most beautiful people, I mean aliens, that I have ever met. They were dressed in glowing white gowns and seemed so wise. This may sound unbelievable but I think

these were the very same beings that interacted with the
Sumerians over six thousand years ago. I truly believe they
were the individuals who were the creators of humanity.
They've been watching over us ever since. Listen to this,"
Wendy looked down at her notes and continued reading.

*We have been watching over you from afar and have
been your guardians since your inception. We have acted
covertly in the development of your planet and your
species. Take heart, we have a vested interest in the well
being of you and your planet.*

"That sounds like good news," Corey said. "Perhaps
they can help us."

"Only indirectly . . . listen."

*Just as Federation Law prohibits the invaders from
using force to secure your planet, we are prohibited from
using force to fend them off. Our only weapon is to
convince humanity and the leaders of humanity to be the
defenders of the planet.*

*It is important for you to maintain your religious and
cultural diversity, but it is equally important that you put
aside your differences and find common ground in warding
off the ensuing silent invasion. Your freedom is at stake.*

End of message.

For a long moment Corey considered all that had been
said. A puzzled look came over his face. "Wendy, I'm still
puzzled. What about the abductions? Which aliens are
doing that and why?"

She paused. "This is getting complicated but I
remember now. They told me it was necessary for them to
create hybrids."

"Hold on," Corey said. "Which aliens are you talking
about, the 'good' ones or the 'bad' ones?"

"I think the 'good' ones. They said that humans were
too emotional and our leaders were too self-serving. They
needed beings who were less emotional who could become
leaders who were less self-serving and who would be more
attuned to their way of thinking. They felt that the hybrids

would be a buffer between them and us. The hybrids would help to launch the new world government."

Corey raised his eyebrows. "Yes, I know all of that too. It will be a new world government. Yes, Quellin told me about what that would be like."

Wendy listened with interest as Corey went on to explain how the new world government would work.

"That form of government sounds very logical to me," she said. "I wonder why we just don't create it ourselves and do away with all of the politics that seem to waste time and money. It is a shame that we need the aliens with their hybrids to make it happen."

"Yes, and I'm concerned about the effect the hybrids and the alien presence will have on humanity."

Wendy studied Corey. "Why are you concerned?"

"Have you ever heard of the report that the Brookings Institution made to NASA in 1960?" Corey asked.

"No."

"NASA was inquiring as to the effect that the discovery of extraterrestrial life might have on humanity."

"What was their conclusion?" Wendy asked.

"The report said that the effect was unpredictable and that certain segments of society would react differently. For instance, they said the scientific and religious community would probably not react well to the discovery."

"That may be why the government seems to be covering up any evidence about UFOs," Wendy added.

"Yes. The report also said a crucial factor would be the nature of the communication between us and the other beings. The really scary comment they made was that historically, societies who were sure of their own place in the universe have disintegrated when confronted by a superior society."

"So, are you afraid that the new society with its hybrids and new advanced technology will lead to the disintegration of humanity?"

"Yes, long term," Corey said. "I think that eventually, the hybrids will win out and individualism, emotion, and free thought will disappear. Our future civilization might resemble a hive community."

Sergi Rachmaninov's "Piano Concerto No. 2" began playing in the background. "That's one of my favorites," Wendy said, pensively. Her thoughts drifted away from the conversation. Corey noticed tears streaming down her cheeks.

"What's wrong? Why are you crying?" Corey asked, as he took her hand and pulled her toward him.

She turned to him and laid her head on his shoulders. "I'm sorry, I don't mean to cry. The music, and something you said, triggered a terribly sad thought."

"What is it?"

"If emotion and free thought disappear, so will music. That would be *so* terrible. I don't want to live in such a world." Wendy held him tightly.

"Neither do I," Corey agreed, as he embraced her. "But, Wendy, try to be more optimistic. Now that we have been warned, I think we can make the new society work for humanity. We don't have to give up our human traits. We can make a conscious effort not to evolve into a hive community. We can keep a free and open society under the one world government. After all, the way Quellin explained, it will be a government of the people, by the people, and for the people. It goes back to the roots of our own society. The really important thing is that we just have to be on guard."

"I hope you're right," Wendy said.

"Wendy, we have no choice. The alternative is to continue down our present path to self destruction." Cory tried to reassure her. *Ironic*, he thought, *these were the very words told to me by Colonel Andrews.*

"I know, it is confusing," Wendy agreed. "Which is the lesser of the two evils?"

"Right. And, who do we trust?"

"I guess I'll put my trust with the ones who claim to have created us and watched over us," Wendy said.

"I agree. I think we have to side with the ones who sent the message," Corey said. The two sat and enjoyed the inspiring music.

Wendy shook Corey's arm. "Corey, somehow we have to make sure this message we got today gets to the people. I'm afraid we can't rely on Pete or the President. The President may actually squelch this and try to keep it a secret."

"I agree," Corey said. "I have the greatest respect for Pete and I trust him. I don't think *he* would harm us but I don't trust those above him. They may try to silence us . . . and if Pete knew as much as we do, they might even try to silence him."

"Do you mean . . . like some sort of accident?"

"Yes," Corey answered softly.

Wendy looked at the device. "So how do we get the message out and still save all of our hides?"

* * *

6:33 PM

When Pete returned to the apartment, Wendy and Corey were sitting on the couch with the device and Wendy's notebook between them.

"Welcome back," Wendy said. "How did the President receive the latest information?"

"Strangely," Pete answered. "That's the best way I can describe it."

"What do you mean?" Corey asked.

"He didn't seem surprised by anything I reported. He simply asked me to get more information."

"I'm not sure we can," Wendy said, as she placed her hand on the device. She did not want Pete to see that the device had been activated. Corey had been watching through the window for the return of Pete's plane. They timed the activation for the moment of Pete's return to the apartment. Now he was here, the device was activated, and things would take their natural course.

"Corey and I were not that hungry so we waited for you to return. Do you want to feed us now?" Wendy asked, with a Cheshire smile.

"Sure, I am hungry, too," Pete said, as he motioned toward the door. Leave that stuff on the couch. I'm too tired to put it in the safe.

They followed Pete out of the suite and crossed the hall to the elevator. As Pete pressed the button to close the elevator door, he noticed a strange light piercing out from beneath the door of their apartment. "What the . . . " He slammed his arm down to block the elevator door from closing. "Something's wrong! Let's go back!" he yelled, as he raced across the hall and fumbled to get the magnetic card inserted in the door lock. The red light came on. "Damn!" He reversed the card and tried again. This time it worked and the green light came on. He opened the door just in time to hear a zip-clap sound as a shaft of light retreated through the ceiling. Pete froze as he noticed the couch was empty. The device and Wendy's notebook were gone! Only a small puff of smoke lingered over the spot they had occupied.

Chapter 21
Return to Normal

State College, Pennsylvania
Sunday, June 15th
2:34 PM

Dr. Robert Greenwith was dozing after having a large Sunday meal when the doorbell rang and Tigger began barking wildly as he ran toward the front door. "Tigger, take it easy. It's just someone at the door. We're not being invaded." As he worked his way through the Sunday paper strewn over the floor he yelled back to the clatter of dishes in the kitchen. "I have it, Lisa. Call Tigger, he's being a pest." By the second ring, he reached the front door and, as he held Tigger back with his foot, pulled the door open. Tigger went wild!

"Hi Tigger," a familiar voice shouted from the front porch.

"Wendy!" Bob shouted. "Lisa, it's Wendy!" Bob embraced Wendy as she came through the door. Tigger went wild, jumping up and down for Wendy to acknowledge him. Lisa came running into the entry.

"Wendy! How have you been?" She asked, as she gave her a hug.

"I'm just fine," Wendy said as she knelt down to let Tigger lick her face. "I see you've taken good care of Tigger. He looks like he's gained a little weight."

Lisa smiled. "You can blame that on Bob. He can't resist Tigger's begging at the dinner table." It was then that a sparkle on Wendy's left hand caught Lisa's attention. "Wendy, what's that on your finger?"

Wendy held up her hand and answered with a sheepish grin. "I met a wonderful person while I was away." She turned, walked back out onto the porch and returned with Corey in tow. "Bob and Lisa, and Tigger, I would like you to meet the man I plan to marry. This is Dr. Corey Newton. We met in Kingman."

Corey's broad chin broke out into a smile as he shook Bob's hand. "I'm pleased to meet you. Wendy has told me all about the wonderful way you both have cared for her."

"Well, come in and sit for awhile," Lisa said. "Would you both like some hot tea?"

"Yes, please," both answered in unison.

Lisa looked at Bob and smiled. "I can see they're made for each other. You all go into the living room and get comfortable while I go and make a pot of tea."

As they were walking into the living room, Wendy's cell phone rang. "Excuse me for a moment," she said as she stepped out onto the porch to answer. "Hello, this is Wendy." A smile appeared on her face. She turned and yelled into the house. "Corey, it's Pete!" Corey came out to share Wendy's conversation. Wendy listened as Pete spoke.

"I'm glad you got my text message," Wendy said. "It was hard tracking down your number but Corey and I wanted to share our good news with you. We just now told my parents. Thank you." Wendy smiled again as she listened to Pete. "That's wonderful! So the next time we see you we'll have to address you as General. That's really great! I guess the President was impressed with the job you did." Wendy listened some more. "Thank you. We were just doing our job. If you ever need our help again, just let us know." She smiled again. "Corey's right here. Let me put him on. Goodbye, Pete." She handed Corey the phone.

"Hi Pete!" Corey said with a smile. "Yes, I can't believe how lucky I am. She actually said yes. Do you believe that? I understand congratulations are in order for you also, General." Corey smiled as he listened. "By the way, send me your email address so I can give you the details of our wedding. We expect to see you there." Corey listened for a moment and then his face took on a more serious expression. "Pete, there's unfinished business in my mind. Have you heard anything from Colonel Andrews?" Corey frowned as he listened. "That is strange. Okay, I'll tell her. You too. Goodbye Pete." Corey hung up and turned to Wendy. "Colonel Andrews is still listed as missing in action. I really hope he's okay."

Wendy stared up into Corey's eyes sparkling in the reflected sunlight. "Corey, don't worry about him. They didn't harm you so why would they harm him? He tried to help them. I'm sure they have other things for him to do to help."

"I'm sure they do," Corey agreed.

"I know you're going to do your best to spread the word." Wendy looked back at the door. "We should get back to my folks. The tea is probably ready by now."

For several hours the two couples chatted. Wendy explained that she and Corey were sworn to secrecy and could not discuss their project. She shared that Corey was going to seek a teaching and research position at the university in the physics department. She hoped Bob could help. She would continue to teach under Bob if Corey could get a position.

"Wendy, you know I'll do everything I can to make that happen," Bob said. "It so happens that a teaching position is open in physics."

Corey pulled out his wallet. "I nearly forgot, I owe you one thousand and twenty-six dollars. The use of your credit card really saved my life. Here, this should cover it," he said, as he handed Bob a roll of hundred dollar bills. He smiled at Bob's surprise. "I was lucky at blackjack."

Wendy smiled. "He was."

"Thanks again for your assistance," Corey said. "You'll never know how much that helped me."

"Think nothing of it. I was glad to help," Bob said with a smile.

"Have you two set a date yet?" Lisa asked.

"Yes, we plan to get married here on the last Saturday in July. We want to have a small wedding." She looked at Bob, "I hope you'll give me away."

Bob winked at her. "You bet."

Wendy looked at Corey and then Bob and Lisa. "Well, we have to head out to Boston now. Corey's going to introduce me to his parents and the people he works with there. And then he has a paper to write." She looked at Corey and smiled. "He's been invited to give a paper the first week of August in Eureka Springs, Arkansas. We plan to honeymoon there. Also, we have some people there we want to meet."

Bob looked at Corey. "What's your paper on?"

Corey looked at Wendy and smiled. "My paper is entitled, 'UFOs and Gravity Drive.'"

Chapter 22
Return to Boston

GraviDyne
Boston, Massachusetts
Monday, June 16th
9:34 AM

Corey drove into the underground parking lot in the twenty-story stainless-steel-and-glass building dominating the research park north-west of Boston. After parking in his assigned spot, he got out and walked around to let Wendy out. "Remember, my cover story for everyone but my boss is that I was on assignment in China. I was visiting the Institute of Theoretical Physics in Beijing to confer on a paper they wrote."

"I'll follow your lead," Wendy said as they entered the elevator. The elevator stopped at the eighteenth floor, marked executive suites.

"My boss has his office here. I think you're going to like Dr. Fox, he's a great guy. He was on my dissertation committee." The door opened and they exited into an expansive and plush reception area. Opposite the elevator was the reception desk. "Come on, I'll introduce you to Judith," Corey said as he escorted Wendy over to the desk.

"Well hello stranger, how was China?" Judith said. She eyed Wendy noticing the engagement ring on her finger. "And who is this bright young lady you brought with you?"

"Judith, I would like you to meet my fiancée, Dr. Wendy Ahearn," Corey said as his face burst into a broad smile.

"I'm very pleased to meet you, Wendy. I have to say, there are going to be a lot of young ladies in the building who will be heart broken when they find out Corey's engaged. Congratulations to both of you!"

"Thank you, Judith," Wendy said with a smile.

"Judith, is Dr. Fox in? I don't have an appointment but I wanted him to meet Wendy and know I am back."

"Sure, let me check. I'll be right back." Judith knocked the door and went into the office behind her.

"Wendy, after I talk to Tom, I'd like to give you a little tour of this place. We can't see it all because of confidentiality but at least you can see where my office was."

"That would be great."

"Hey, Corey! Come on in here!" Tom said as he peaked around his door. He was beaming.

"Sure," Corey said as he led Wendy into his office.

"Have a seat, both of you," Tom said as he pointed to the two chairs in front of his desk. "When did you get back, Corey? Judith tells me your brought someone special."

"I got into town last night and yes, I do have someone special I'd like you to meet. This is my fiancée, Dr. Wendy Ahearn." Now Corey was Beaming.

Tom got up from his seat and came around to Wendy. "Don't get up, I just wanted to shake the hand of the person who stole the heart of my ace scientist. It's a real pleasure meeting you, Wendy." He grabbed her hand and began pumping it.

"Well, thank you, Dr. Fox," Wendy said with a grin.

"Please, don't call me Dr. Fox, call me Tom." He said as he returned to his chair. "Well Corey, how was your project and how on earth did you meet this fine lady? It was on earth wasn't it or was it in heaven?" Wendy began to blush.

"She is an angel but I met her on earth. We were together on the project. I can't say anything about what the project was or where we were but it is my opinion that she was the key player. I was just there for technical support."

"Stop being so modest, Corey. You were as important as I was, you know that," Wendy said as she jabbed Corey in the arm.

"So, Corey, are you finished with the project and can I expect you to report for work?" Tom asked.

"Yes and no."

"What do you mean?"

"Yes I am finished with the project but sort-of-no to the second question."

"What!"

"Well, as you know, Wendy and I are getting married. She teaches at Penn State University and her boss says he can get me a teaching position in the physics department there. We want to be together and I think I would like teaching so I guess what I'm saying is I'm giving my two weeks notice."

"But, Corey, what about your project? You love that project. You *are* the project. Without you, that project will die!"

"I know you are disappointed but I think I have a solution that will make all of us happy," Corey said as he leaned over the desk toward Tom.

"I'm listening." Tom was not surprised that Corey would have worked out solution.

"Well, in addition to teaching, I will need to conduct a certain amount of research to get tenured. My expertise is quantum gravity. You need research done in quantum gravity and in fact my project *is* in quantum gravity. So, why can't you fund your project through the school and to me?" Corey grinned with satisfaction.

Tom rubbed his chin as he pondered what Corey had just said. "You know, I think you just might have something there.   You would have to maintain confidentiality on the project and could not publish your results you know."

"Well, perhaps I could publish the non-critical and confidential portions. You could review my papers before I publish. That's done all the time in academia."

"Yes, I think that would work and what you do publish would give us some good PR."

"Yes, that's right," Corey agreed.

"Sounds like a plan," Tom said. "So, when and where are you two getting hitched?"

"We plan to get married in State College on the last Saturday in July. We're just going to have a small wedding but I hope you can be there," Corey answered.

Tom looked at his day-planer. "That's only about six weeks from now." He studied the book. "Count me in!"

"Great!" Corey said as he and Wendy got up to leave. "Tom, is it okay if I give Wendy a short tour, I want her to see where I worked?"

"Certainly! Have fun. I see you tomorrow. By the way, James has been asking about you. His curiosity has been killing him. He asks what you are doing in China every time I meet him in the hallways. His nose has been bent out of shape ever since you left. Please, make sure you touch base with him before you leave today so I can walk the halls in peace."

"Sure, I'd go out of my way to search him out, Tom. My old buddy, James," Corey smiled as he led Wendy from the office. As they entered the elevator, Wendy's curiosity go the best of her. "Who is this James character?"

"You got that right," Corey said.

"What do you mean?"

"He is a character. You know me as a gentile person but that man has tried my patients so many times. Every time we have a conversation, I just have to walk away just to keep from decking'm."

"Now I *have* to meet him. Anyone who can upset you is a must-see. Please introduce me to him."

"Okay, but if I deck him it will be your fault."

Corey took Wendy to his office and showed her some of the research he was doing. He picked up a copy of an article he had written for a UFO magazine and showed it to Wendy. "This article is one I wrote on my own time. James got a copy and tried to get me fired for, as he called it, 'dragging the company through the mud with such nonsense.' I tried to convince him that I wrote it on my own time and did not even mention GraviDyne in the article but he went to Tom and complained."

"What did Tom say?"

"He laughed. He said I should write bogus articles and shove them under James' door just to get him riled up."

"It sounds like Tom has him pegged too," Wendy said.

"Come, James is usually hanging out in the library, bugging anyone who happens to be there. I take you to meet him." Corey led Wendy down to the second floor library and began searching between the stacks. Wendy was the first to spot him.

"Is that mousy looking guy with horn-rimmed glasses, James?" She asked. Corey turned and looked in the direction she was pointing.

"Sure enough," He smiled. "And he's coming our way. Hold on to you hats!"

From twenty passes out they could hear his squeaky voice. "Dr. Newton, I presume. How your paid vacation in China?"

"James! I've missed you and the enlightening conversations we always have. I'd like you to meet my fiancée. This is Dr. Wendy Ahearn. Wendy, this is James Atherton the third."

James looked up at Wendy who was at least six inches taller. Pulling his glasses halfway down his beak nose he smiled. "Do you believe in UFOs?" Wendy pulled back her outstretched hand as it was obvious James was not in the mood to shake her hand.

"Yes, I do," She said with a sinister smile. "You appear to be highly educated so I assume you also believe."

He turned to Corey and smiled. "It figures, as they say cooks of a feather flock together."

Wendy fired back. "Because you work here I though you were well educated. Obviously, I was wrong." Her blood pressure was beginning to climb. "Corey, I think we're late for our appointment. Let's go," she said as she turned her back on James and began walking away.

REFERENCES

For the reader whose curiosity is piqued by this book, I have included a list of references that will be helpful for doing more research. They are organized by chapter and in the approximate order their material was used. Extensive research can be done through Google, Wikipedia, Filers Files, Huey helicopter UFO websites.

Prolog
Randle, K., *A History of UFO Crashes*, Avon Books, New York, 1995

Randles, J., *UFO Retrievals: The Recovery of Alien Space craft*, Sterling Publishing, New York, 1995

Randles, J., *Alien Contact: The First Fifty Years*, Barnes & Noble Books, New York, 1997

Spighesi, S. J., *The UFO Book of Lists*, Kensington Publishing, New York, 2000

Stevens, Wendelle,   www.ufophotoarchives.org

Stringfield, Leonard H., *Situation Red, The UFO Siege*, Doubleday & Company, Inc., Garden City, New York, 1977

Friedman, Stanton T., *Flying Saucers and Science, A scientist Investigates the Mysteries of UFOs*, New Page Books, Franklin Lakes New Jersey, 2008

Chapter 1
Farrell, Robert E., *Alien Log, R. E. FARRELLBOOKS, LLC, Peoria, Arizona*, 2004

Chapter 2
www.bellhelicopter.textron.com

Sparks, Jim, *The Keepers*, Wile Flower Press, Columbus, NC, 2006

Romanek, Stan with Danelek, J. Allen, *Messages, The World's Most Documented Extraterrestrial Contact Story*, Llewellyn Publications, Woodbury, Minnesota, 2009

Chapter 3
Redfield, Dana, *Summoned, Encounters With Alien Intelligence*, Hampton Roads Publishing Company, Inc., Charlettesville, VA, 1999

Chapter 5
Adamski, George, *Inside the Spaceships*, The George Adamski Foundation, Vista, CA, 1953

Corso, P.J. and Birnes, W., *The Day After Roswell*, Pocket Books, New York, 1997

Hesemann, M. and Mantle, P., *Beyond Roswell: The Alien Autopsy Film, Area 51, & the U.S. Government Coverup of UFOs.*, Marlowe & Company, New York, 1997

Berlitz, C. and Moore, W., *The Roswell Incident: The Classic Study of UFO Contact*, Berkley Books, New York, 1988

Brunswick, R., *UFO*, Goliath, Frankfurt, 1999

Good, T., *Alien Base, Earth's Encounters With Extraterrestrials*, Century Random House, London, 1998

Good, T., *Unearthly Disclosure*, Arrow Books, London, 2001

Adamski, G., *Inside The Spaceships*, The George Adamski Foundation, California, 1955

Adamski, G. and Leslie, D., *Flying Saucers Have Landed*, The British Book Centre, New York, 1953

Romanek, Stan with Danelek, J. Allen, *Messages, The World's Most Documented Extraterrestrial Contact Story*, Llewellyn Publications, Woodbury, Minnesota, 2009

Filer, George A., *Filer's Files: Worldwide Reports of UFO Sightings*, Infinity Publishing, West Coshocton, PA., 2005

Chapter 6
Cannon, D., *The Custodians "Beyond Abduction"*, Ozark Mountain Publishers, Arkansas, 2001

Cannon, D., *Jesus and the Essenes*, Ozark Mountain Publishers, Arkansas, 1999

Lewels, J., *The God Hypothesis*, Wild Flower Press, North Carolina, 1997

Downing, B., *The Bible and Flying Saucers*, Marlowe & Company, New York, 1968

Ross, Hugh, *The Creator and the Cosmos: How the Greatest Scientific Discoveries of the Century Reveal God*, NavPress Publishing Group, Colorado Springs, CO, 1993

Turnage, C.L., *New Evidence That The Holy Bible Is An Extraterrestrial Transmission*, Timeless Voyager Press, California, 1998

Tolman, Richard C., *Relativity Thermodynamics and Cosmology*, Dover Publications, Inc., New York, 1987 (Oxford University Press, 1934)

Chapter 8
McGehee, Bobby, *New Universe Theory With Laws of Physics*, Authorhouse, Bloomington, Indiana, 2005

McGehee, Bobby, *Model of the Universe With Laws of Physics*, Authorhouse, Bloomington, Indiana, 2010

Singh, Simon, *Big Bang The Origin of The Universe*, Harper Perennial, New York, 2004

Guth, Alan H., *The Inflationary Universe*, Helix Books, Reading, Massachusetts, 1998

Barrow, J., *The Origin of The Universe*, Basic Books, New York, 1994

Rees, M., *Before the Beginning, Our Universe and Others*, Perseus Books, 1997

Hill, P., *Unconventional Flying Objects: A Scientific Analysis*, Hampton Roads Publishing, Virginia, 1995

Watts, A., *UFO Quest: In Search of The Mystery Machines*, Sterling Publishing, New York, *1994*

Cramp, Leonard G., *Space, Gravity and the Flying Saucer*, British Book Centre, New York, 1955

Chapter 10
Mitchell, Edgar, *The Way of the Explorer*, New Page Books, Franklin Lakes, NJ, 2008

Talbot, Michael, *The Holographic Universe*, Harper Perennial, U. S. A., 1991

Jones, Marie D., *PSIence, How New Discoveries in Quantum Physics and New Science May Explain The Existance of Paranormal Phenomena*, New Page Books, Franklin Lakes, New Jersey, 2007

Noory, George, and Birnes, William J., *Worker In The Light*, Tom Doherty Associates, LLC., New York, 2006

Chapter 11
Fuller, J.G., *The Interrupted Journey*, Berkley Paperback, California, 1966

Mack, J.E., *Abduction: Human Encounters with Aliens*, Ballantine Books, New York, 1994

Jacobs, D.M., *Secret Life, Firsthand Documented Accounts of UFO Abductions*, Simon & Schuster, New York, 1992

Jacobs, D.M., *The Threat*, Simon & Schuster, New York, 1998

Hopkins, B., *Missing Time*, Ballantine Books, New York, 1988

Strieber, W., *Communion: A True Story*, Avon Books, New York, 1988

Fowler, R.E., *The Watchers* ,Bantam Books, New York, 1991

Hill, B., *A Common Sense Approach to UFOs*, Betty Hill, New Hampshire, 1995

Walton, T., *Fire In The Sky*, Marlowe & Company, New York, 1996

Fowler, R.E., *The Andreasson Legacy*, Marlowe & Company, New York, 1997

Fowler, R.E., *The Allagash Abductions*, Wild Flower Press, Oregon, 1993

Haley, Leah A., *Unlocking Alien Closets: Abductions, Mind Control, and Spirituality*, Greenleaf Publications, Murfreesboro, TN, 2003

Jordan, D. and Mitchell, K., *Abducted!*, Dell Books, New York, 1994

Walden, James L., *The Ultimate Alien Agenda*, Llewellyn Publications, St. Paul, Minnesota, 1998

Chapter 13
Leir, R., *Casebook: Alien Implants*, Dell Publishing, New York, 2000

Hawker, Gloria Ann, *Diary of An Alien Abductee*, Write to Print, Merrimack, NH, 2001

Chapter 18
Saussure, F., de, *Course in General Linguistics*, Open Court, Illinois, 1996

Walker, C.B.F., *Reading the Past Cuneiform*, University of California Press, California, 1987
Jean, G., *Writing The Story of Alphabets and Scripts*, Harry N. Abrams, 1992

Keith, Jim, *Saucers of The Illuminati*, Adventures Unlimited Press, Kempton, Illinois, 2004

Chapter 20
Boulay, R.A., *Flying Serpents and Dragons: The Story of Mankind's Reptilian Past*, The Book Tree, California, 1999

Summers, M.V., *The Allies of Humanity: An Urgent Message about the Extraterrestrial Presence in the World Today,* The Society For The Greater Community Way of Knowledge, Colorado, 2001

Crystall, E., *Silent Invasion,* St. Martin's Press, New York, 1996

Walden, J.L., *The Ultimate Alien Agenda,* Llewellyn Publications, Minnesota, 1998

Krapf, P.H., *The Contact has Begun,* Hay House, Inc., California, 1999

Dennett, P., *Extraterrestrial Visitations,* Llewellyn Publications, Minnessota, 2001

THE AUTHOR

Dr. Farrell has been involved in technology most of his adult life. He holds a B.Sc. in Mechanical Engineering, a Masters Degree in Business Administration, and a Doctor of Engineering. For twenty years, he worked in industry, designing plastics processing machinery. For fifteen years he was a Professor of Engineering preparing students for the plastics industry.

During his entire professional career, Dr. Farrell has been fascinated by the UFO phenomenon and has done extensive research through the literature to formulate his view on the topic.

This book is the result of an effort to combine science with fiction to enlighten and entertain the reader. He would greatly appreciate any feedback you are willing to give him as he continues to research and write more books in the *Alien Log* series.

Contact the author at: author@alienlog.com